INTER ANGELIS ET PUERIS

FIDELES INVENIAMUR

FURIOUS ANGELS

BY

DAMIEN MAC NAMARA

FURIOUS BOOK PUBLISHING
NCI Research and Business Centre
Mayor Street
IFSC, Dublin 1
Ireland

This edition published in 2016 by Furious Book Publishing

A CIP catalogue record for this book is available from
the British Library.

ISBN-13: 978-0-9954760-0-4

This is a work of fiction. All of the characters, organizations and
events portrayed in this novel are either products of the author's
imagination or are used fictitiously.

www.furiousbooks.com

books@furiousbooks.com

DEDICATED TO A.C AND A.F AND S.M.K.

ACKNOWLEDGMENTS

I would like to acknowledge the kind and patient editing work of: Alix Reid, Cherry Mosteshar and Angela Brown. To my beta-readers Damien Lyne, James Moore and Jamie Mollaghan, thanks for reading the same chapters over and over.

All artwork by Rhett Podersoo. A talented man.

1 NEW YEAR'S DAY

Dark, sunken eyes peer back through the bathroom mirror, and they're not mine. The flesh is eaten away, faded against the protruding bone, my cheeks gaunt and grey. I don't move another muscle, I'm rooted to the spot. Everything goes blurry as my breath fogs up the glass. This has got to be some kind of hallucination.

I wipe my palm quickly across the mirror, and my sixteen-year-old face suddenly returns to normal. Just to be certain, I lean in closer and inspect the details; spikey fringe, blue eyes and a few hairs at the base of my chin, nothing unusual. The stress of coming back to Tara Hill after four years has finally caught up with me...but a hallucination? I must be more stressed than I thought.

I hear the kitchen door open and a light from the driveway shines through the pixelated glass of the bathroom window. My uncle James hums to himself as he takes my suitcase from the car, scraping the little plastic wheels along the gravel.

He thinks he's doing me a favour but he's not. This isn't how I want the rest of my Christmas holidays to go. I'm supposed to be at home, playing games all day on my new PC, but I was too polite to refuse my mother when she asked me to stay at my aunt and uncle's. So I'm stuck now in this remote Irish village, out of politeness and misplaced guilt—to hang out with a cousin I don't remember at the worst time of his life.

When I make my way back into the kitchen, two curious smiles greet me.

'Thanks for coming William,' says my aunt Marie.

'It's no problem,' I lie.

I start to play through all the different excuses I can use to get out of here. I screech my chair on the tile floor, and my aunt carefully wedges some cake off an overloaded plate, landing it in front of me. I don't remember her being this nice when I was younger. In fact, I think I'm still a little afraid of her. She has this natural air-of-authority with her white blouse buttoned up to the collar and her hair in a tight bun.

'Now, William,' she says, pleased with herself and wearing a warm grin. The type of warm grin aunts wear when they're giving you cake.

James takes a slurp of his tea and exhales with relief. His attention bears down on me, like I'm a curious specimen.

'Your cousin is next-door in the cottage,' he says, then casts a glance at his wife and his weather-beaten smile fades to something sterner. 'We would have preferred to keep him here a while, but he wanted to stay in his father's old room. He's barely left it since the accident.'

I find it odd Andrew wants to stay in my grandmother's old house, because if I had just lost my father, I'd want more company and not less.

About a month ago, my uncle Ken was killed outside Dublin Airport when he lost control of his rental car and smashed into a traffic-barrier. He left behind my fourteen-year-old cousin Andrew, who grew up in a New York suburb. Ken moved there years ago for work, but shortly afterward Andrew's mother died of cancer. So now I guess he's got no one left except our aunt and uncle. They have their own kid, Sarah, but she's away at college.

'It must be three or four years since you last saw your cousin,' says Marie.

I tell her it's been at least eleven years.

She raises her eyebrows and spends a minute working out the math. The truth is, I was never around during the few times Andrew was here on holiday and Ken never stayed for very long anyway. I put down my cup and look at them both; the question nagging away at me finally forces its way to my mouth.

'I don't really know what I'm supposed to do here.'

James smiles sadly. 'Just be there for him. That's all you can do, William.'

I have a vague memory of meeting Andrew when I was five and he was three—a grey, blurry memory of standing outside a church in the rain while a priest said prayers over his mother's coffin as it was lowered into the earth.

I stayed away all these years because there's nothing to do out here but go on country walks or hang out by the Loch or climb trees. There are no distractions in the countryside, meaning there's more time to think about stuff. When I have time to think, I think about my past, and this place reminds me of a part of myself I've ignored for a long time.

Hopefully Andrew was too young to remember his mother, just as I was too young to have remembered my father, Patrick, who's buried next to Ken's fresh grave. I suppose in a way we have some kind of common ground, if you can call it that.

It's going to be a strange start to the New Year.

***

After all the cake I can eat, I call it a night. At eleven thirty it's a little early for me, but there's only so much small talk I can make with my aunt and uncle.

I drag my suitcase into the cold night air along the broken garden path between the house and my grandmother's cottage, and I remember back to some summer day about five years ago when I came to visit my gran. She always used to sit out by the garden in the mornings if the weather was fine. Looking at the closed doorway, I can almost see her there, which makes me a little sad.

In the silent thought, I notice the quietness of Tara Hill compared to what I'm used to in Limerick city, and the silence of the place magnifies how far from home I feel.

I lower the telescopic handle of the suitcase. A subtle click of the motion sensor above the aluminium door switches on the back-porch light. There's no sign of life from inside the cottage and again I wonder how Andrew stays up here in the darkness by himself.

I clumsily tug on the brass handle. It takes two attempts for me to open it, as if the door is too big for the aluminium frame. The smell of musty dampness rushes up my nose. I fumble around and flick on the light. It's a little too bright in here for what the old kitchen offers in terms of visual appeal. A small dining table with four woodworm chairs pushed underneath a torn Teflon tablecloth eats up all the space in the room. I edge on past, up a few stone steps, and push through a narrow green door that leads to a sitting room; it's colder in here than it is outside.

A closed sketch pad sits on an old, torn, leather couch across from a large fireplace that's burning embers with balls of paper scattered on the floor all round it. Some of the papers are partially burnt, as if they had fallen out of the fire after someone threw them in from a distance. Two wooden doors stand at the end of the room, one in each corner.

Remembering what Marie told me, I make my way into the bedroom on the right. A pleasant rush of warm air hits my face in the lamp-lit room. It's barely big enough for what's in it: an electric heater someone switched on earlier, a single bed, an old wooden wardrobe, a small bedside cabinet, and, over the bed, a picture of some holy person whose eyes seem to follow me around. Faded cream wallpaper covers the place, with strips hanging down in places. It's an old person's place for sure, like anything I touch could fall apart at any minute.

I relax a little and kick off my shoes, only realising now how tense I've been all day. On the drive over, I thought about what I was going to say to Andrew to break the ice, but right now nothing I can think of sounds genuine. What do I say to a kid who just lost his father?

James says Andrew needs me, but I can't think of why he would…and me of all people, a cousin he hasn't met in years. I doubt Andrew even remembers me, because I barely remember him, and I know I'm not going to find the right words when the time comes.

I turn off the lamp and slide open the curtains a little, but absolutely nothing from the outside shines through—no streetlights, just emptiness. The silence and complete darkness feel weird because in the city my bedroom overlooks a busy road, and my brain is finely tuned to the white noise of traffic. The electric heater switches on with a gentle hum, and the noise gives me some comfort, so I decide to make an attempt at sleep and lie down. The old mattress creaks in response to my every movement.

I stare into the blackness and remember the distorted image of myself I saw earlier in the bathroom: sickly and gaunt but so vivid, as if my own deathbed were playing out in front of me. I know it wasn't a hallucination because I never hallucinate.

2 JUNK WEIGHING

I hear the creak of a door opening and what I think is the sound of clanking glass bottles. Light seeps into my bedroom from outside and it looks like Andrew is up after all and in the sitting room. This is just the distraction I need, and curiosity prompts me to open my door. A skinny kid in a white hoodie, his black hair flopping down over both ears, sits on the couch, holding a bottle of something. An empty bottle sits on the floor next to him.

His eyes widen like he's been caught red-handed.

'Shit, you're here already!' he says in a New York accent.

Not the greeting I was expecting.

'Came a day early. Couldn't get a lift out here tomorrow,' I say

He makes no acknowledgment. The seal of the bottle top cracks as he opens what looks like a fresh bottle of Scotch. It seems Andrew found my grandmother's secret stash or somehow bought alcohol in a place that doesn't require ID. He brings it to his nose for a closer inspection.

I smile. 'Ringing in the New Year?'

A voice in my head repeats my opening sentence with a sarcastic, mocking tone. What a dumb thing to say. So much for my practiced little speech.

'I thought you were taller. James said you were tall!' he says.

I give a nervous laugh. 'I think everyone is tall compared to James!'

Andrew stands up in front of me; his forehead reaches about my eye level. He grunts out a 'Yeah, I guess' then takes a swig from the bottle. He forces it down and gives me the once-over. Neither of us says anything, and he gulps down another swig of Scotch, maintaining eye contact. I don't know how he's drinking that stuff straight down. He must be depressed.

'Aren't you supposed to mix that with something?' is all I can offer, intimidated by a fourteen-year-old.

He throws back an identical swig to the one before. 'Takes too long,' he says.

Maybe I'm being paranoid, but I feel like my junk is firmly on some imaginary weighing scale he's placed between us. As he raises the bottle for a third time, a thought in the back of my mind kicks its way down unexpectedly to my mouth.

'Can I have some?' I ask, my voice breaking midsentence.

Andrew raises the bottle as if he's going to have more, but then he pushes it against my chest.

'Don't drop it,' he says, and heads for the kitchen.

I hold the bottle in my hands and look around the sitting room in all its glory: worn faded-red carpet, a torn couch with a matching torn armchair, no sign anywhere it was Christmas recently. An open drinks cabinet sits next to the green door, undoubtedly stripped bare by my uncle before Andrew moved in. Obviously James didn't factor in the resourcefulness of his nephew to drink away his misery. I bring the bottle closer to my nose and the smell reminds me of the Christmas cakes my grandmother used to bake.

Andrew comes back with two porcelain cups.

He shrugs. 'No glasses.'

We sit down on the couch, and I take a cup from him; a piece is chipped away from the blue rim, and the base looks a little dusty.

'I might give this a wash,' I say, scraping away some dust with my finger.

Paying me no attention, Andrew pours a shot to the quarter mark then pours his own.

'Cheers,' he says, before drinking his Scotch straight back.

I look at the brown stuff in my cup with little pieces of dust from a hundred years ago floating around. I take a breath and look up at him. 'Man, I was sorry to hear about your dad.'

'You gonna drink that or what?' he snaps like his voice is on fire.

I feel I've just said the wrong thing again. I brace myself, swirling the dark-brown liquid in the cup.

'This is my first time drinking alcohol,' I say.

He rolls his eyes and gestures impatiently to give him the cup.

'No, it's alight!' I say firmly, and throw it back in one quick movement. It instantly burns everything inside me—from the back of my throat to the pit of my stomach. The sensation is bad enough to force my eyes closed. It tastes like something that shouldn't be consumed by humans; like I've just drank the liquefied remains of one of my ancestors. My mouth twists downward as the Scotch lodges in my stomach like a weight.

Andrew smiles. 'You really shoulda washed that out. Didn't you see all the dirt in there?'

I feel like I'm the most naïve person on the planet. I hit my cup off his and stupidly gesture for another. The imaginary people in the control room of my head frantically press buttons and wave their hands in the air, telling me to stop what I'm doing. I don't stop, though, because now I feel I have to keep going.

He starts to pour, all the while looking at me and not the bottle, like he's trying to see when or if I'll tell him to stop. I leave him to it, and he fills my cup to the brim then pours himself the same amount but this time takes a more measured gulp. I do the same, trying to force a straight face, like the disgusting taste doesn't bother me, but my mouth gives the sensation away.

He looks at me with a sombre expression, like there's more going on behind it, like I'm being sized up. His stare wills me to say something to break the awkwardness.

I gesture towards the sketch pad behind him. 'So you draw?'

Andrew's eyes narrow again, like I've hit a nerve. 'I don't wanna draw. I have to draw.'

I have no idea what that means.

'What do you like to draw?' I say, digging a bigger hole for myself.

He grunts and takes another gulp but doesn't answer the question.

I try match the amount he just took, coughing down the contents.

'How come you've never drank before? You *are* Irish right?'

I guess that was some kind of joke.

'Not all Irish people drink, you know.'

'So why you drinkin now?' he asks.

I hear the undertone of a challenge in his voice, like he knows he's making me do this. I take another gulp like it's no big deal and think about the answer. I wonder why I asked him to pass the bottle in the first place—maybe this felt like the place to take my first real drink, considering this place is part of the reason I tend to avoid alcohol.

I shrug. 'Bored. Where do you keep the stuff anyway?'

Andrew raises an eyebrow and throws back some more. 'Gonna tell on me?'

'Maybe,' I say, throwing back a shot.

'There's a false compartment in my closet.' He starts pouring again. 'How long you stayin', Cousin William?'

I shrug. 'For a while. You can call me Will. I kinda prefer it.'

As I take another gulp, I feel my head get a little fuzzy.

He takes a measured sip this time. 'So why did you come?'

I try to guess what James and Marie told him about me being here. I suppose they made up some story so he wouldn't feel awkward.

'I spend my holidays here,' I tell him. 'It's nice to get away from the city, you know? Catch up on some studying.'

Three lies, one after the other.

He looks down at his cup as he swirls the contents. 'Yeah. This place is so awesome,' he says drearily. He throws the entire quarter glass back then coughs and clutches his chest. He nods at my glass, telling me it's my turn. I throw the whole thing back; it burns into my soul. I lean forward like I'm going to heave, but my stomach settles just in time. Andrew pats me on the shoulder. 'See? It aint so bad!'

As I look up at him and exhale, a slight disconnect exists between my brain and my movements. For the first time in my life, I'm a little drunk. I take the bottle from him, and surprisingly he lets it go. I pour us both a regular shot.

We both drink some back at the same time; I wait for a few seconds in the silence and look around the fireplace for some kind of conversation starter. Then I look at him again. 'Were you close to your dad?' I hope it isn't a dumb question.

'Don't,' he says, shaking his head.

'Sorry. I'm terrible at this stuff,' I say, trying to backtrack.

'When he was alive, we weren't close. That answer your question?'

I suppose it does.

He takes a swig straight from the bottle, maintaining eye contact. Then he holds out his hand, waiting for me to do the same.

I take the bottle from him and do just that; this is much much worse than drinking from a cup. Andrew takes the bottle from me and throws back another swig. After wiping his mouth on his sleeve, he gestures again that it's my turn. This time I make sure to take an even bigger mouthful, and my face shakes as the liquefied evil goes down my throat in a trail of fire. Andrew immediately follows this with another gulp then another in quick succession.

'Likewater!' he slurs.

Less than a fifth of the bottle remains. Without giving what's left of my brain any time to think, I let the Scotch bounce off my lips but without swallowing any. At the limit of my tolerance, and with a burning in my stomach that feels like the Scotch is trying to drill a hole through my skin, I slam the bottle down on the couch and keep my hand around the neck, hoping Andrew hasn't noticed the volume in the bottle is still the same.

He grabs the bottle near the base and sways a little from side to side like he's psyching himself up. A fully dimpled smile breaks out, and each of his brown eyes looks off in different directions. I laugh at him, and neither of us can stop ourselves from laughing as the bottle shakes in our hands.

His smile lessens as quickly as it appeared.

'I know're fulla shit, William!' he says.

'What?' I say, confused.

He points to me. 'You…you…wanna know how I know?'

I shrug. 'What are you talking about?'

'You don't spend your vacations here. You never spend any time here!'

Looks like I'm not as good a liar as I thought.

'Yeah, I do. I swear!' I say with absolutely no confidence.

Andrew falls stubbornly quiet.

Leaning forward, I take one of the scrunched-up balls of paper from the floor. He quickly grabs it from my hand and throws it into the fireplace.

'I asked James if you could come,' he says softly.

I didn't expect him to say that. I figured my mother and Marie arranged this. Suddenly I feel bad for thinking the way I did earlier.

He sways a little. 'You lost your dad; I lost mine. I figured you could tell me what I'm supposed to do.'

I lean against the backrest of the couch; he does the same.

'I lost my dad when I was really young,' I tell him. 'Maybe I was lucky, you know?'

My eyelids suddenly feel too heavy.

'Lucky?' he says, surprised.

'I mean, too young to remember him. You can't miss what you never really had.'

'What age were you?'

'Almost two.'

He smiles. 'That's pretty young.'

A memory—no, not a memory, more like a feeling—pushes up from the back of my mind. 'That's why I never drink.' I close my eyes and start to speak before I even know what I'm saying. 'My dad was an alcoholic, had a fight with my mother one night, went to drink it off, and drove his car into a tree. He was killed instantly.'

I open my eyes, expecting myself to be upset, but I'm not.

Andrew diverts his gaze and avoids eye contact. 'I just wonder how I got here, you know? One day I'm in high school, hanging out with friends, doing stupid stuff...' His voice trails off to a whisper.

'And the next you're here in the middle of nowhere?'

He gives a tired laugh. 'Welcome to my life.'

3 The Image

Noise, like a compressed language, rings in my ear—too many words to recognize in too short a time.

My mouth is dry, and it's painful to swallow. All the fun of the alcohol has worn off and left me with a throbbing brain, I guess this is what they call a hangover. I hunch forward, take my head in my hands, and wait for the bedroom to stop spinning. The little window next to my door is still pitch-black, but it feels like I've been asleep for longer. As I step into the sitting room, Andrew is lying in the foetal position, facing the backrest of the couch, his mouth open and drooling a little. I feel sorry for him now, and it never occurred to me he might have asked James and Marie to arrange my visit. He must have gotten pretty lonely out here.

I make some clumsy steps to the freezing kitchen and drink straight from the crusty brass tap. I dip my head into the sink and breathe, mentally telling my body if it wants to throw up, now would be a good time. Looking down the drain, I dare my stomach to heave, but nothing happens, and I can only imagine how stupid I look with my head shoved into the kitchen sink. I edge myself upright and make my way back to the living room, tripping over a little ball of paper on my way. It's one of Andrew's drawings. I glance over him, making sure he's still out cold, then take the scrunched up ball from the floor and carefully unfold it, one little bit at a time, trying not to make too much noise.

The image is surprisingly vivid   a fusion of blue, green, and a little yellow. The lad's definitely got talent, and I wonder why he threw this away. A forest sits nestled at the end of a green field with speckles of wildflowers here and there. A blue expanse runs adjacent to the field; a brown—possibly wooden—pier stretches out into the water. It's peaceful; I wouldn't have expected he'd draw something like this—maybe it's his happy place. I carefully scrunch it back up and place on the floor.

Figuring I might as well see what's in the sketch pad near the door, I flip open the cover—the same image is on the first page. This time it's not such a happy scene: darker shades, a sense of foreboding coming from a greyer sky, no flowers either. This drawing triggers an unexpected memory, something from a long time ago. Casually I flip to the next page; it's the same image. I flip again, and an identical scene greets me: field, lake, pier, trees. The theme continues, although each picture has a varying mood—some happy and bright, some dark and sad. The darker ones resonate with thoughts in the back of my mind, something from my childhood maybe.

'What the fuck are you doing?' says an angry voice from behind.

I turn around. Andrew stands blurry eyed behind me. I didn't even hear him move.

'Why do you draw the same picture over and over?' I ask, caught off guard.

He knocks the pad out of my hands. 'It's private!' he shouts with a little slur in his voice.

I'm surprised at his outburst because I thought we kind of bonded earlier. I think about what I can say to make this right, but I'm interrupted by a hard but clumsy shove to my chest, the impact knocking me backwards.

'You shouldn't have done that! It wassssn't cool.' Andrew says, slurring again.

I make a 'calm down' gesture. 'Relax—that's the drink talking…'

His breathing deepens like anger is about to erupt from somewhere. He pushes me again, and I fall back towards the mantelpiece above the fireplace, the stonework grinding into me. I tell him in a raised tone not to do it again. I take a step forward to try to steady myself, but he pushes me even harder this time.

'Andrew! Knock it off!' I shout.

He shrugs and pushes me again. 'Why? You ain't gonna do anything about it. You're jusss a little pussy.'

I push him back onto the couch without even thinking. Before I know what's happened, I'm falling against the mantelpiece, knocking framed pictures of our grandparents to the floor. Andrew moves in quickly and sweeps my legs from under me with some clumsy martial arts move, and I fall to the floor, dragging him down with me. He recovers quickly and pushes his palm into my face, forcing my head into the musty carpet. Clawing his fingers into my skin, he tightens his grip even more, and I return the gesture forcefully, locking us into a face-gouging contest we're too stubborn to give up on. He throws a few angry jabs at my chest with his free hand, expelling the air from my body, and it hurts like hell. I react immediately and land an equally clumsy but hard punch right in his eye; he breaks his grip on my face and turns away from me towards the floor.

Andrew doesn't try to retaliate this time; he just holds his head in his hands and breathes deeply.

I remind myself that this lad has just lost his father under tragic circumstances.

'You all right?' I ask, catching my breath.

I feel like I've picked on him even though he started it, and suddenly I wish I didn't just win this fight. I get up and stand over him, extending my hand.

'Truce?' I say.

He lets one hand drop from his face and looks up at me with a red, watery eye. Any sense of victory sinks to the pit of my stomach.

'I'm sorry,' I tell him. 'I didn't want to fight.'

Suddenly I'm folded over after a sharp kick to my balls. I fall on my knees and spit up some brown stuff onto the floor. Andrew retreats backwards, scrambling along the floor, and I give him a look that says I'm going to kill him.

'OK, truce,' he says, like he knows he's gone too far.

I wait a moment for the pain in my lower abdomen to go down a little. This is exactly why drinking is a bad idea. Over a few deep breaths, I let go of my need for revenge.

'All I did was look at your stupid drawings!' I say, still winded.

He doesn't respond; he just looks on, blinking an excess buildup of water from his eyes and rubbing it away with a sniffle. It seems like tears, but I have my suspicions because I doubt he cries easily.

'The pictures were just for me, Will,' he says, in what feels like an attempt to diffuse the situation.

'And how was I to know?' I snap.

'Every night it's the same dream,' he says. 'It's the same place.'

'Just sleep it off, Andrew!' I say dismissively.

He laughs under his breath. 'Sleep?' he says incredulously. 'I keep having the same dream about my father every single night. I wish I could sleep! I haven't slept in weeks! You know what that's like?'

His shoulders sink, and his arms fall down by his side. Maybe his defensive wall is coming down a little. I move next to him and sit on the floor against the couch; it takes the pressure off my stomach, and I feel a little better. Andrew looks down at his intertwined fingers resting on his lap. I feel like I'm in one of those situations in which someone really needs to talk, and it might actually matter what I say next. I'm no good with this stuff.

'So what's this dream about then?' I ask. He looks at me, and I raise my hand as if to stop him from speaking. 'You don't have to tell me if you don't want to.'

He swallows hard. 'Me and him…me and my dad…we're walkin' along this road. It's got to be Ireland because of all the green, and the road is narrow. He takes me by the hand, and we walk through a gate. There's a lake to the left of me and a slope that runs down towards the bank. The grass is tall…'

Andrew looks straight ahead like he's imagining the whole scene play out in front of him.

'It's the scene from your paintings,' I say.

He nods. 'I want my dad to take me down by the pier, but he doesn't move. He shows me a forest in the distance and tells me to go wait for him in there. I look at the trees, and it's all so dark. I don't wanna leave my dad. I don't wanna go into the forest without him, Will.'

'It's just a dream,' I say softly.

'It's more than that. It seems so real to me…' He stops himself from saying any more.

Something becomes clear in my mind, a very old memory.

'That's when you wake up?' I ask.

He shrugs. 'That's when I wake up, and I draw what I remember. I know there's somethin' in that forest my dad wants me to see, but the dream always ends in the same place.' He looks up at me. 'You gonna tell Marie and James? They already think I'm unstable.'

I smile. 'You're not unstable. Besides, that eye is gonna tell its own story in the morning.'

Andrew smiles back. 'I'm gonna say you beat me up!' He hits the palms of his hands off his knees, sniffles back some emotion, and stands up. 'I'm sorry,' he says. He turns and makes for his bedroom. 'See you tomorrow, man.'

'Andrew, I think I know that place.'

He stops and turns around fast.

'I think your dad took us fishing there years ago. You must have been, like, three or four. I think it's the only memory I have of your dad actually.'

'Where is it, Will?' he asks eagerly.

'It's called Loch Jordan, and it's right next to that forest you were talking about. It's sort of a tourist attraction around here.'

Andrew turns and heads for his room again.

I shout after him, 'If you showed James those pictures, he definitely would have known it!'

Andrew returns with a black jacket donned over his white hoodie. 'You gotta take me there right now.'

I can't help laugh as I nod towards the window. 'Look outside, man. It's pitch-black. You see any street lights around here?'

He zips up his jacket. 'Look, I'll owe you one, OK? And believe me…I don't like owing people. We can use the lights on our phones.'

'First thing in the morning, I promise.'

He shrugs 'Please?'

'As soon as it gets bright, we'll—'

'Then give me the directions,' he interrupts. 'Draw a map! I don't care!'

'Andrew…'

'It's the same damn dream every night, Will!' he persists, getting emotional again. 'And every single day, I wake up to the same shit, drawing the same stupid thing over and over.' He holds out his arms. 'They're gonna send me to a fuckin' shrink, Will!'

'Who are?'

'James and Marie,' he says, dropping his arms to his side.

I realise how exhausted he looks, and a pleading in his eyes tells me he's desperate for closure. I can't let him go by himself, so whether I like it or not, I guess this is happening.

4 Feelings

This is all part of the grieving process; I think I read about it somewhere online once. Andrew doesn't want to believe his dad is gone, and the isolation is driving him crazy. I don't want to leave Tara Hill until he's feeling better. I'm not sure where this new sense of responsibility for him comes from, but I feel a little guilty for not wanting to come out here in the first place.

I break out of my little thought bubble and try to get my bearings as we descend Tara Hill.

'It's about two k from here,' I say, shining the light from my phone down to the crossroads.

I think back to that day Andrew's father, Ken, took us fishing, looking for anything unusual or even traumatic in the memory, anything that could make Andrew stress out. Unfortunately most of the memory is a blur of fuzzy colours and blank faces. All I know is Ken took us to the loch once when we were kids, not long after his wife, Elizabeth, died. If I can't remember anything about that day, I wonder how Andrew could.

'You don't remember ever going to the Loch?' I ask.

Andrew shudders from the cold and puts his hands in his pockets. 'I was three; I barely remember things I did last year.'

I look back up the hill; the faint light from the porch shimmers in the distance.

'Gotta be a reason you're OCD'ing like this,' I say.

He shines his phone at me. 'You think this is OCD?' he says sarcastically.

'I think you've latched on to a thought and can't let it go,' I tell him, squinting my eyes.

'You don't believe my dad is tryin to tell me something?'

And there it is—the connection to his dad he wants to believe in.

I blow into the hollows of my hands to warm them up. 'Is that what you think?'

He says nothing. We walk on for a bit in an awkward silence towards the village without meeting a soul; everything in the only street is closed up and tidied away. In fact, this place barely qualifies as a village; a few old cottages, a large stone church and a store all squished together. Some dogs bark in the distance, like they know someone is disturbing the peace of this sleepy place.

Andrew shines his phone at a small store and gas station to our left. 'Is that Marie and James's place?'

I'm surprised he doesn't know, considering he's been here almost a month. James built the store after he became redundant a few years back. He used to work on a production line in the city before Ireland became an expensive place to make things. His store is probably the only business in all of Tara Hill. Petrol pumps sit outside the little store, and metal bars guard the windows, though that hardly seems necessary around here.

'Yeah. How come you haven't come down here yet?'

Andrew waves the torch around the forecourt. 'I haven't left my room in weeks, man.'

A tension suddenly hits my chest as the church steeple comes into my peripheral vision. This is the place I most want to avoid when I come out here. The statue of some winged creature kneels near the entrance to the graveyard, and it makes me think of my own father and how I never visit his grave. I always figured I'd develop a connection to him as the years passed, but nothing ever came. I'm also all too aware of Ken's fresh grave metres away. That's the problem with villages; everything is nearby. The silence between Andrew and me becomes deafening, and we both know our fathers are over there, but neither of us gives any acknowledgment.

After a minute or so, I nudge him to a stop when we reach the crossroads.

'We almost there?' he says.

I look on down the pitch-dark roadway to my left.

'Halfway down that tunnel,' I say, pointing ahead with my phone.

'Tunnel?' he says, confused.

'It's what our cousin, Sarah, used to call it.'

The road quickly narrows into a single lane with thick hedge growth on either side. The trees from both sides of the road arch over us and touch in the middle, blocking out the night sky. I feel their presence smothering me, even though I can't see them. I need to keep the conversation moving just to keep my mind occupied.

'I saw something really weird in the bathroom earlier today,' I tell Andrew.

He grunts. 'Too easy.'

'Seriously,' I say. 'I looked in the mirror above the sink.'

He stops in his tracks in front of an old metal gate. 'What was it?'

I can barely make out the shadowed outline of his face, but his tone tells me I've hit a nerve. He speaks again before I can reply.

'Same thing happened to me the day of my dad's funeral. I saw the dream—the whole thing—play out in the reflection in the mirror.'

What he says takes a moment for me to digest, and I wonder if this is some kind of weird joke.

'What did you see, Will?' he persists.

Branches creak above our heads as I point my phone directly at his face. 'Why did you bring me out here? Answer me honestly.'

He quickly moves my phone aside. 'I asked you what you saw in the mirror!'

'Myself!' I snap. 'I saw myself, but I was a little older, and I looked sick. I feel like there's stuff you're not telling me!'

He shrugs. 'I only know as much as you do! Think about it—it's my dad…he's trying to tell us something, Will.'

I'm starting to think Andrew somehow made this whole thing happen to get some sort of closure surrounding his dad's death. I have no idea where all this is going but he gets full marks for creativity.

He nods towards the gate behind me. 'This looks just like the place.'

He's right—this is the place Ken took us to years ago, but maybe he already knew that.

'There's nothing in there, Andrew. It's just a field and a lake,' I say bluntly.

'And a forest!' he snaps. 'That's where we gotta go. That's the place I can't reach in my dream.'

'Why now? Why not tomorrow?'

He exhales through his nose like I'm starting to piss him off again. 'I told you already. I'm not going through another night of that shit, Will.' He brushes past me and makes for the gate. 'I'm done with sleepless nights.'

He climbs the gate, jumps down to the other side, and walks into the darkness waving his phone in front of him. I'm torn between doing nothing and giving him the benefit of the doubt that he knows as much about this whole thing as I do.

'I don't know what to do!' I shout after him.

Andrew makes a half turn. 'Just wait for me here. I won't be long,' he shouts back.

I try to connect the dots between our mutual apparitions in the bathroom and Andrew's recurring dream. I can't find any pattern, and none of this makes sense. Right now, however, I have to believe there's some logical explanation for all this, because the thought of

Ken speaking to us from beyond the grave is freaking me out. I finally jump the gate and catch up beside Andrew.

'You think I'm crazy, don't you?' he says.

He has a slight limp that wasn't there earlier. 'The thought crossed my mind. Something up with your foot?'

'Weak ankle. Not supposed to land hard on it.'

We move until the rustling of leaves tells us we're approaching the forest. I can just about see a dense clustering of trees ahead.

'It's like I'm having the dream again, but I'm awake this time,' he says, a little out of breath, like he's not used to walking fast.

'That must be kind of surreal,' I say trying, to diffuse the tension I'm feeling.

He stops and stares dead ahead. 'What do you see when you look down there?'

I stop and focus in as best I can along the semi-lit path in front of us. 'Same as you. Some kind of forest.'

'It's more than that,' he replies.

Andrew's words do nothing to settle my nerves, and the last thing I want to do right now is go into that dark place and find out if his feeling is right or wrong. I just don't have the junk, but here it is, on the imaginary weighing scale again: I'd rather have stayed at the cottage and finished off the Scotch.

I try to find a logical reason why Andrew and I both experienced weird visions in the same bathroom mirror. Stranger still is how he was able to draw pictures of this place even though he allegedly doesn't remember coming here when he was a child.

He puts his arm around me for support. The move takes me by surprise, but he doesn't notice my nervousness.

'I'm gonna put an end to this once and for all,' he says.

He edges forward, but I stay still; he immediately senses my hesitation.

A flick of his eyes checks me up and down. 'We cool?'

I swallow hard. 'Yeah,' I say unconvincingly, and grow a bigger pair. Andrew's walk is reduced to a hobbling as we crunch over the frozen grass, the only thing making any sound. I can't help feel like I'm marching into some kind of ambushed doom, but I don't know how to stop myself.

A chorus of branches creak overhead as we find ourselves metres away from the forest, each tree in a strange unison with the next. It's like we're standing on the edge of Tara Hill, bordering another place. The cold breeze stops for a moment, and I hear something else—a faint humming in the distance. I follow Andrew's light-trail to a silhouette partially obscured behind the trees; it looks like it doesn't belong here.

We push our way deeper through the trees, and the silhouette takes shape. Sharp metal edges cut their way out of the darkness as our phone lights reflect off the shiny metallic surface; this thing definitely isn't part of nature.

Andrew and I quickly reach a clearing in front of a large container-like structure about three metres tall and fifteen metres or so wide. The metal has a smooth polished finish, like chrome, and looks clean and brand-new, with no signs of rust or damage from the elements. Something like an electrical current buzzes from beneath the surface and tells me this thing shouldn't be messed with. The fact that this structure is here at all only confirms Andrew's intuition that something was down here in the first place. Again there's no logic to this, and I need a logical explanation. Thoughts creep into the back of my mind that Ken is actually trying to tell his son something; these thoughts make me want to leave.

Andrew moves forward and reaches out.

I grab his arm 'Don't! We don't know what this is.'

He shakes off my hand and places his palm on the surface. 'Feels like static on an old TV screen.'

The panel suddenly comes alive. In white lettering against a gloomy red background, it displays:

TACTICAL UNIT LANDER

[DEPLOY]

Andrew shines his phone at the screen; the beam flickers momentarily then goes out. A part of me wants to forget this thing exists.

'This screen wasn't here a second ago, right?' he says.

I give it the once-over. 'No, it wasn't,' I say nervously.

The red glow from the screen engulfs one side of his face. 'You think this belongs to my dad?'

He's looking for answers I can't give him, but whatever it is—his dead father or something else—seems to have led him right to it.

He raises his arm with an extended finger.

I lower his arm immediately. 'Seriously. We don't know what this does. We should go!'

He ignores me, and before I can do anything, he touches 'Deploy' on the screen. It immediately switches off, leaving us in darkness again. I can't believe he just did that.

The buzzing from within the structure turns to a higher pitch, like something inside the container is about to overload. Andrew takes a step back. 'Okay. Maybe that was a mistake.'

The screen suddenly lights up with a high-definition aerial shot of the forest shrouded in a night-vision green. The image is overlaid with a fine yellow grid, dividing it into about fifty little squares; a red dot pulses impatiently in the centre, as if it's counting, counting down…

'It's a map of here,' he says.

The low buzzing sound turns into a rapid beep, and a young female voice says, 'Auto-deploy initiated' in an American accent. The same words flash in red on the display.

I know we should go, but I'm practically hypnotized by the red flashing text. Although my brain says, *Run!* my body does nothing. Andrew nudges my shoulder to get my attention. He looks upwards and says something, but there's no sound coming from his mouth. A sudden flash of light a million times stronger than lightning engulfs everything around us and freezes Andrew's image in my brain like a picture negative. Ringing in my ears forces me to my knees—at least I think I'm on my knees; I don't really know what position I'm in. I can't see or hear anything.

5 Revelation

My eyes open to find Andrew standing over me. His voice breaks through the ringing. 'Talk to me!' he says with wide-eyed concern.

As I slowly sit up, the sudden rush of blood from my head makes me dizzy. The forest comes back into focus, but the structure we saw moments ago somehow has doubled in size, as if it ate up all the trees around it.

An opening directly in front of us leads into a narrow but bright corridor; its brilliant white walls project a path to its perimeter.

Andrew helps me up. 'C'mon. We gotta check this out.'

Despite my attempt to pull him back, he steps inside the corridor. Through squinting eyes, he looks all around then turns his back to me, his black jacket contrasting with the intensity of light around him. 'There's nothing in here,' he says.

Branches break from somewhere behind me, triggering a defensive urge that makes me quickly step into the corridor after him. I turn around and look into the forest, but nothing stirs on the outside, and everything is perfectly still among the frozen trees. In fact they don't even sway, as if their leaves have been suspended in a vacuum.

A little triangular button catches my attention near the doorway, slowly pulsating amid a soft blue light.

'What do you think it does?' asks Andrew over my shoulder.

I think it probably closes the door, but I don't press it. 'We should go, come back tomorrow,' I say.

'After you then,' says Andrew after a moment.

I step out again into the cold air and realise I didn't even notice the chill inside the corridor. I blow into the hollows of my hands again to keep warm. 'Someone has to know about this place,' I say, thinking out loud.

'See you soon, Will.'

I turn around, and everything is dark, the doorway inexplicably replaced with a solid metal panel. Looks like Andrew pressed the stupid button! I kick the bottom of the exterior in frustration and curse him in my head. Another branch breaks from somewhere behind. I close my eyes tightly, feeling exposed and vulnerable. I don't dare turn around because I keep imagining awful things right behind me, and I can even feel their imaginary presence. I hate the countryside; I hate everything about it: the remoteness, stillness, lack of noise, lack of people. I want the comfort of my own bedroom in Limerick city.

Light penetrates through my eyelids, and I quickly snap them open again. The door has reopened, but the corridor is empty. I step inside and debate whether to press the button. I look to the darkness of the outside in all its weird stillness. Another branch breaks, and I lose my nerve. I press the damn triangular button.

The outside is immediately gone, as is the white light of the corridor. I yell out as my stomach heaves with a sudden free-falling sensation, and I try reach out, but there are no walls to grab on to. I'm in a black, empty limbo. A faint green light closes in quickly from beneath my feet until I'm surrounded entirely by its glow. My yell echoes against the walls of what appears to be a cavern beneath the surface of the forest and I'm suddenly standing in the centre of a large circular platform. I compose myself a little, and everything returns to silence.

'Weird, isn't it?' echoes Andrew's voice from behind.

Startled, I turn around. 'Very! What is this place?'

'It must be my father's.'

I throw a glance around me, and it's as if we're standing on an island in the middle of this dark cavern. I can just make out the rocky ceiling a few metres above us, and by the looks of it, we're about ten metres below ground. There's no sign of the bright corridor or anything that may have been used to get us down here, and the place is empty, apart from this strange platform. I test the consistency of the floor with a little kick, and it looks to be made of hard glass. My little kick seems to trigger a wave of green light to pass over our bodies, as if the platform is scanning us.

Some flicker of blue catches in my peripheral vision.

Andrew turns around and walks towards what look like two large display screens floating in mid-air. The image of a circle is displayed on both screens, with its circumference divided into four coloured segments: green, orange, red, and white.

When we get closer, I realise the screens appear to be made up entirely of light, with no mounting fixtures or frames. They distort briefly when I pass my hand through, sending an odd tingling sensation to my elbow.

'If your father was involved with this, he was into some interesting tech,' I say.

'He used to freelance with a buddy a' his,' says Andrew. 'They did some work for the military. I guess this place could be something to do with that.'

He sounds a little unsure of himself, like he's trying to piece all this together. This is news to me, but I never really knew what my uncle Ken worked at.

'If this place is military, then we should probably leave,' I say.

Andrew throws me a look. 'My dad wanted us to find this place. Isn't it obvious after everything that's happened tonight?'

I shrug. 'That's the problem; I don't know *what's* just happened tonight! Look, we still don't know the connection between—'

'My dad brought us here!' he interrupts. 'Think about it: you came here for a reason, to help me find whatever this is.'

'That's harder for me to accept than it is for you.' I look around me. 'Any idea how we can get out of here?'

Andrew makes a fist and holds it out in front of him. 'Rock, paper, scissors?'

'What?'

'What colour should I press?' he says, looking at the screen.

'None of them!' I exclaim.

Andrew flicks his eyebrows. 'How about…red?'

'Not red!' I say, pointing at the screen. 'Never press the red button on anything!'

He smiles and touches the green segment of the circle.

The circle rotates fast then disappears. It seems to be an interface of some kind.

The following appears across the top of the screen:

[MATERIALISATION LIBRARY]

I once read that military tech is light-years ahead of anything in the civilian domain. Disappearing doors that morph into solid walls and crystal clear screens made entirely from light give some credibility to Andrew's idea this is all part of some military operation.

'Materialisation Library. Military books or something?' says Andrew.

Five columns of alphanumeric codes appear underneath the following subheading:

[NEUROTACTICAL]

The first code in the first column reads, 'GX-100' and goes all the way down to 'GX-150.' The next column starts with HX-1 and goes to HX-7; the third column, in the middle, has just three codes: AR-1 to AR-3.

'Classified files maybe?' says Andrew.

'May-be,' I say, moving a little closer. 'But why would your dad want us to see them?'

Andrew raises his right hand as if to touch the GX-100 code.

I quickly intercept and move his hand away. 'As far as I remember,' I say in a pseudo calmness, 'our grandfather owned a lot of the land around the Loch. So this place could be on our family's land. So how about we find a way out of here, go home, talk to Marie and James, and find out what they know?'

Andrew shakes his head. 'I don't think so. What if my dad didn't want Marie and James to know about this place? If James knew anything, he could have brought me here instead of watching me go crazy in my room for the past month. You said yourself James would have recognized the forest from my drawings. Marie and James don't know anything, Will, and you know it!'

I think it over. Unfortunately he's right, but I'm still anxious to leave.

Andrew gestures with a flick of his head towards something on the floor behind us. 'Look, that part of the platform is a lighter shade of green. It ascended towards the ceiling right before you followed me down here. It's probably our ticket back to the surface. In any case we can figure it out later.'

'This is still a bad idea.' I say.

'Life is full of bad ideas.'

He touches the GX-100 code. The columns quickly clear away, revealing a detailed 3D graphic of a handgun with labels referencing different parts of the weapon. The language in the labels is strange, nothing I can read or recognize. Andrew wastes no time in pressing a pulsing blue dot underneath the weapon, causing a perfectly straight beam of orange light to shoot upwards behind the screens, hitting the rocky cavern ceiling. The centre of the beam expands briefly then rapidly disperses again. A solid object is left behind, slowly rotating on its horizontal axis in mid-air.

'That's messed up!' Andrew whispers.

He slowly circles around the object, which is clearly the GX-100 weapon we just saw on his screen. Its glossy surface reflects the green light of the platform, and it looks pristine, like it just came out of a weapons-factory production line. The weapon is similar to a handgun, with a charcoal-grey one-inch barrel and a padded grip that looks like rubber. A small dark-blue display, back mounted on the rear of the weapon, shows some numbers I have no idea about.

Andrew takes the weapon in his hand. 'Assigned,' he says, reading from the mounted display. A white projectile shoots forward and dissipates into the darkness of the cavern, hitting the rocky walls with a loud snap. He looks at me and shrugs as if apologising.

'I take it your dad designed weapons for the military?'

'Honestly, man,' he says, 'I don't know what my dad did. I drew pictures, and he liked to do math.'

The closest thing I can compare this to is 3-D printing. When our school organised a trip to the university last year, they took us to this cool lab the engineering majors use to design simple shapes and tools on a computer then print them out in a plastic resin using a special printer. The printers I'd seen, though, were pretty slow and could only make simple objects, nothing complex with moving parts. The computer in this place just made an entire weapon out of light in less than a second. I can see why the military would want this.

When I examine the weapon, the mounted display changes from blue to red and tells me I'm 'unauthorised.' I guess it binds to the handprint of whoever gets assigned to it.

After touching on a few more random codes, it appears we've stumbled into a vast weapons-making machine with enough firepower to take out a small country. I can't believe this place has been left here unguarded.

Andrew touches the code AR-1, which is one of only three codes in the middle column. A schematic of an armour suit rotates on the screen, with labels of text in the same strange language I can't understand. Next to the image is a semi-circular, visor-like object that reminds me of the augmented-reality visors I've seen advertised on TV.

I'm surprised to see two names appear beneath the armour schematic:

OFFICER WILLIAM OAKLEY, GRADE 5

OFFICER ANDREW OAKLEY, GRADE 5

This is odd—really odd—and I don't like it when the computer I'm using knows more about me than I know about it.

'Looks like my dad put me in the computer,' says Andrew, 'but why would he put you in here too?'

He asks me that question like I should know the answer.

'That's not even my legal name,' I say.

'Whaddya mean?'

'My mam never married my dad, so legally my name is William Anderson, not William Oakley. I'm surprised your father didn't know that.'

'*Mono-tro-pus, Om-nis,*' says Andrew, as he muddles his way through the strange text. 'My dad hadn't seen you in years, though. Maybe he forgot. You got any idea what this means?'

'I'm no good with languages,' I say, 'but if we can identify the language, we might be able to—'

Suddenly my body tingles from head to toe; I feel like I've just been jabbed with an electric current. A white glow momentarily consumes my body then leaves behind a rigid, black, vinyl-like material that covers my skin. My temples tighten with a strange pressure, and everything in the room is now in perfect clarity, as if my vision has been upgraded somehow—the colours are more vibrant; the text on the screen is clear and sharp. I feel around my eyes and find a smooth plastic housing.

Andrew is also covered from head to toe in the black armour suit. It seems to be in one complete piece, like a jumpsuit but with a tighter fit. The collar is high and extends the length of his neck to the base of his chin. His eyes look back at me with a bright shade of yellow behind the visor that's wrapped around them.

'So that's what that does,' he says, examining his outstretched arm.

The computer somehow morphed the armour suit from our screen straight onto our bodies with a perfect fit.

'There isn't a 3-D printer in the world that can do this,' I say.

Andrew looks up at me. 'Your eyes are yellow.'

I nod. 'You too.'

Something on the shoulder of his armour catches my eye. I raise his arm a little and turn what looks like an insignia towards me: two small spheres sit inside a grey-filled circle—one black and one white. The spheres look like atoms ripping apart from each other with streams of blue and green energy clinging between them. It's a symbol that wouldn't look out of place on an astronaut's space suit. Some kind of engraving lies underneath:

INTER ANGELIS ET PUERIS, FIDELES INVENIAMUR

'You think this suit would protect me against that gun?' Andrew asks.

I roll my eyes at him. 'We're not finding out!'

I turn and look at my screen, my curiosity wanting to interact with it. I press the red segment, ignoring my earlier advice to Andrew to avoid anything red:

[G-COMPILER]

ADITUS NEGETUR

(LUKA GUDJOHNSEN)

That's as far as I get on the red screen because there are no further options.

'Gudjohnsen, sounds Scandinavian,' says Andrew over my shoulder.

I move my attention to the white segment and try to make sense of the unreadable language and submenus.

'I remember a lad called Gudjohnsen,' I say. 'He used to play in the English premiership. I think he was Icelandic.'

'The buddy my dad used to freelance with lives in Iceland,' says Andrew. 'I can't remember his name, but James might.'

I nod. 'First thing in the morning then…'

I prod around the screen, trying to figure out exactly what's selectable and what isn't.

'I bet this won't hurt one little bit,' says Andrew.

I turn to find him aiming the GX at my leg. Before I can yell at him, a white projectile hits me in the inner thigh just below the balls. A delayed impact stings my skin, like getting hit by a paintball at close range. I 'uh' through the brief pain and cover the spot where it hit with my hand then shift my weight to my other leg.

'Not cool!' I groan, annoyed.

'I know. Hold on,' he says, turning the weapon towards his chest then pulling the trigger. He groans as his body jolts from the impact. Then he presses the trigger again, as if he enjoys it. My cousin clearly has issues.

'I'm sure that thing isn't a toy,' I say, making a painful effort to remain upright.

'Maybe it is a toy,' Andrew mumbles, examining the weapon again.

'I doubt that.' I groan again and turn my attention back to the garbled text. The information on the white screen is organized neatly, but it's not one bit readable. I press some text near the top left of the screen, and a long list of names appears—my name and Andrew's are first on the list.

The first name we find after our own is 'Gudjohnsen, Luka: second executive officer,' the lad whose name appeared on the G-Compiler screen.

'Keiko, Hiro: systems officer, grade one…Beech, Chris: tactical officer, grade one… Casey, Sam: AI lead officer, grade one…Must be two or three hundred people on here,' Andrew says, muttering his way through the rest of the list.

He impatiently touches his own name, and a profile appears, complete with a picture that looks like it was taken when the scanning beam passed over him. I can't but feel paranoid, as if eyes are watching me from somewhere in the room.

Andrew mumbles through the odd text of his profile:

18:37:40 SYNAPTIC GRAFT FROM OFFSET 15X10FF—SUCCESS

00:05:00 SYNAPTIC GRAFT FROM OFFSET 16X10FF—SUCCESS

01:30:14 TALOCRURAL JOINT REASSEMBLY—SUCCESS

EOF

He squints at the screen. 'What the heck is this?'

I put my paranoia to the side and take a look at the text.

'A graft…isn't that like a transplant or when something is put on top of something else? Like a skin graft?'

'I think so, and I remember hearing about synapses before,' says Andrew. 'Something to do with the brain isn't it?'

'Or memory maybe?' I suggest.

Andrew stares at the screen, compulsively tutting, like he's thinking something over.

'Will,' he says after a moment, 'what if we didn't see those visions in the mirror? What if we just thought we saw them?' He slides his finger down the list of events and taps on the first line. 'See the time? 18:37—that could've been when I saw my dream in the mirror play out.' He moves is finger to the next line. 'And maybe it was midnight when I started to draw, just after I had my first reoccurring dream.'

It isn't a bad theory: two memory grafts—the first one forces him to see the vision in the bathroom mirror, and the second makes him dream it over and over.

'Do those times add up?' I ask. 'I mean, do they match what actually happened to you that night?'

He shrugs. 'The day of the funeral is mostly a blur.'

I scan my brain for a link between the first two lines of Andrew's profile and the third—talocrural joint; that's got to be a body part, a limb. Something was reassembled, but what? I take out my phone and do a quick search; the reception should be awful underground, but it works like normal. A few seconds later, I have a definition of 'talocrural.'

'How's your ankle?' I ask.

His mouth opens, but he then hesitates and looks down at his foot. 'I haven't felt any pain since I came down here.'

'The time,' I say. 'Half past one in the morning—that's about when we arrived here. If this thing fixed your ankle, then we're way beyond 3-D printing.'

Taking over, Andrew eagerly navigates back to the list of names—which I suspect is some kind of crew manifesto and selects mine. I instantly relive my earlier moment, as the face I saw in the mirror comes flooding back with its hardened expression and scar line running down the cheek. It's like someone has stolen my body and decided to damage it. Someone obviously wanted to get our attention, and whoever it is has succeeded in getting mine. I've held on to the belief that finding this place was the latest in a chain of unrelated coincidences. But there's obviously a connection between them all, and I'd be pretty naïve if I thought otherwise. Everything that's happened tonight feels eerily planned by something or someone, and I don't like it one bit.

Andrew squints and looks closer at the screen. 'It's you, but it's not you.'

'I knew I didn't hallucinate it,' I say, thinking out loud. 'That's what I saw yesterday.'

I read the one event listed:

21:10:00 SYNAPTIC GRAFT FROM OFFSET 15X11FF—SUCCESS

If Andrew is right, then a memory somehow was implanted in each of us when we first arrived at Tara Hill. In Andrew's case, something else was implanted hours later that caused him to draw the memory compulsively, but in my case there were no further implants, no further memories, and no repairs to any of my body parts.

Since Ken was already dead when these memories were allegedly implanted, I reason that these events could have been triggered by some kind of automated computer program. But this still brings us no closer to figuring out why we were brought here in the first place. The scope of this technology surprises me, even for something in the military domain. This is one powerful field bunker; it not only can resupply units but also can heal them. This thing has to be worth trillions or whatever number comes after that.

Next we move on to the profile of Luka Gudjohnsen: a blond twenty-one-year-old stares back at us in a cold, almost dead manner, as if his picture were taken in a morgue. There's some sadness in his expression I can't put my finger on.

Andrew calls up the next profile and the next, looking for anything familiar. We spend an hour browsing through the rest of the crew manifesto, and a pattern becomes blatantly obvious: none of the crew are much older than maybe twenty-five, and all of them, except for us, Luka Gudjohnsen, Hiro Keiko, Chris Beech, and Sam Casey, are marked as deceased.

Tactical-unit lander—that's the name I remember from the panel on the outside of the structure. I guess that's what this place is: some kind of tactical-bunker thing, a resupply centre and field hospital for the military.

Andrew and I spend more than four hours building weapons and trying them out. With a little trial and error, I'm able to determine a rough classification for the different codes: the HX codes are for mounted weapons that get fixed onto the heaviest of the armour suits, the AR-3. I say 'heaviest' because they're really heavy to wear, and it's a chore to move around with the suit on. Exploring the entire list of weapon codes eventually brings us the IX range—these are drone units, like those little crafts I've seen people flying on YouTube. The drones are flat, disc like devices about the size of a car wheel that have some kind of antigravity property that allows them to float in mid-air.

Unlike other drones, though, they don't use propellers to move; instead they use three beams of blue light on the underside to silently keep them in position. No moving parts! Stranger still, the drones are controlled with a visor, a kind of neural interface that interprets thoughts as commands. I was able to move the drone around the cavern and fire off a few shots just by thinking about where I wanted it to go. Playing around with this stuff is like being at our own private technology exhibition. Now I know what to expect over the next ten or twenty years.

At sunrise Andrew and I head back to the surface using the part of the green platform that looked a little different. Andrew was right about it being our ticket home. We need to get back because James gets up early for work, and it's probably better we're home before he goes snooping around the cottage.

The walk home is a lot less mysterious than the walk to get here, although the forest around the tactical-unit lander—or TUL— still emits an eerie stillness around the structure. All the mystery of the field, the narrow tunnelled road, and the church are cast away by the dawn. Those surroundings are friendly to me now; the tunnel of trees isn't claustrophobic, and the graveyard by the church is peaceful.

Around 6:00 a.m. I fall into bed, and my head races with images of everything I've seen. I think about the dead crew and what might have killed them. I know I definitely won't sleep.

6 The Loch

A grinding vibration drills into the side of my head.

I open my eyes to flowery, sun-filled curtains. I fumble for my phone on the small bedside cabinet:

Incoming Call

Uncle James

It's ten thirty. I answer the phone, my voice barely sounding out 'Hello.'

'Good morning, William! Did you sleep well? We have some breakfast here for ye!' says James in one big, long sentence that takes a few seconds for my sleepy brain to process.

I make some weary form of acknowledgment.

'Drag that cousin of yours out of his bed and come down to the kitchen,' he continues.

I hang up and make for Andrew's room, still wearing yesterday's clothes, with little bits of twigs clinging to my hoodie. An open red suitcase almost jams the door when I push it in. T-shirts and socks are thrown everywhere; a fairly untouched-looking easel sits at the far side of the room, facing the window over Andrew's bed. Probably a Christmas present from James and Marie. His sock-covered foot hangs over the side of the bed, and he obviously hasn't heard me come in, because his breathing follows the same sleep-driven rhythm. I wedge my way between the built-in wardrobe and his double bed. A mountain of clothes covers most of his greasy hair, which is strewn over his face. My foot hits something hard on the floor, and I look down to find the empty bottle of Scotch. Maybe it's not the same one...

'Andrew,' I say softly, and nudge his shoulder.

One brown eye opens wide and peers out from under his hair. I brace myself for an outburst about my having invaded his privacy, but his eyes relax.

'Time's it?' he slurs.

'Half ten. James and Marie—'

'Fuck no...' And the rest of the sentence becomes a long, tired mumble. He sighs then sits up, throwing back the covers to reveal his clothes from last night. A dark-coloured stain, like spilled liquid, trails down his white hoodie. He rubs his eyes, moans in pain, then takes his hand away from his face quickly.

'Oh, man look at that thing,' I say, laughing out my words.

Andrew looks up at me with a dark-yellow bruise around his eye. 'It really fuckin stings, man!' he groans.

I laugh. 'Yes, it's a bit of an eyesore, all right.'

He exhales a tired grunt, and a faint smell of Scotch breath hits me.

'Tell me you didn't finish that off this morning?' I ask, nodding towards the empty bottle on the floor.

'Takes the edge off the day.' He groans.

I can't turn my head quickly enough from the stench of his breath. 'Go brush your teeth or something,' I tell him, and make for the door.

I can't believe Andrew finished the bottle at six in the morning, although part of me is a little annoyed he finished it without me and I can't explain why.

'Will!' he says in a suddenly upbeat tone. 'I didn't dream about anything last night!'

I'm happy for him, though I doubt it's just a coincidence. The dreams probably switched off when we checked in at the TUL. I get the feeling something is monitoring us—maybe some kind of computer program, perhaps the same one that gave us those weird reflections in the mirror. I can't help wonder what's next on its list of things to do.

After freshening up a little and washing the sleep from our eyes, we go to the house and sit across from James and Marie at the kitchen table. The ticking clock on the wall is the only sound filling up a very awkward silence. The pancakes Marie has made—no doubt for Andrew's benefit—smell so good, but she doesn't get them from the cooker or offer us any. She sits in a chair next to her husband, tapping her fingers on the wooden table, with a tea towel thrown over her shoulder, her suspicious eyes darting from Andrew to me and back again.

Her husband's expression is much different. James is barely able to keep his face straight. I catch his eye, and he throws me a wink, as if he's subtly congratulating me on punching Andrew in the face.

Andrew slides a yellow plastic bottle towards him. 'I walked into a door. Is this maple syrup?' he asks in an awkward attempt to change the subject.

Marie nods judgementally in my direction. 'Were ye fighting, William?'

'I've been meaning to fix that kitchen door now for a while,' James interrupts, then takes a sip of tea from his 'Best Dad in the World' cup. 'Did you find it a bit sticky when you tried to open it, William?' he continues.

I raise my eyebrows and nod like a simpleton. 'Um, yeah, uh, very sticky.'

Marie sighs and scrapes her chair along the tile floor then moves to the cooker.

James coughs. 'Now, lads, I thought we might take a trip down to the lake for a spot of fishing. How does that sound?'

His timing is a little unfortunate. If he had taken Andrew back there sooner, it might have saved my cousin a whole load of sleepless nights.

'We kinda got plans...right, Will?' says Andrew.

Marie carefully places two pancakes on Andrew's plate. 'Your plans can wait.' She throws a glance at her husband. 'James has taken the afternoon off especially.'

James smiles. 'Great day for it too…first bit of sun we've had in months.'

I remember their daughter, Sarah, once telling me there were absolutely no fish in the loch. Maybe James just wants to bond or something.

Andrew doesn't persist with Marie about our plans, which surprises me a little. I guess he doesn't want to argue; probably learned from experience. He and I make some small talk with our aunt and uncle until both our plates are cleared.

✦✦✦

After a short drive to the loch in James's red van, the three of us climb into a small wooden boat James has tied to one of the piers. The loch is peaceful and nestled in a golden reflection of the sun. We seem to have the whole place to ourselves and not surprisingly because early January is probably off-season with tourists and locals around these parts. With some effort, James rows out a little into the calm water, but he looks like he hasn't done this in a while because his face is all red and he's a little out of breath. He seems happy to be here, though, and he hums an upbeat tune while he locks the oars into place. Then he carefully shows Andrew how to attach the bait to the end of the fishing hook while Andrew pretends to be interested.

'For years me and yer fathers used to come here during the summer.' He stops briefly to break from his baiting and gives a quick glance at Andrew. 'We never did manage to catch anything, though.'

He hands Andrew the baited fishing rod then starts work on mine, taking a little plastic worm from his fishing box. 'We should stop by the butcher's on the way home, lads, if we don't catch anything.' he says. 'Marie will be dumbfounded!'

I laugh out of politeness.

'So who won the fight anyway?' he asks.

'We called a truce in the end,' I tell him.

'Hmm,' says James, handing me my fishing rod. He then takes a breath like he's about to make a little speech. 'I thought we might take a trip into Limerick later. You haven't been to the city yet, Andrew, have you?'

'No, not yet,' says Andrew, who's focused on applying another artificial worm to the end of his hook. 'We could go to the mall or somethin', I guess.'

'Good man,' says James, a little nervously, and clears his throat. 'Now me and Marie thought you might like to drop in and have a chat with Father Manning at the Franciscan church.'

Andrew looks up at James with a stare that could kill him. 'What?' he snaps.

James puts up a hand. 'It would only be for a half hour. He's a bereavement councillor, and we were told he's very good.'

Andrew throws the rod to the floor of the little boat. 'You fuckin' serious?' he says, in an angry, high-pitched tone.

'Andrew,' says James calmly. 'It might be a good idea to talk to someone is all I'm saying.'

Andrew gives a matter-of-fact gesture. 'Will is here now! I don't need to see some stupid shrink!'

I feel the need to say something to ease the tension a little, and it's obvious James doesn't want this confrontation. I figure seeing the councillor was probably Marie's idea.

'He'll be fine, James, really. We've got a whole week planned.' I glance at Andrew. 'Don't we?'

'Lads,' says James, calmly looking over the loch, 'I told Marie to wait and see...how things worked out but...' He looks over the both of us. 'But arriving down to breakfast this morning with a black eye and the smell of drink off ye didn't exactly do either of ye any good. I thought you didn't drink, William?'

My face flushes with embarrassment. James must think I'm pretty two-faced or just a pushover.

'It's not how it looks, James,' says Andrew. 'Just tell Marie I'm gonna be fine and to wait and—'

'I understand that boys will be boys,' he interrupts, 'but you're booked for an appointment this afternoon.'

Andrew points to James. 'I'm not talking to some priest, man. Just leave me alone.'

James removes his tweed cap, wipes his balding forehead, then puts the cap back on. 'You'll go with him, won't you, William?'

I feel like I'm in a difficult position, and I know I have to agree with him. 'Yes,' I tell him. 'I'll go.'

'Good man,' James says, and casts out his line. 'Ah, it'll be grand, Andrew. He's just there to listen…that's all. You don't have to say anything if you don't want to.'

Andrew shakes his head dismissively.

A family of ducks swims by in a V shape, quacking away to themselves and providing a welcome distraction.

'James?' I say.

'Hmmm?'

'Did Ken ever say anything about a military contract he was working on?'

James recasts his line. 'A military contract?' he says, clearly surprised. 'Not that I remember. I know he used to go to Iceland from time to time. Ah, there was a good pal of his up there…What was his name now…?' He looks out over the loch as if the answer is out there somewhere. 'Ah, yes, Alan…Alan Dalton. As far as I know, Alan worked in a military base there, but I don't know if Ken ever did.'

'But he used to freelance with Alan sometimes, right?' asks Andrew.

'That's right,' says James. 'I didn't see Alan at the funeral. He mustn't have been able to get off work.'

Now Andrew and I have a name, something we can work with. Maybe this Alan person can tell us more about Ken's research and what we're supposed to do with it.

7 The Church

I get the feeling Andrew's pride is a little bruised from the whole bereavement-councillor thing, but after a month of him behaving the way he did, I can't really blame James and Marie for sending him. If I were in Andrew's shoes, I think my pride would be bruised too, and I definitely wouldn't want anyone to know I was going. Maybe it's a macho-male thing—not being able to admit something is wrong when we need help. On the other hand, I think finding the TUL has done more for Andrew than any therapy session could. This is just very bad timing.

Right after returning to James and Marie's house from the loch, we're on the road again. Andrew is pretty quiet during the entire journey to Limerick City and gazes out the window from the backseat of Marie's small car. One of those little pine-tree-shaped air fresheners dangles from the rear-view mirror, and I catch Marie's eyes in the reflection. She knows well that I was the one who gave Andrew the black eye. I smile at her sheepishly and look away.

After a half hour of driving, we arrive along the banks of the river Shannon on the outskirts of Limerick. Small groups of teens skateboard along the promenade while a few well-to-do people sip coffee in the café smoking zones across the street. Before long, we pull up outside the Franciscan church for Andrew's appointment. I grew up just across the river, not far from here, and sometimes I come to this church after school. Not because I'm a devout Christian or anything—it's just more of a spiritual insurance policy I take out at exam time. Maybe it's more of a ritual than anything else: putting the money in the coin slot at the altar, kneeling, asking for a favour, then heading home, though, if I admit it, I do like the feeling of Zen in the place.

We get out of the car and wave Marie off before the stalled line of traffic behind her gets any longer. She's going to busy herself in the shops for a while.

'This place looks pretty old,' says Andrew, looking over the four large stone pillars that support the roof overshadowing the entrance.

The building is the biggest church in the city by far, seven-storeys high and extending all the way back about two-hundred metres in one large grey block to the river behind it. The absence of any windows on the front-facing part only reinforces its dominance. Four weather-beaten stone angels sit on each corner of the roof, holding spears and shields and looking downward towards the passing cars in the busy street as if judging them. A large red wooden door guards the entrance.

I push it open using two hands to counteract the weight.

'The church is about three-hundred years old,' I say. 'Gran used to bring me here a lot actually.'

We're met by the smell of burning incense, which instantly makes me aware this is a holy place and brings the memories of taking school exams last summer right back to me.

Rows of varnished wooden pews sit on both sides of a central aisle. Large wooden framed holy pictures depicting scenes from the crucifixion adorn the yellow wall on my right. Along the left are pictures of saints displayed in alcoves that are decorated with a multitude of flowers and electric candles flickering as if they were real.

Halfway up the aisle, the pews break into narrow pathways that lead left and right towards oak confession boxes. A lad in a brown hoodie sits next to one of them with his hood disrespectfully raised over his head. Years of going to mass on a Sunday taught me something about church etiquette, and leaving my hood up or a hat on or picking your nose was usually enough to earn a scowling look from my grandmother. Gran took me most places on weekends while my mother was putting herself through medical school.

Andrew and I walk towards the altar as the high-pitched singing of a school-choir echoes out. The choir sits down and leafs through their music sheets while a posh looking middle-aged lady calls out the title of the next hymn. My eyes drift to an open tabernacle behind a large flat granite table with the bible open in the centre, a red-cloth bookmark keeping the page. I try to remember the last time I attended a full Mass. I didn't keep going after Gran died, even though I told her I would. I've forgotten the smells and how the world outside becomes a zillion miles away in here.

We stop near the altar, and Andrew's tension is evident by his rigid shoulders and clenched fists. I suspect this is the last place the poor lad wants to be because it's probably digging up memories of his father's funeral.

He looks at me with wide brown eyes and takes a breath.

'It's OK. I'll be right here,' I say as reassuringly as I can.

He sighs and makes his way into the room at the side of the altar through a small wooden door. I sit down on the creaky bench, observing the exaggerated facial expressions of the choir as they start up a new chorus of some vaguely familiar hymn from my childhood.

'Quem quaerimus adjutorem, nisi te Domine, Sancte Deus, Sancte fortis, Sante Misericors Salvator, amarae mort ne tradas nos…'

I remember some of the words—*sancte* means holy; *Domine* means God. I guess some of the Latin did stick in my brain. The boys sing the first verse, and then the girls sing the second, while the teacher directs with waves of her hand. The language sounds familiar to me, as if I've heard it before recently.

Another creak from the wooden bench I'm sitting on snaps me out of my thought bubble. From the corner of my eye, I glimpse a shade of brown from a raised hood. It seems the disrespectful lad from farther back has moved up next to me. I wait for his inevitable question where he asks me for spare change.

The question doesn't come, however, and he just sits with both hands in his hoodie pockets with shoulders hunched while staring up at the altar as if waiting for something to happen. There's a slight tremble in his body like he's freezing with the cold, which is strange because it's quite warm in here.

The chorus sings out again, and the words grow more familiar to me. The stranger beside me hums along to the tune then laughs under his breath.

'Do you think they understand the words?' he says, turning towards me. His accent isn't Irish; it's more of a mix between American and Eastern European. There's a sharp coldness to his piercing grey eyes peering out from under his hood.

I briefly try to figure out if I'm going to respond but decide it's easier not to be rude.

'I suppose so,' I say with little enthusiasm.

He leans back against the creaking wooden pew. 'Lambs, following along,' he says, and intermittently hums to the tune again.

If he doesn't like the choir, maybe he should leave. I face forward and gaze up at the pine wooden cross hanging over the altar. It takes me a moment to realise his humming has stopped, and I feel his eyes on me once again.

'Can I help you with something?' I ask, still fixated on the cross.

'How would you help a dying man?' he offers bluntly.

I dart my eyes to him but don't know what to say. The gaunt shadows on his face magnify the protruding bones underneath his skin and tell me he isn't physically well.

'Why are you here?' he asks.

He shivers again, and I wonder what's wrong with him. I briefly think about his reasons for being here and talking to me, and I can't help feel a little sorry for him.

'Waiting for a friend. His dad just died.'

He laughs subtly. 'Ironic isn't it? People coming here to grieve the dead…when this place is a symbol of eternal life.'

I turn my head a little to take a better look at who I'm talking to. His words don't match the youth of his voice. He keeps his focus on me and takes down the hood to reveal untidy blond hair that looks like it was once spiked up but has fallen out of shape due to neglect. He must be about twenty or so, but he's a pale, sickly twenty-year-old. His grey eyes are his healthiest-looking feature.

'I guess people need to believe in something bigger than themselves,' I reply, trying to offer him something meaningful.

He diverts his focus to the old wooden cross. 'Believing in God is better than believing in human nature. Humans are weak and they ruin perfection,' he says with a hint of superiority, like he's speaking about humans as if he wasn't one himself.

The rest of church fades away from my attention. He's obviously terminally ill with something and maybe came here for some inspiration. The moment is a little surreal, and my mind flips to thoughts of my mother, working with terminal patients every day. Maybe he knew her; maybe she treated him.

'How did he die? Your...friend's father?' he says quickly, with a sudden energy.

It's a blunt question, but it doesn't matter. 'Car crash, about a month ago,' I reply.

He looks me up and down like he's sizing me up. 'People die all the time, I suppose, hmm?'

Something almost sinister creeps into his expression; maybe he's angry.

I shrug. 'Yeah, but it's still tough when it happens.'

'You're taking care of your friend now?' He nods towards the door Andrew walked through. 'That why you're here'

'Trying my best.' I say, breaking eye contact. 'What brings you here?'

He laughs a little too loudly then coughs uncontrollably, as if it were a consequence, and wipes something from his mouth that could be blood.

'Oh, forgiveness. Forgiveness for all my sins,' he says, and slides a little towards me through a grunt of discomfort. 'My sins brought you here too, William,' he whispers.

I never told him my name. Some adrenaline kicks in and makes my heart race. Up close something about his face is terribly familiar, like something I dreamt had just jumped into real life.

He lets a half smile creep out the side of his mouth. 'Didn't expect that did you?' he whispers. He glances at the altar briefly, as if searching for what to say next. 'I think William…I think you have reached a crossroads in your life…and you have to decide *this way* or *that way*. You need to choose what path to walk, and unfortunately when that decision is made, there may be no way back for you.'

I look right into his cold grey eyes, and a feeling of anxiety sinks into the pit of my stomach. 'You're one of the officers. From the tactical-unit lander.'

He nods gently. 'It's not a toy William and if you hesitate, your path will just come and choose you, dragging you along its course like an unwilling participant.' He stops himself from coughing again, barely regaining his composure. 'I'm glad to be here with you now, but the next time we meet, I may not be so glad of you.'

He falls clumsily back against the pew.

'I can help you!' I say.

Andrew comes out of the side office by the altar and walks towards me with purpose.

'I, Myself, am the Light,' whispers the familiar stranger beside me, his eyes still fixed above the altar. 'And the Light cannot be confused with—and still less blend Itself with—the darkness. Where I am found, the darkness is dissolved.' Something falls from his hand and echoes against the tile floor.

His head falls forward.

Andrew sits down beside him. 'He don't look so good,' he says, and squints a little, trying to figure out something.

The stranger's eyes are half open, but he's awfully still.

'Hey, man,' I say with a gentle nudge to his arm.

No response. I look up at Andrew, and he knows what I'm thinking.

Andrew slicks back his hair. 'Oh, shit...'

I pick up the object he dropped on the floor—it's a visor, a neural interface just like Andrew and I have at the TUL.

'I think that's Luka Johnson,' says Andrew nervously, 'the third name on the crew list!'

8 The Hidden Room

Luka Gudjohnsen, to be more precise. Father Manning, the priest who met with Andrew, gives Luka the last rites where he sits. The choir mumbles in shocked awe behind us and tries to get a look at the poor dead lad. When the police arrive, we tell them we don't know Luka, but they don't care much and routinely write down everything we say in little notebooks.

It's sad he died the way he did by clinging to life on a wooden church bench, but I'm sure it's no coincidence he just happens to be at the church when we were there. Why he saved his last words for me I'll never know.

I think back on what he said: telling me about his sins, telling me about crossroads and decisions. But then I think of how his expression changed, how his words twisted. I realise he didn't speak to me in a kind way or even as an acquaintance. When he said he was dying, I was too busy feeling awkward to truly notice the tone of his voice or the words he was speaking, but one sentence out of all of them repeats over and over in my mind: that he was the one responsible for the two of us being here. Worse still, his 'sins' were responsible for us being here.

Luka may have been the one pressing the buttons all this time. I suppose he could have been the one who brought us here by giving Andrew the vague memories of the loch and the forest; maybe those were the sins he was talking about.

After Marie picks us up, it takes us another two cups of tea and the compulsory cake to fill her in on the afternoon's events. We don't tell her the whole truth, of course; we just tell her some young homeless lad died in the church. Marie blesses herself and asks God to have mercy on his soul. Andrew uses as little words as possible to fill Marie in on his talk with Father Manning. He seems to have just sat there and stared defiantly at the poor man.

Before dusk we brave the cold again and escape back to the TUL. I study Luka's profile, and it looks like I got the Icelandic origin of his surname right. He was born in Reykjavik and his date of birth tells me he's twenty-one but I can't determine anything else because I can't read the language. His skin is an unhealthy shade of pale, and he has those same cold grey eyes that look at the camera like he didn't want his picture taken at all.

Andrew examines the object he dropped, swiping his thumb across the liquid glass, which sends momentary ripples across the surface before it reforms perfectly again. After last night's little experiments, I know the visor is a type of interface that can be used to control the drones. It's able to read thoughts, so I guess that makes it a neural interface.

Andrew pushes his hair back behind his left ear and slides the device over his eyes, immediately engulfing them in a dark red. In fact it's a gloomy, demonic-like red that changes the entire look of his face.

'What?' he asks, reading my body language.

'Is it doing anything?'

He gives a downturn of his mouth. 'Nah.' He looks around the cavern as if he's searching for some kind of change. He stops suddenly when he looks to his left. 'Huh,' he says, taking off the visor. 'Whaddya make a' this?'

I slide on the device, and immediately a white path illuminates to my right, leading to what looks like a door embedded into the cavern wall about ten metres ahead. I bet whatever is in there was for Luka's eyes only.

'You think he wanted us to find it?' asks Andrew.

'Maybe, but why hide it in the first place?'

We walk down the new pathway, and I open the door via a small triangular button, identical to the one on the surface. We're immediately greeted by a soft orange light that shines from the ceiling and illuminates what looks like a medical bay. A long metal table sits underneath the orange light, and my hand glows in a fluorescent hue as I glide it over its frictionless metal.

Gentle whooshes of air inhale and exhale in some kind of synchronous breathing; the unsettling sound appears to be coming from three chamber-like objects lined up side by side along the back wall. Curiosity brings me closer to a transparent oval dome that stretches across a solid white chamber full of blue goo. It reminds me of the stasis chambers I've seen in the movies when a crew needs to enter deep sleep for a long space journey. The sound of breathing disturbs me. The goo in the chamber on my left is perfectly still and aligns with the top of the rectangular base. The one directly in front looks exactly the same.

'Giant empty baths of goo,' I say.

'Not empty,' says Andrew, pawing the glass of the chamber to my right.

I move next to him and cast a glance inside. For a moment I can't make out the form, but then the breathing within the unit grows louder, and the surfaces pulse—fast pulses and breathing. I realise the tiny form is alive. A miniscule embryo in a foetal position, its little heart beating underneath the blue goo. The embryo is only a few centimetres long, but I see it clearly now as the goo tightly engulfs the child like a second skin.

I instantly wish I'd never come in here. It's becoming clear Ken's research goes far beyond weaponry, and whatever that thing is, it makes me very uncomfortable. I no longer know what we're dealing with—resupply bunkers and field hospitals are one thing, but this is out of my comfort zone. I take a step back from the chamber.

'You think that thing is alive in there?' asks Andrew.

I hesitate as I think about what Ken could have been up to in this place. On one side we have an almost-dead crew, and on the other we have the growth of new people.

'It can't be that simple,' I say under my breath.

'What can't?'

'Is this place growing new crew members to replace the dead ones?'

'Or cloning them!' says Andrew.

'You must know something about the research your dad—'

'I don't know any more than you do,' he snaps.

Andrew paws the dome of the chamber and fixates on the goo. He seems as surprised as I am to see that tiny person in there. The way it's lying in the foetal position, the sound of its breathing, the pulsating movement—it makes me want to run a mile from here. The pulse is the worst part of it all. I present myself as deceptively casual, but I'm not at all. This room freaks me out.

Just what is this place supposed to be? Part weapons factory, part medical lab? I can't imagine how those two things work together. Maybe the crew died protecting whatever is growing in those chambers, or maybe, as Andrew says, they contain the clones of the dead crew, who are now being reborn after their untimely deaths. There's the other problem—just what exactly killed them and Luka Gudjohnsen in the first place?

We make our way back to the green platform, and on a hunch I ask Andrew to go back to the red screen that was previously locked out by Luka.

This time the screen displays [G-COMPILER], just as it did before, but now something else is visible: a huge list of four-character codes, each organized neatly into alphabetical columns. After a little investigating, we figure out each code represents a subprogram—like an app on a mobile phone.

Each app has a description, but just like the profiles in the crew manifesto, we can't read them because of the language barrier. Suddenly my mind is cast back to the church and the language the choir sang in.

'I knew I recognized that from somewhere,' I say, thinking out loud.

I take out my phone and load up a translator. It takes a few seconds to process the image of the screen, but I eventually get a broken, partial translation of the words. Looks like I was right

'Latin?' says Andrew, after I fill him in. 'Where do they speak that again?'

'Nowhere, it's a dead language. Why would anyone encode such an advanced computer system in a language few people can read?'

'Maybe that was the point, Will...to keep people out.'

'Or slow them down,' I say. 'Latin isn't hard to crack.'

I read over the badly translated text of several applications, and eventually I put together a crude pattern—some of the apps are used to read or modify human memory. The remaining apps are used for things like communication, 3D printing, and genetic engineering.

For instance [IR15] can be used to launch communication probes. [MA27] is an object printer that can be used to print things such as weapons. [OP67], according to the text, is an app for decoding and sequencing genetic material.

The further down the rabbit hole we go, one thing becomes clear: this place isn't just about making weapons.

Two hours pass—two hours of scratching our heads and looking at long lists of letters and numbers and files. My best guess is this G-Compiler thing is an advanced programming language, and by the looks of the history folder, three programs were made recently: Finder.src, Annex.src, and Seven.src.

Andrew sighs. 'I hate this techno-nerd stuff.'

'It's just like that easel in your room you never use,' I say. 'The G-Compiler allows us to create things…like, ah…' I scratch my head and wonder where I'm going with this.

'Your attempt at dumbing this thing down is blowing my little mind, Will.'

I scroll through a few apps on the screen. 'Say you wanna build a new type of weapon or armour suit,' I say, trying to recover my confidence. 'I'm pretty sure you could just give the computer the specs then use the object printer to print it out in that orange beam.'

He smiles. 'You don't know that!'

He's right—I'm just taking my best guess, but I'm pretty sure we could use the G-Compiler to build anything that's not already in the library.

Thinking of the armour suit reminds me of the inscription I read yesterday underneath the insignia. I'd give pretty good odds that text is in Latin too and decide to run it through the translator on my phone.

Inter Angelis et Pueris, Fideles Inveniamur

The translation is surprisingly straightforward:

With the Angels and the Children, We Find the Faithful

I study the symbol again. It shows two atoms ripping apart; one is black, and the other is white. Perhaps darkness and light? I remember what Luka spoke of in the church before he died, about how he was the light scattering the darkness or at least something along those lines. He spoke those words like a prayer as he looked up at the cross above the altar.

The computer library is vast, containing a multitude of things able to manipulate memory and matter, and maybe even grow human life. It makes me wonder what Ken's research is really about. Perhaps it's destructive, symbolized by the dark side of the symbol, or perhaps it's like the light in the other half of the symbol, the side of this place that can create life as well as take it away. The two atoms pull away from each other as if they symbolize two opposite uses of his technology, but right now all I can do is take shots in the dark.

10 Fragments of AI

I moan and 'hmm' over the decision I'm about to make.

'Just press it already!' says an impatient Andrew.

We've stumbled across an interesting app on the list. At first I didn't pay much attention to it, but after I read the description, it was worth another look. The partial translation mentions an artificial intelligence subsystem. Other words that jump out at me are *human-computer interface* and *command module*.

'It probably does nothing by itself,' I say.

'Good. Press it then!' Andrew persists.

'Haven't you seen every sci-fi movie ever? AI always tries to kill you.'

He rolls his eyes. 'That's just a bad sterotype!'

I shrug. 'There are life forms growing in the other room, and we just watched Luka die. Maybe we shouldn't turn on the killer AI system today is all I'm saying.'

'And I'm the one seeing the shrink!'

I smile. 'Well, that's just bad luck.'

'If you don't run that program, I'm just gonna do it later. You know it and I know it!'

Sighing, I look over the broken translation again. 'Fine, but it gets to kill you first.'

I compile the program. A few seconds later, a message appears, telling me something about a neural net and a memory file that can't be found. I keep touching 'Agree' to dismiss each message as it pops up on the screen.

'Looks like this thing is broken or missing files,' I mumble.

'Oh, shit, Will...' says Andrew beside me.

'Hmm...' I say, partially ignoring him.

Andrew punches me in the arm, and I look up from my screen. It takes me a moment to realise a person on the opposite side of the platform is walking towards us.

'You've got to be kidding me,' I say, instinctively grabbing Andrew's shoulder.

We back away from our screens in synchronous movement as the figure of a young woman moves closer.

'Where's the fucking gun?' whispers Andrew nervously.

'Forget the gun,' I say through gritted teeth. 'Let's just get out of here!'

We move to the edge of the platform and realise we've somehow missed the mark to ascend back to the surface. The young woman walks straight through our display screens, causing them to flicker momentarily.

'She's small. I can take her,' Andrew whispers.

The young lady, about my age and a little shorter than Andrew, stops a few metres in front of us. 'Officers Oakley,' she says with a nod.

I pull Andrew steady before he charges at her.

'How may I be of assistance?' she says in an American or Canadian accent, placing her hands behind her back and standing perfectly still. Her slender frame is rigid with an at-ready stance, showing off her well-formed chest. She doesn't appear at all angry or threatening and wears the same insignia on her black short-sleeve T-shirt as the one on our armour. She looks a little familiar to me—clear unblemished skin with short, dark, red hair nerdily combed to one side and stuck into place. She looks like any regular human kid who could be living next door, with the exception of her eyes, which have a glaring greenness about them. She's beautiful.

'I think she's one of the crew,' Andrew says softly.

'Officer Sam Casey, human AI interface,' she offers politely.

I remember her name from the manifesto; she's one of the few crew members still alive. I think she's the communications person or something like that. An emotionless expression gives nothing away about her character. I don't know if she's going to take out a gun or offer to take my jacket, though her small stature and slim build are at least disarming.

'Where did you come from exactly? I didn't see you come in,' I ask with a nervous break in my voice.

Sam looks at me from head to toe as if studying my body language. 'Perhaps you misunderstand, Officer Oakley. I'm an AI persona, a computer simulation. I was brought online by you moments ago when you activated the AI subsystem using Officer Gudjohnsen's clearance codes embedded in his optex.'

She smiles but otherwise remains perfectly motionless and doesn't even appear to be breathing. After a little dialogue, we figure out that an optex is the visor. Presumably Luka's visor gave us the security clearance to switch on the AI.

Andrew cautiously moves a little closer and scans her up and down, like he's checking her out. He takes a quick look behind her then smiles up at me.

'So you're some kinda hologram?' I say.

Sam turns her head calmly, following Andrew as he moves to her side. 'I consist of a generic AI pattern—extended, using certain personality traits specific to Officer Sam Casey. I have a solid outer structure and aesthetic properties similar to your own; however I do not possess any internal structure.'

'Nothing on the inside, huh?' Andrew mutters, continuing his thorough walk around.

Sam nods. 'You could say that, sir.'

'Prove it then,' he says.

'I do not understand.'

Andrew persists. 'You said you have an outer structure but nothin' on the inside...' He flicks his brown eyes up at her and waits for a response.

It takes a moment before Sam figures out what Andrew is asking. In an instant wave of light that engulfs her body, her skin and facial features erode until she becomes pure light in human form.

'Is this sufficient?' her voice says from within the light.

Fixated on the image standing before him, Andrew is uncharacteristically rendered speechless. I can only guess this is some kind of twist on the materialisation tech. How anyone ever created such an advanced AI I can't even begin to imagine, never mind the display systems needed to make her look and move like a human. Andrew pokes her side with one finger, like he's testing for substance.

'It feels so real,' he says.

Sam morphs back to her human appearance, and I move a little closer to study her for myself. It's hard to believe she isn't human; these military people certainly have been busy, and if we're ever going to get answers about the TUL, she's probably our best bet. Andrew, on the other hand, looks like he's just won the lottery as he looks her up and down with a grin on his face. I guess in a way a cute girl hologram is every boy's dream come true.

I decide to ask the questions first and marvel at the 'technology' later. My first question is pretty obvious; I ask her why Andrew and I have profiles in the computer.

'You're both assigned to this installation, are you not?' she says matter-of-factly, her eyes flicking from me to Andrew then back again.

Her accent could be American or Canadian—I can never be sure. Her speech is mundane, almost deadpan…devoid of expression, excitement, or emotion, like a lack of character I can't put a finger on. There are no imperfections on her face, no spots or scars; her hair is perfectly positioned, as if she were sculpted out of the air. When I speak to her, she listens intently, with 100 percent attention—not judging and not flinching, with no body language. I can't see the stuff going on under the exterior that helps me size someone up, and it's unsettling. The darker part of me wonders about things I shouldn't be wondering about.

'Who assigned us here?' asks Andrew.

'Your security access codes have always been assigned,' Sam replies. 'There is no information on who assigned them or when they were assigned.'

'What do you know about Ken Oakley?' asks Andrew, immediately after Sam stops speaking, as if this is some kind of interrogation.

'I am not familiar with a Ken Oakley, sir,' she replies politely.

Andrew smiles, but it's a sarcastic smile. 'Bullshit.' He throws a look in my direction. 'I think she's broken.'

I wonder if Sam is able to lie, though neither of us would know by looking at her because she has no body language. All the same, part of me finds it difficult to believe she doesn't have knowledge of Ken, although right now the only link we have to Ken is Andrew's recurring dream.

I wonder if someone could have used that memory purposely, to make Andrew believe it was his father calling him. This makes me think of what Luka said again, about his sins being responsible for us being here; the image of his dead body makes me shiver on the inside.

Sam doesn't react in any way, as if the sarcasm goes over her head or she doesn't find it relevant. Her nonhuman parts are beginning to gradually creep through. She gets to the point quickly and speaks when spoken to.

'Sam, have you ever met either of us before?' I ask.

She shakes her head slightly. 'This is our first meeting, sir.'

Getting a little defensive, Andrew folds his arms. 'Whaddya know about Luka Gudjohnsen?'

'Luka Gudjohnsen is the executive officer assigned to this installation,' she says, as if she were reading from a script.

Andrew shrugs. 'He's dead. Didn't you know?'

Sam doesn't flinch. 'I will update the personnel file immediately, sir. Has the cause of death been ascertained?' she asks, looking straight at me.

I look at Andrew, who shrugs again, like he doesn't care. He's not hearing the answers he wants to hear.

'Not yet, Sam,' I say. 'At least not that I know of.'

Andrew gestures to the insignia on Sam's black T-shirt. 'What does that symbol mean?'

She looks down at her uniform. 'This is the symbol of the Furious Angels, the organisation that designed and built this installation.'

There it is, finally, a name. Something we can work with. *Angels* is the same word I translated from the text under the insignia. I run it over again in my brain: *Children...angels...faithful.* From the looks of the manifesto, the crew looked to be pretty young, too young in fact for the titles and jobs they had (or have) in one of the most advanced military or research structures on the planet. Maybe the crew are the children the motto refers to.

'What's the average age of the crew?' I ask Sam.

Andrew gives me a confused look, probably wondering why I asked that.

'Excluding recently deceased Officer Gudjohnsen, the average age of the crew is fourteen point four years.'

I glance at Andrew. 'Too young to be officers in a military installation.'

'There're chambers in that room over there,' says Andrew, gesturing towards the cavern wall, 'full of blue stuff. What are they for?'

Sam looks at him. 'I have no idea, sir. The program that created those incubation chambers doesn't provide any supporting documentation.'

'Which program is that?' I ask.

'Seven.src is the name of the program that created and currently monitors the incubation chambers in the medical bay.'

'And you have no idea why those chambers are there?' Persists Andrew.

'No sir.'

'Maybe we're asking the wrong question Andrew,' I say. 'Sam, are the contents of the chambers alive? I mean are there people growing inside them?'

Sam responds in a matter-of-fact way. 'Yes sir, the incubation chambers are designed to act as an artificial womb.'

11 Mobility

That's pretty much all Sam knows about the Furious Angels. She doesn't remember any history or known address or contact details...nothing! Maybe our new AI friend has a selective memory, or maybe her memory was wiped somehow. It doesn't make any sense to me, and either the Furious Angels are the most careless organisation in the world for abandoning this place or something more sinister is going on. I find it odd that Sam has no idea about the TUL's origins or its purpose. Equally strange, she has no recollection of herself or the unusually young crew and why most of them are dead. On the upside, she translated the Latin text on the displays back into English...I guess that's a start.

The three of us stand over the goo-filled incubation units. The liquid in the first of the units from left to right pulses with a fast heartbeat. I don't want to look at it, but at the same time, I can't turn away.

'So these are, like, clones of the crew?' asks Andrew.

Sam scans the displays on the back wall. 'Unknown,' she replies. 'Seven.src will not share its data with my program.'

It would seem Luka didn't even share his data with the AI. That doesn't give us much hope that we'll figure out what's going on anytime soon. I hate looking at the chambers—that rapid pulse is still too surreal for me—but Andrew insisted on coming in here and quizzing Sam some more.

If the crew are dying, maybe this is some strange way of backing them up. I focus in on the scrolling data of the overhead displays to purposely avoid the sight of the pulsing embryo. Just what was Luka up to in here?

Andrew sighs. 'Wanna get outta here for a while?'

'Definitely,' I say.

'Do you wish to take the RMN to your destination?' Sam asks unexpectedly.

We both look at her. She reads the ignorance from our expressions then asks us to follow her back to the green platform, where she navigates to a screen I've never seen before:

[TERRAIN ARTEFACTS]

This screen divides into two columns, with hundreds of codes on the left and just one code in the right: [RMN-T-2].

After Sam selects the code, a high-definition blue schematic resembling a concept car rotates on the screen. She reaches into the screen and extracts the image; it hovers in mid-air in front of us.

The featureless exterior of the car has no obvious lighting or handles on the doors, no exhausts, no mirrors. Textual labels appear around the rotating 3-D schematic, showing indecipherable acronyms.

'This is a standardised template for an urban-terrain vehicle.' Sam pauses. 'Have you been briefed on the vehicles and weaponry in the materialisation library?'

'Why haven't we seen this before?' I ask.

'We gotta make one a' these!' Andrew says, in admiration of the thing.

'The RMN would not have been available if the AI module was inactive,' continues Sam.

Andrew squints as he studies the drawing. 'Looks like my dad's Corvette...kinda.'

The vehicle's smooth, curved body flows seamlessly; it's carved out of a single piece of material and not assembled in panels like a traditional car. Metallic alloys surround the slim-depth tyres, making it appear as though this car has been built for speed.

'What's under the hood?' Andrew asks Sam.

She narrows her focus as if she doesn't understand.

'What are the specifications of the RMN?' I clarify, speaking Sam's language.

The image of the car expands into a larger section that shows a complicated-looking triangular machine with large cooling fins on its surface.

'The RMN features a self-regenerative fuel cell, with a regen index of 0.05 over 1. The vehicle is equipped with a standard AI-drive module and four expansion bays for additional modules. It is capable of light armament that incorporates a matter-deflecting pulse weapon...'

The rest of her sentence trails off into something I can't follow. From Sam's little speech, we eventually figure out that the car doesn't take any gas, and its fuel cell can self-replenish at a rate of 5 percent per minute at a certain power usage. After that, Sam pretty much loses both of us.

'Put in all the stuff you just told us about,' says Andrew, like he's just won the lottery. 'All the weapons and armour!'

'Yes, sir,' Sam says without hesitation.

'Andrew, neither of us has a driving licence,' I say. 'Do you really think we should just take this out for a spin...with on-board armour and weapons?' My voice reaches new levels of pitch.

'The on-board AI can drive if required, sir,' interrupts Sam.

Sam isn't helping my case. Playing with the technology in here is one thing, but taking it out onto the road is something entirely different.

'No weapons, no guns, nothing that can kill anyone!' I say, feeling a little like a babysitter for these two.

'The pulse disruptor is designed only to neutralize power systems,' says Sam. 'It is not designed to kill.'

Andrew smiles. 'Relax, man. This is gonna be great!'

I rub my forehead. 'How do we get the RMN outside exactly?'

'Indeed,' says Sam, as if she expected the question. She clears away the RMN schematic with a wave of her hand and navigates quickly to the G-Compiler. 'We will need to construct a vehicle bay and connect it to the east wall of the tactical-unit lander.'

A stream of hexadecimal text scrolls fast on the screen. I presume this is all coming from Sam's AI brain, as her bright-green AI eyes stare at the code without blinking.

'Coding complete,' she says after a moment. 'Shall I commence construction?'

'Construction of what!?' I exclaim.

'Do it!' says Andrew.

Sam nods. 'I may go offline temporarily during the construction process. I will meet you in the bay once the materialisation is complete.'

The green lights of the platform immediately extinguish; both screens distort then lose cohesion. Sam suddenly disappears, and Andrew and I are left in darkness.

'Lockdown in progress,' echoes Sam's voice in a mundane tone from somewhere within the walls of the cavern.

A vibration under my feet quickly intensifies and shakes my bones. The grinding grows louder until it's the only sound filling my ears. A vast multitude of white grid lines superimpose over the cavern wall behind us, which until now I hadn't realised was only ten metres or so from the green platform. The jagged, rocky surface suddenly loses its structural integrity and spontaneously morphs into a wall of red, sending a heat wave over my body. We take several steps back, but the heat intensifies. The enveloping light edges closer to our position, encompassing everything in its path from floor to ceiling, all the time growing hotter and brighter.

I grit my teeth to try to fake a calmness that gets harder to maintain. I raise my hand to eye level, but I don't look away while little fragments of rock fall to the floor from the ceiling above us. The vibration worsens again, but worse still is the deafening sound, and I curse myself for trusting an AI. I'm about to be phased out of existence by the encroaching wall of fire. Andrew quickly takes another step back, but my legs stay firmly rooted to the ground.

'What's going on, Will?' he shouts.

'Never trust a computer!' I reply, backing into his shoulder.

This is all getting a little tight, and it reminds me of some old movie where the walls come together and squish anything unlucky enough to be on the inside. I bet everything in this bloody place can kill us. Even simple computer commands like 'build a room' are dangerous. I hate it here.

With that thought, the room suddenly falls colder and silent. Everything returns to the familiar surroundings: the platform illuminates; the screens flicker on; and a new white path illuminates ten metres to the new door embedded in the surface of the wall. I feel both relieved and stupid. Andrew tries to catch his breath.

'Relax princess,' I say, briefly inhaling my own farts.

A faint smell of something resembling burning plastic grows stronger as we get closer to the new extension. Andrew opens the door, and four rows of bright light thud on in the new room, revealing a large open space underneath us. The ceiling of the new vehicle bay is at the same level as this cavern, but the floor is about twenty metres lower. We walk out onto a balcony and look down over a polished grey floor reflecting the white lights from the ceiling. A spotless RMN-T-2 sits on a hexagonal platform in the centre of the bay with a couple of blue display screens suspended in mid-air at its left and right side. My anxiety is replaced with a sense of awe.

The balcony unexpectedly jolts and begins to descend towards the ground to the beep of a low warning tone. Turning fans whoosh into earshot from the ceiling above, like someone has just switched on the air conditioning, and gives our surroundings a heightened feeling of importance. Abruptly we come to a stop at ground level. The chrome railings of the balcony release with a clicking and open outward.

Our sneakers screech against the hard grey floor. The potent smell of rubber becomes stronger as I crouch down and run my fingers over the perfect tyre grooves of the RMN, its wheels resting on metallic alloy spokes. The light of the room glides over the flawless, smooth bodywork with a texture like a hardened plastic. There doesn't look to be any obvious way in, with no grooves for the doors, hood, or trunk; no lights on the front or rear; no wing mirrors; and no exhaust.

'Do you require any further assistance?' asks Sam all of a sudden from behind me.

I twitch when I hear her voice at such proximity.

'Could you please not do that?' I bark, throwing her an annoyed look I'm sure she doesn't understand.

Andrew opens the passenger door somehow, and it disappears in a sliver of white light. I touch the vehicle where I'd expect to find the handle on a regular car, and my door vanishes in the same way.

The interior is surprisingly minimal, with two dark-grey leather seats positioned at either side of a centre console that displays the familiar circular interface. I notice the absence of any steering wheel, gas pedals, or brakes, and I wonder how this thing is actually supposed to drive. The last thing I want to do is eject myself through the roof or fire off whatever that pulse-disruptor thing is. I bet with a few misplaced commands the car can kill us too—nice and easy.

'We're good, Sam. We'll call if we need you,' Andrew says dismissively from inside the vehicle.

The doors rematerialize as I sit down beside him in the car. Only three segments are visible on the navigation interface this time: one green at the top of the circle, one red at the bottom, and one blue at the left.

Andrew hovers a finger over the interface as if he's deciding which colour to select. 'Green means go, right?'

I roll my eyes at him.

He touches the green segment; the display in front of him activates in a bright red of analogue meters all resting at zero. I hate it when he's right. With a little tinkering, we figure out the RMN's satellite navigation system, and in this mode it appears the car drives as well as navigates.

We confirm a destination through Tara Hill along a route that consists mostly of deserted back roads. The RMN's supercar-like features aren't something that belong in Tara Hill, and we don't need the attention, so it's better to keep a low profile. A jolt from beneath the platform sends us into a slow ascent to the backdrop of a two-tone warning that echoes around the empty bay. We pass the door to the upper cavern and keep ascending about ten metres to surface level.

As the platform slowly edges its way forward, the outer wall of the TUL dematerialises in a haze of white light. The interior of the car dims as the windscreen comes to life in a high-definition night-vision green, and seat belts shoot across our bodies, making us both swear. Andrew and I look at each other and laugh at our edginess. With a sudden acceleration, the car moves along a straight, ready-made path through the trees—a path I didn't realise existed.

A force from the rear of the car pushes us forward with an accelerating hum, and we quickly clear the forest. The RMN accelerates hard yet glides smoothly over the uneven surface of the field. The metal gate at the perimeter shrouds in yellow before vanishing out of our way.

The RMN moves to the right and accelerates off again as we leave Ken's field behind us. One of the red displays on Andrew's side reads, '480 pars/second,' but it feels like we're doing about sixty. We decelerate as we approach the tree-overshadowed 'tunnel' bend in the road, and our speed drops significantly. As the car moves unexpectedly to the left and hugs the overgrowth, branches scrape against my window. Bright lights of an approaching car momentarily engulf our display, and it beeps its horn in one long pissed-off note as it passes.

Andrew looks over his shoulder. 'What's their problem?'

I grit my teeth and dig my fingers farther into the seat. I can't look anywhere but straight ahead because I don't trust this thing. I realise we're driving on the wrong side of the road and remember I didn't see any headlights on the front of the RMN; the night-vision makes them obsolete for us but also makes us invisible to every other car along this pitch-black road. If we meet the cops we're screwed.

The car resumes its previous position and pulls away at a speed much faster than we were going and heads straight for the junction dead ahead.

'Whaddya think this red button does?' asks Andrew.

I'm too preoccupied with monitoring everything the car is doing to really pay attention to what he's saying. Andrew seems to have a lot more trust in this thing than I do.

The RMN slows a little then turns right at the junction before pulling off again, quickly passing the shop. The car glides silently over the tarmac of the road as hedgerows and a neighbour's driveway fly past in a green blur. We slow down again and make the left turn up Tara Hill. I feel a little safer here because I know this road is hardly ever used by anyone except James and Marie.

'I guess it stops us maybe?' says Andrew, answering his own question. He presses the red segment on the centre display.

A steering wheel suddenly materialises in front of him, resembling an airplane flight-control column. The car veers a little to the right and scrapes against the hedgerow. Andrew grips the column with both hands and tries to straighten up. As we accelerate forward, the force throws us back against our seats as we speed up the hill.

'Uh, I think I just switched us to manual drive. There's a gas pedal under my foot!' Andrew says, shuffling around with his feet underneath the dash. 'I can't find the stupid brake!'

Not the most reassuring words I've ever heard. I don't dare take my eyes off the road in front of me.

Andrew speeds off along the single-lane country road with just enough space for us to pass. I can tell from his body language he loves the thrill of speed, and I've never seen him so relaxed in the short time I've known him. He clumsily takes corners, driving like a kid playing a computer game with no fear of real consequences. I bite my tongue because I don't want to be a backseat driver, although I would like to continue living.

'Whaddya think the blue button does?' he asks, throwing the car's centre display a casual glance.

I tell him I don't want to know.

He makes a gesture to press it, but I intercept his hand. 'Just drive,' I say, my eyes catching his briefly.

Hedgerows and tall arching trees fly past as the RMN's suspension system keeps us from feeling much of the terrain. Andrew speeds up again along the narrow roadway to what feels like well over a hundred miles an hour.

'Find that brake yet?' I say, trying to keep my composure; I'm not as comfortable as he is with the speed we're going.

'It's got some kind of safety feature. It won't let me veer off too much.'

I give him a wide-eyed look. 'Are you actually trying to crash the car?'

As we ramp over a small, humpbacked stone bridge, the contents of my stomach reach the base of my throat, and whatever is in there gets thrown up and down. It feels like the RMN just lifted off the road and landed again with a soft thud. A small pop-up screen appears on the windshield near the centre of the dash. It shows an approaching main road with no way forward, only left and right.

'Caution! Collision!' Sam's mundane voice sounds out over the car's internal speakers.

The roadway comes into view dead ahead, with stop signs on both sides of the road. Andrew accelerates again like he's playing chicken with the oncoming motorway.

'Caution! Collision!' repeats Sam, but in a louder, more urgent voice this time.

Andrew maintains a steely focus with both his outstretched arms gripping the wheel.

My pulse is racing. I look at the flurry of green and the fast-approaching stop signs.

'Dude, slow the fuck down!' I yell.

Andrew smiles. 'I've never heard you swear before.'

As we're about to reach the stop signs, [OVERRIDE] appears in yellow text across the windscreen. The car's computer repeats the same thing in Sam's voice, and the steering column disappears, leaving Andrew's hands in mid-air. The RMN accelerates even harder, defying every logical decision I would have made if I were driving. Bright lights from an oncoming vehicle envelop us from my side, and we shoot across the motorway as the inevitability that something is about to smash into us careens through my brain.

The contents of my stomach heave up again like we've just left the ground, and the night-vision green of the windscreen changes briefly to a gloomy red then shuts off, leaving us in darkness. We're now driving blind; the vehicle shakes with a sudden braking force that pushes my body forward. The seat belt holds me steady as the car grinds to a halt. The doors dematerialise while the humming of the car's motor dies away.

'Safety module exit code nine-nine-seven,' says the car's computer. 'Override system initiated. Return to base. Standby for rescue.'

As I fall back against my seat, the belt releases from around my body.

Andrew looks at me and smiles.

I could punch him right in the mouth or better yet give him another black eye.

I stagger out of the RMN and the night air hits me like a cold wall. My legs immediately collapse, and I fall to my knees, heaving up a chunky mess in front of me; I puke up all the tension in my stomach with each repeated hurl.

Andrew puts a hand on my shoulder. 'Relax, princess!'

'You got a death wish, man?' I say between breaths, and shrug his hand away, spitting out the last of the vomit before making an attempt at standing upright again.

A quick look around tells me we're in a field just off the motorway, and fortunately it appears to be empty. A damaged hedgerow borders the perimeter, and a section of it is now hacked away because the RMN ploughed right through.

From the looks of it, the on-board computer did just enough to get us clear of the bushes and onto the grass for a safe landing. It wasn't pretty, but it did its job. The road is deserted ahead, so whoever almost hit us has long gone or never saw us in the first place.

'I don't have a death wish,' Andrew says from behind me. 'I just knew everything would work out.'

I turn around. 'Based on what exactly?'

'You've seen what the technology can do,' he says. 'The car's computer wasn't gonna just let us crash!'

I'm too annoyed right now to get involved in this conversation, so I ignore him. I scan the vehicle, looking for damage. The body looks like it just rolled off the factory floor, but something on the inside is definitely messed up. Right now the car is sitting lifelessly with a trail of tyre tracks in its muddy wake, and I've no idea how we're going to move this thing before someone finds it in the morning.

'Tara Hill isn't too far a walk from here, but we can't leave the car behind,' I say.

Andrew sits on the hood and leans back against the windscreen with one leg hitched up. 'The hood is nice and warm,' he says, looking up into the night sky.

I can't believe how unbothered he is. 'Have you any idea how we're supposed to move this thing? You think we can just leave a priceless piece of equipment sitting in an empty field?'

'You heard the computer. We're supposed to sit here and wait to be rescued, remember?' His voice trails off into a low sarcastic tone. He looks back into the night sky. 'I just wanted to feel something. Feel a rush, you know?'

'A rush, is it? We find a machine that can build weapons and cars out of nothing, and you want to find a bloody rush!'

He throws me a look. 'You think this all one big coincidence? That we just happened to find this place and our names just happened to be in the computer and my dad died for nothing? Is that what you think?'

'No, Andrew,' I say quickly, and move next to him. 'Look, you're right, man—something brought us to the TUL, but there's a logical reason for it, most likely some kind of computer program set to run after your dad died.' I lower my tone and remind myself that he's still grieving. 'Your dad left you a great legacy. Don't disrespect that by doing whatever you want. You're not invincible, and neither was he.'

'I wonder where they're gonna bury Luka. Probably an unmarked grave or somethin',' he says softly, apparently ignoring everything I've just said.

I sit down next to him on the hood. 'Andrew, we can't draw attention on ourselves like this. We can't afford to attract the wrong type of people, OK?'

I wait for a reply, but it never arrives.

Exhaling out my frustration is easier than having an argument, and I'm not as confrontational as Andrew is. The countless stars of the night sky provide a brief distraction—I'm distracted because in the countryside the sky looks so much clearer at night than it does in the city, where the lights drown everything out.

'Someone has to be missing Luka,' I say, thinking out loud. I begin to wonder again why he came to meet us before he died but my train of thought is interrupted when I realise the flickering star above me is getting surprisingly larger.

Andrew takes out his phone. 'We should go talk to Alan Dalton in Iceland.'

The light from the star intensifies, like it's descending towards us.

I nudge Andrew's the shoulder. 'What is that?'

He puts down his phone and looks up. We both scramble off the hood.

The descending light suddenly engulfs everything, as if we're standing under the floodlights of a stadium. I raise a hand above my eyes to get a better look at the object in front of me. A large wing-shaped aircraft with an ominous stealth-bomber form descends, and the air suddenly becomes warm around me. An orange beam from the rear of the craft intensifies as the plane rotates ninety degrees and the wing lowers towards the ground.

12 66 Degrees Parallel North

Looks like Andrew was right about the rescue, but landing an ominous-looking aircraft right next to the M7 motorway isn't my idea of discreet. When we—or I should say Andrew—wrecked the RMN, the on-board computer sent an SOS back to the TUL. Sam was able to materialise what she called a terrestrial-class transporter and use the craft to repair the RMN, before sending it back to the TUL on self-drive.

For the rest of the night, all Andrew can talk about is meeting Alan Dalton, and he's got an intuition that Alan must have a connection to the TUL. After all, Alan worked with Ken for years and maybe he was the one who recruited Luka at his company in Iceland.

What bothers me is that Alan probably does know something about the Furious Angels, and I'm guessing the last thing he's likely to do is leave the TUL in our incapable hands. Once Alan knows we have the TUL, he'll probably want to secure it, and that's a shame because regular life will be pretty dull after seeing what that technology is capable of. Weighing it all up, I guess I don't want to talk to Alan Dalton, but I know Andrew needs answers and Alan's the best lead we have.

***

After a patchy sleep back at Tara Hill, we head straight down to the vehicle bay early the following morning. Andrew and I stand at the nose of the transporter as it sits, defying gravity, in an eerie silence about two metres off the ground.

The craft resembles a large triangular stealth bomber. It has a flying-wing design, but the fuselage is more pronounced —like a tube—stretching down the centre of the V-shaped body. The rear of the fuselage slopes downward into a shiny surface reflecting the lights in the room. Except for the dome-like cockpit above the nose, there are no windows, no visible doors on the fuselage, no jets, no turbines or weapons. Like the RMN, the transporter is the only ready-made aircraft in the library, although I'm guessing different types of craft can probably be configured using the G-Compiler.

Sam materialises at our position and waits with her hands patiently behind her back.

'You sure about this?' I ask Andrew.

He looks upwards at the aircraft. 'Gotta do something,' he says softly.

'You know this could change everything. If Alan knows we have this place, he just might want it back.'

'Let's just find out what he knows first,' Andrew says, then shifts his gaze to Sam. 'How tough is this thing anyway? What're the specs?'

Sam politely responds, 'The craft can serve as an AI-piloted transporter when human pilots are not available.' She says this like she's mundanely reading from a script. 'The sloped armament of the outer shell comprises an illerium-based alloy, making it undetectable to radar. I estimate one hundred percent avoidance with known missile technology and targeting systems. Indeed the probability of a successful lock by available laser and thermal-scanning technology is significantly unlikely when the unit is controlled by an AI subsystem'.

Andrew smirks as he looks up at the craft. 'Sometimes I don't wanna know the answers to my own questions.'

'How fast can this thing get us to Iceland, Sam?' I ask.

'Approximately four minutes, sir.'

'*Minutes*?' I say, not sure I heard her correctly.

Sam gives me an affirmative nod then makes her way towards a short metallic stairway that materialises near the rear of the craft. Her uniform morphs into a heavy grey armour; multiple circuit pathways etch down along her right sleeve.

'The craft can reach speeds exceeding twenty times the speed of sound,' she says as we follow her. I catch Andrew giving an affirming nod to himself, like he's just judged Sam's AI rear end. I do my best not to notice it because I'm sure it's not right to notice, no matter how well sculpted some programmer made it. He was a talented programmer, though, whoever he was.

We follow Sam into the craft towards a cockpit that's larger than it seems from the outside. No mechanical levers, buttons, or obvious controls are aligned inside the grey dome-like interior. There are four chairs, two at the front of the cockpit right behind the dome windows and two more a little farther back.

I take a seat and lean forward so I can see the empty vehicle bay. The RMN is sitting like new on the platform to my right. Sam sits down at the right-hand station, where a co-pilot normally would sit on an airplane. She swings around in her chair. 'Diagnostics have been completed. Ready to depart.'

'But you didn't do anything!' I say.

'We're going right now?' asks Andrew.

Sam looks at us both, apparently wondering which stupid question to prioritize. 'I am requesting the departure time from you, Officer Oakley.' She flicks her green eyes at me. 'And I can assure you that I have completed the diagnostics. You are welcome to review the log files.'

I kindly decline Sam's offer, but I don't exactly trust an AI pilot to fly us at Mach 20 over an ocean to Iceland! Andrew takes a seat behind Sam and peers over her shoulder. I can tell he's eager to go, and part of me is too, but I wonder if Andrew only sees the opportunities in things, whereas I think of all the stuff that can go wrong.

'What are the coordinates, sir?' asks Sam, interrupting my train of thought.

Andrew runs a finger down the middle of his chin as he pieces together the answer in his head. 'Well, I guess, take us to Iceland's capital,' he says. 'We can call Alan when we get there and tell him to meet us at the airport, so it'll look like we came in by plane.'

Sam's eyes dart to mine.

'As long as no one sees us flying in,' I add.

'There are two airports in the vicinity, Officers Oakley,' says Sam. 'The smaller of the two is in the centre of Reykjavik and is used more for domestic travel, based on the flight numbers that service this airport. The other is on the outskirts in a satellite town called Keflavík. I believe this is the international airport, and it has several vacant industrial allotments nearby—I could conceal us in one of those.'

Andrew clicks his fingers. 'Keflavík, that's the place I heard Dad talkin' about!'

Sam extends a hand towards me, and a visor materialises in the centre of her palm. 'Please put this on, sir. It well help us to communicate with each other during the mission.'

She gives Andrew an identical one.

I put on the optex and try my best to adjust to the tightness at my temple.

Sam rotates in her chair to face forward and asks us to assume flight position. I don't know what that is, so I just copy what she does. A belt materialises in front of my body while the craft glides effortlessly to the centre of the bay.

'Flight plan confirmed, sirs. ETA four point two minutes.'

The nose arches silently upwards, as if we're about to take off, but we keep tilting back—past thirty degrees, forty degrees, and then sixty degrees! Sam reads my body language and assures me it's a standard procedure.

I slide into the back of my seat as the plane arches to a full ninety degrees. We face up at the black-panelled ceiling of the vehicle bay, and it dissolves into a fragmented blue until I realise I'm looking into a distant sky. My pulse races because I get the feeling this won't be a gentle ascent. It's the same feeling I get when I slowly climb to the top of a hill on a roller coaster.

Too quickly I realise that my instincts are right. An immense force from behind causes unsettling creaking and moulds the shape of my body into the seat padding. I know the TUL is long gone, and my view changes from a blur of green to dark grey.

In a few moments, we're clear of the cloud cover and break through to clear-blue sky. The vibration increases beneath my feet and climbs up through the chair, making my hands shake in the padded armrests. I feel completely at the mercy of this thing, and our journey seemed a whole lot easier last night, when we were just talking about this. It all sounded great then, but now I feel like an idiot for strapping myself into this flying tomb. I think I would prefer Andrew's death-chase through Tara Hill in the RMN, at least then I was still on the ground.

I try to relax, but most of my stomach is hurling to the pit of my throat. I curse myself for doing this and sit perfectly rigid, like I could break into pieces at any minute. I don't blink or breathe. The craft makes a steep adjustment—a sudden push from the tail section—and the clouds and sky move fast in front of us as the horizon appears dead ahead. We're back at level flight.

Thirty thousand feet—that's how high up we are, according to Sam. A vast expanse of blue comes into view below us as the nose pitches downward a little. Slivers of clouds fly past over the ocean, and it's all oddly beautiful. The craft banks steeply to the left while my insides bank just as equally with our every movement.

'You OK back there?' I say, looking over my shoulder.

Looking as rigid as I do, Andrew grabs on to his seat tightly. 'I'm OK,' he groans, trying to put on a brave face.

He looks pretty pale, though, and I think he might be doing even worse than I am. I figure I'll get him talking and ask if he wants to give Alan a call. He yanks off his optex then leans forward with his head between his legs and breathes out like he's going to throw up, but nothing comes out after a few heaving gestures.

As I look out over the blue horizon, Sam does a brief scan to her right, and I wonder if I should ask her the question on my mind.

'So you like flying?' I say.

'Alan? Hey, it's Andrew…Andrew Oakley,' Andrew says from behind me.

Sam swivels a little towards me. 'I believe Sam Casey is afraid of heights,' she says matter-of-factly.

'Yeah, Ken Oakley's kid,' says Andrew. His voice fades away as I try to figure out if Sam is making an attempt at humour.

I squint my eyes. 'Really?'

'Yes,' she says bluntly.

'And how do you deal with that?'

The craft banks to the right a little. 'Through a simple isolation of that particular personality trait.'

I take a moment to figure out what she just said.

'Of course,' I mutter. 'The old personality…isolation…'

The craft straightens back up.

Andrew's voice comes back into earshot. 'OK. See you then. Bye.'

'He's available?' I say over my shoulder.

'Yeah, same ol', same ol'…"Sorry for your loss," et cetera, etcetera.'

The blue ocean disappears into a rocky, jagged coastline, becoming a dark-grey landscape devoid of any green, as if we're looking down on the surface of a barren planet. We're descending, and I can feel the descent as windy roads and scattered tiny houses dot the terrain below us.

'Where's the ice?' says Andrew, with a little stress in his voice, probably caused by the descent.

Sam banks steeply to the right and lifts the nose. A column of water erupts out of the ground in the distance. I think it's one of those natural hot springs I've heard about, and it reminds me of what's going on in my stomach. I breathe through the rapid descent.

Sam levels up about two thousand or so feet above the ground and begins a low, short approach on the outskirts of the airport. We're coming in over some kind of plane junkyard with pillars of metal coming rapidly closer. She weaves through them like a pro, which is equally impressive and terrifying.

We come to a smooth, calm stop between two columns of crushed metal. The humming of the transporter drops to nothing as our seat belts disappear.

'Keep the optex on at all times,' advises Sam. 'It allows me to monitor your vital signs and communicate with you more effectively.'

With all the tension of flying, I'd forgotten I was wearing the damn thing, but the tight sensation immediately returns on the side of my skull, as if I've just remembered I'm supposed to be uncomfortable. I stand up as much as I can without hitting my head against the domed fuselage.

'We can't wear them, Sam'—I pull off my optex and turn to Andrew—'unless you want to explain why our eyes are a bright shade of yellow.'

Sam persists. 'Then I advise to keep them with you. They are beneficial for interrogation situations.'

I glance at Andrew. 'Is that what you told her this was?'

He shrugs. 'It aint far from the truth!'

Andrew and I exit the transporter with our optexes stuffed into our jackets and our normal eye colour restored. A dry, bitterly cold wind hits us when we step onto the pavement, but at least the bite is partially lessened by the pillar of scrap metal at my side. We walk a jagged path back through the junkyard, twisting and turning around corners of wreckage and empty aluminium-panelled hangars.

Our walking is brought to an abrupt end by a mesh-wire security fence standing about five metres high. A mess of bundled razor wire coils along the top, which can't be fun to climb over. By the looks of it, there's a road leading to the airport at the other side.

'This place is a maze,' says Andrew, peering through the aluminium gaps.

I shake the fence pointlessly.

Andrew dons his optex. 'Sam, if you can hear me, we're kinda locked in. Can you get us outta here?'

The wire fence vibrates momentarily, and then a large section disappears, as if it's melting into the air. Sam is turning into a handy person to have around.

Andrew and I step through and turn off to the right. The chill in the air worsens, and I realise why they call it Iceland. There's something different about the wind here; it's piercing and extremely dry. As it cuts through my clothes, I realise I might as well be wearing nothing.

Walking through the grey, rocky landscape feels nothing like home. There's not a green field in sight, and snow-capped hills sit in the distance. It's hard to believe that less than ten minutes ago I was in Ireland.

Eventually we weave through the warmly cladded tourists outside the airport terminal. Everyone's covered from head to toe in brightly coloured jackets as they wait to board a nearby bus. A large half-hatched egg made of stone, with a claw breaking through its metallic shell, rests on a pile of stacked rocks at the entrance. I'm oddly fascinated by the weird monument, but Andrew doesn't pay much attention.

The automatic glass doors of the airport welcome us inside the warm interior, and after a little bit of walking, we find some seating space in a waiting area next to a gift shop draped in the red and blue of Iceland's flag. People stroll along dragging tagged suitcases on shiny polished floors with little bags of duty-free goods sticking out. Everyone looks blond haired and blue eyed; they're smiling, excited about their vacation or hugging relatives who've just returned home. Even the security people look friendly and chat idly while they walk by in armoured vests.

No one seems to be in any rush as they amble through the spacious layout of the lobby. Announcements come over the intercoms, which are buried in oak panels in the wavelike ceiling. Everything is spoken in Icelandic, and each word sounds the same, rolling into one big mess of r's.

Andrew sits on his hands and leans forward, pensively scanning the automatic doors. He's spoken maybe a single sentence since we got here, and I'm nervous for him in a way, but maybe this is the last day of the mystery. Maybe Alan will fill in the blanks; Andrew will get closure; and we'll get some sort of normality again.

As soon as I think of normality, I know I don't want it. I remember how awkward I felt my first day at my aunt and uncle's and how seeing that distorted vision of myself made me want to run a hundred miles from Tara Hill. Then I met Andrew, and he's everything I'm not: impatient, impulsive, artistic. Still I feel like I've known him longer because of everything that's happened in the past few days. Sometimes change creeps in without you even knowing change is happening. If we lose the TUL to Alan, Andrew and I will still have our friendship, but I know I can't forget what I've seen, and I can't walk away from something that could change the world. I'm becoming as apprehensive as my cousin but for different reasons.

Andrew checks the picture on his phone and it obviously matches the man who just walked in. He stands up and raises a hand to get the guy's attention: a heavily built forty-something in a navy suit with no tie and an open jacket, letting it all hang out like he doesn't care. He walks with purpose towards us; a few loose grey hairs wave in the air-conditioned breeze from the overhead fan and ruin his attempt at a comb-over.

Andrew greets him with an extended hand.

'My God, Andrew. I don't believe it, son.' Alan places a firm palm on Andrew's shoulder as he shakes hands with the other. 'What's it been? Eight, nine years?'

Andrew smiles. 'Try ten!'

Alan looks at me and no doubt wonders who I am.

'This is my cousin, Will,' says Andrew, like he just remembered I'm here.

'Pleased to meet you, son,' he says in a soft Southern-American twang.

He gestures towards an empty table behind us. 'Siddown.'

Andrew and I sit beside each other, and Alan sits opposite then leans in closer. 'Your father was like family to me, and I can't tell you how sorry I was to hear about the accident. I wasn't able to get to Ireland for the funeral, but it was my intention to come and pay my respects in the next couple of weeks. I just regret you came out to see me before I got to see you.' His eyes shift to mine. 'Where you guys stayin'?'

'Uh...we're uh—' I say, fumbling over my words.

'We're movin around for a couple a' days,' interrupts Andrew.

Alan smiles. 'Plenty to see around here. They got this, ah... really famous...' He clicks his fingers like he's thinking about the words. 'Lagoon! That's it! About fifty miles from here...I can take you and, ah, Will's parents out there if you're around a couple a' days,' he says, obviously assuming we're here with my parents.

Alan is wide-eyed and friendly, his tone and body language relaxed. If he's missing a tactical-until lander, he probably doesn't think we have it. After several of our politest declinations, Alan insists on taking us for a late lunch in the outskirts of Reykjavik. After we leave the terminal, he drives us twenty minutes through a flat, rocky landscape dotted with small, brightly painted houses until we climb up a steep road to a large dome-shaped glass structure that rests on four large chrome-facade cylindrical supports.

He tells us the cylinders are tanks full of geothermal water filled from a local hot spring, and the dome is a revolving restaurant. It's an odd combination for sure but no less impressive as we ascend in the glass elevator at the front of the building to the top level. The bustling restaurant is full of suits and well-to-do Icelanders having animated conversations or more reserved business-type meetings over coffee and light desserts. We're greeted by a trendy dessert bar full of fresh pastries and other pretty concoctions. A hot, young, curvy blonde knows Alan by name and escorts us to a table near the glass wall of the dome. It offers an awesome panoramic view of the capital a few miles beneath us; it's populated with narrow streets, and a large granite church sits like a centrepiece designed to resemble a column of lava, Alan tells us.

To the east of the city is the sea, housing dozens of boats bobbing up and down on the choppy surface. The weather outside worsens as a misty rain shrouds the dome. It's nice to look out at it from the comfort of this place, which is shielded completely from the nature at work outside.

Andrew sips some coffee as a waitress places a local chocolate speciality on a plate in front of us. I certainly feel much more at ease than I did on the short flight over here. Alan's character is completely disarming and seems only concerned with making us comfortable, like an uncle or a good family friend would.

'So my dad worked with you as a contractor?' asks Andrew.

Alan's phone rings, but he quickly turns it off and puts it in his pocket. 'That's right…Um, your father oversaw the installation of a backup system. Uh, we call 'em disaster-recovery units. Your dad was one of the finest engineers I've ever worked with.'

Andrew interlocks his fingers and looks pensive, with a slight stress line cracking out on his forehead. 'You guys work in…ah…in the military base here?' he says, though it's not the question he wants to ask.

Alan nods and sips some coffee. 'Mmm-hmm. Fifteen years.' He places his coffee cup back on its saucer. 'Well, I've been stationed here fifteen. Ken would come work with us every now and again.' He scans the room briefly. 'Between you and me, I dunno how much longer they're gonna keep us here. There's a whole heap of pressure comin' from the politicians not to renew the lease.'

'The lease on the base?' I ask with my mouth half full of cake.

'Yessir,' he says in a single breath.

Andrew chops up his cake slice into little chunks with his fork. 'You guys ever work on military stuff...you know, weapons systems...or...'

Alan smiles at the nature of the question and shakes his head as he takes a bite of his dessert. 'Hmm, you gotta have special military clearance for that kinda work.' He shrugs. 'It can be tough for a non-US citizen to get that.'

That makes a lot of sense in hindsight, and I'm surprised it didn't occur to me before now. Ken was of course an Irish citizen.

'Why do you ask, son?' says Alan.

Andrew diverts his gaze to the window as downtown Reykjavik comes back into view. 'We found the tactical-unit lander,' he says bluntly.

I quickly swallow what I'm eating.

Alan looks over our heads. 'Tactical...unit lander...' His eyes search his brain briefly. 'I'm not too clear on what that is exactly,' he says with a downturn of his mouth.

Andrew wipes his mouth with a neatly folded white napkin. 'Another selective memory,' he says under his breath.

Alan seems not to hear him. 'We worked on this long-range guidance system a couple a' years back. They wanted to improve the effectiveness of bringin' in aircraft…' He makes a gesture with his right hand like a plane coming down to land. '…you know, in adverse weather conditions." He pauses. 'You found some of the old sketches?'

Andrew smiles, but I can feel the tension starting to build in him. He leans forward and reaches behind him, taking out the GX 100, and puts it on the table between us.

Alan coughs and calmly takes the stun weapon off the table, studying it discreetly over his lap. His eyes narrow. 'Looks like some kinda lightweight composite material.' He diverts his blue-eyed stare to Andrew. 'What's this all about son? Your dad build this?'

Andrew leans back against his chair while the waitress comes and removes our plates. Alan smiles falsely at her and nods.

'He worked on it with you, man!' says Andrew.

The waitress leaves us in an awkward silence. Alan looks at me.

'Alan, we know you and Ken worked with the Furious Angels,' I say, taking a little gamble.

Alan laughs to himself. 'Sounds like a biker gang!'

'With Luka Gudjohnsen,' adds Andrew abruptly.

'I never worked with Luka Gudjohnsen on anything, son,' says Alan.

Andrew points to him. 'Don't lie to me. You were my dad's best friend!'

'Dude, go easy,' I say softly.

'This is all bullshit, Will. You know it as well as I do,' Andrew says, raising his voice.

Alan leans in with a look of gentle sympathy. 'Tell me what all this is about, guys.' He flicks his eyes to mine. 'Did you find something back at the house, something Ken was working on?'

Andrew lets out an emotional exhale. 'Sam Casey…' He shrugs. 'The materializer, the RMN, the fucking incubation chambers…ring any bells?' he snaps.

Alan makes a calming gesture with his hand. 'Start from the beginning. What exactly did you find?'

I interrupt before Andrew can speak. 'Alan, are you saying you've never heard of the Furious Angels or the tactical-unit lander or any of the stuff Andrew just mentioned?'

Alan doesn't blink; he just sighs and shrugs. 'I'm sorry…I've never heard of any of that stuff.'

Andrew stands up abruptly. 'Screw you, Dalton!'

Alan is briefly taken aback by the reaction and calls after him, but Andrew walks off towards the elevator.

Alan looks on at me as if he's expecting some sort of explanation.

My ears burn with embarrassment. 'He's a little all over the place right now, you know, with the funeral and everything.' I make a gesture to stand up.

'Listen, son' says Alan, as he reaches into his pocket and takes out a card. 'Give me a call anytime if you wanna talk. If there was something Ken was working on, I'm sure I can find out what it was.'

I take the card from him. 'Thanks.'

'One more thing,' he says. 'Did you mean Luka, my stepson, when you mentioned working with Luka Gudjohnsen?'

I hesitate. 'I…I'm not sure…is your stepson named Luka Gudjohnsen?'

Alan shrugs. 'He hasn't gone by "Luka Gudjohnsen" since I married his mother ten years ago. It's Luka Dalton these days.'

'Do you have a picture of him?'

'Sure.' He takes out his phone and scrolls through some stuff until he finds what he's looking for. 'His twentieth birthday last year,' he says, turning the screen towards me.

I recognize him instantly—the kid is a healthier version of the Luka who died next to me in the church. He has the same sandy-blond hair and grey eyes and is uncharacteristically smiling in front of a lit birthday cake between Alan and a woman I presume is his mother.

'That's him,' I say.

I look at Alan and wonder what to do next.

'Have you two met before?' asks Alan with a surprised inflection, like he's genuinely curious.

'When was the last time you two spoke?'

Alan flicks his eyes towards the glass wall. 'Uh, couple a' days ago. Why?'

I take a breath. 'Alan, I met him in the Franciscan church in Limerick two days ago. He talked to me about forgiveness and belief and...' I lose my voice, getting choked up on my own words.

Alan squints and leans forward. 'You met Luka in Ireland?'

'Alan, Luka passed away...sitting next to me in the church...'

'*What!?*' says Alan in a raised tone. He hesitates like he's waiting for me to respond, but I don't have the words and just sit there with my mouth open. He moves his thumb over the screen of his phone and dials a number. I hear the ringtone from where I'm sitting as he puts the phone up to his ear.

'What's up?' says a young voice on the other end of the phone.

Alan's face softens immediately to a wide smile. 'Hey, buddy. I'm just checking in with ya. Listen, I'll call you back. I gotta take care of something here.'

He hangs up and looks at me blankly, all signs of sympathy faded from his face. 'What the hell is all this about, Will?'

I don't know what to think, but I know I have to get to Andrew.

'I'm so sorry, Alan. I must be mistaken,' I say, quickly standing up.

Alan grabs my arm and pushes the grip of the GX-100 into my hand. 'You tell that cousin of yours to call me.'

I shove the weapon under my hoodie and walk away quickly from the table, left with even more questions than I arrived with.

13 Akureyri

'You took your time!' Andrew barks when I reach the end of the stairs at the restaurant's entrance.

He pushes himself off the wall he's leaning against and walks ahead without saying a word.

I shout after him, 'You're the one who left in a hurry! It was rude.' I quicken my pace, though I'm not that pushed about dealing with him when he's like this.

'Rude?' he snaps. 'He's full of shit, Will, and you know it! This is my dad's supposed best friend—you're telling me he knows nothing—*nothing*—about the TUL? He gave my dad the contract to work with him, Will!' He uncharacteristically stumbles and stutters over his words as if they're too big to fit in his mouth.

We come to the end of a narrow, sloped path that leads into a car park, and neither of us has any idea where we're going.

'I think he's telling the truth, Andrew.'

'Well, then you're dumb!' he snaps.

I pull him to a stop; he turns and shrugs me off, suddenly looking at me like I'm his worst enemy.

'Luka Gudjohnsen is Alan's stepson,' I offer bluntly. 'He changed his name to Luka Dalton after Alan married his mother. If you had stayed longer, he could have told you himself.'

Andrew looks up the hill but doesn't say anything.

'And Luka is still alive apparently.'

His focus quickly shifts to mine; the anger on his face changes to confusion.

'Alan called him. I heard him speak. Luka isn't dead...at least not the Luka I saw in the picture Alan showed me.'

A quick search for 'Luka Dalton' on my phone brings up his Facebook profile, and it doesn't take long to find out he's a student in Akureyri University in northern Iceland.

Andrew scrolls through the profile. 'It's him, but it's not him! Just like it was almost you in your profile picture. We gotta go to this Akureyri place and find out what's going on.'

Another pattern perhaps: two people who have near doppelgangers. Maybe Andrew was right about the incubation chambers producing bad copies of people listed in the crew manifesto.

I put the thought to the side to get my bearings. We're on the edge of a large, open car park with about two hundred spaces, many of them occupied with people coming and going. A busy main road with a bus shelter lies opposite, nestled among the grey rocky landscape. We can't bring the transporter down here because it would attract too much attention, so we arrange to meet Sam a few kilometres outside Reykjavik.

Andrew leads us out along the main road and follows the directions the visor is giving him to Sam's rendezvous coordinates. The open landscape rolls on forever and leaves us exposed to the bite of the cold air. As uncomfortable as it is, the walk gives me some time to put together the pieces we have so far. So what exactly do we know? We know I saw a sicker version of myself in the mirror the very first day I arrived at Tara Hill. We know the Luka we met in the church was also sick and frail, unlike Luka Dalton. We also know there must be some connection between Luka and Ken, presumably through Alan. So in a way we know Ken is connected to the TUL, and so are Alan and Luka.

The problem is, there seems to be—or at least were—two Lukas. One running around Ireland and the other in Iceland.

So it looks like Andrew was right after all, and the incubation chambers are cloning the crew. That means the Luka we're about to go see isn't the same person we met in the church. The question remains, though: who else is inside those chambers? Copies of us? Other crew members? And why is everyone dying?

***

Andrew and I sit in the canteen of Akureyri University, a modest campus set in the rural outskirts of one of Iceland's most-northern cities. I sip my second cup of coffee ever because the buzz from the first one in Reykjavik was just too good, and I wonder why I didn't start drinking coffee sooner. Our table is just big enough for two and rocks a little from side to side, like one of the legs is shorter than the others.

Through a large glass wall, I look down over the main concourse, where twenty or so young Icelanders sit in a circle and look to be debating the finer points of something. Most of them dressed in trendy woollen fleeces, happily letting the world walk around them, though no one seems to mind they're taking up so much space.

A small group of older students, or maybe teachers, are the only other people in the canteen and sitting at the other side of the room near a well-used notice board. A hot blond girl walks by our table and drops off a leaflet with what looks like information about an upcoming student election. Andrew and I smile, and she smiles back but gives us a look that says she knows we're not from around here. I guess in a small community it's easy to spot the outsiders.

I flick through Luka's online profile again and run some of the text through a translator as best as I can on the small screen.

'Says he's studying biology,' I say, 'specializing in equine science. He's been in a relationship with a local girl for about six months.'

Scrolling down through pictures of him, I quickly realise this Luka is a lot more Zen than the one I sat next to in the church. There are entire albums dedicated to happy Luka and his girlfriend working on some farm and lovingly huddled together in cosy-looking rural pubs with groups of friends on college nights out.

'Equine science?' Andrew squints down at the students below us. 'Is that something to do with genetics?' he says, half paying attention to what I'm saying.

'Well,' I say, taking another sip of black coffee. 'that depends on whether you're talking about horse genes or not.'

Andrew flicks his eyes to me. 'Horses?'

'Yep,' I say, putting my phone in my pocket. 'Happy Luka specializes in horseys.'

Andrew takes an extended gulp of juice from the carton. 'You can major in *horse studies* here?'

'Mmm-hmm, there's a lot of pictures of Luka and his missus working on a horse farm.'

'*Horses?*' interrupts Andrew again, like he's stuck in a loop. He focuses his gaze over the concourse again. 'How stupid is that?'

I pretend to cough. 'Says the prospective art student.'

He drains the last of his juice through his straw and squeezes the carton dry then clumsily throws it at me. I look him in his black-yellow eye and finish my coffee.

The canteen starts to fill with loud groups screeching back chairs and forming an orderly queue at the food counter. It seems some classes have finished.

'He may not even be here,' I say, looking down over the crowds of students now moving in and out of hallways beneath us.

'We'll know soon enough,' says Andrew. 'I had him paged at reception.'

I have to admit I'm secretly impressed at Andrew's improv. 'Is that why you took so long in the bathroom?'

He raises an eyebrow. 'It's half the reason.'

Luka comes in through the double doors behind Andrew, wide-eyed as he hesitatingly scans the room, looking for someone familiar who might have paged him here. I catch his eye, but he glosses over me like he has no idea who I am.

'He's here,' I say softly.

Andrew looks around quickly, subtle as a jackhammer. Luka waves at some friends across the room and goes to join them. He walks right past us, looking baby faced in his untidy sandy-blond mess of hair with a green rucksack strewn over his shoulder with various badges pinned to the fabric.

'No way that's the same Luka from the church,' says Andrew, leaning in closer. 'Can't be. He's too healthy looking.' He narrows his eyes and taps his chin with his finger like he's thinking something over. 'Why would someone bother to clone that guy? He looks like a hippie tree hugger.'

I turn down my mouth and can't help laugh at the irony of that statement with Andrew's artistic temperament and long, messy hair flopping down over his ears. 'Not exactly a million miles from a hippie tree hugger yourself,' I say.

Andrew subtly gives me the finger. 'Make a plan.'

I turn around as discreetly as I can. Luka is in the queue for the deli, pointing at something inside the glass food display. I put on my optex and tell Sam we want to keep an eye on him.

'I could launch a communications relay from the tactical-unit lander,' says Sam. 'However, this can only provide sporadic geospatial information and will not be effective when the target is indoors. I recommend attaching your optex to the target for a few moments sir. It will enable me to implant a small tracking module just beneath the surface of his skin, providing complete surveillance of the target.'

Easier said than done. I hesitate to tell Andrew what Sam just told me, as I imagine him diving across Luka's table and smacking the optex to the side of his skull or something equally as messy. However I reluctantly fill him in after a few moments.

'The GX-100 is a stun weapon, remember? We'll just take him out and let Sam do her thing,' Andrew says.

'Take him out? Are we on a SWAT team now?'

Andrew peers over my shoulder then stands up, taking the optex out of his pocket.

I stand up immediately after him. 'What are you doing?' I say in pseudo calmness.

'He just sat down. His friends are at the deli counter. He's by himself.' Andrew screeches his chair back and walks past me.

'Don't...'

I realise the rest of the sentence is useless, as he's already out of earshot.

Andrew turns around and beckons me to follow him. He moves to Luka's table and sits across from him. I join him, and Luka gives a greeting with a flick of his head as he puts some salad into his mouth and chews slowly, no doubt wondering who the heck we are. I screech back the wooden chair next to Andrew and scan Luka's fresh looking face. I find it strange to see him again, looking so different this time. He greets us at first in Icelandic but I make a brief apology that we don't speak the language.

'Oh, okay. Happy New Year!' Says Luka, with his mouth half full in his Scandinavian twang. 'Are you new students? I haven't seen you around the campus before.' His tone is very well mannered, as if he were speaking to friends.

Andrew leans in towards Luka, looking him straight in the eyes. 'You ever heard of a guy called Ken Oakley?'

Luka pauses his chewing and rolls his eyes to the side like he's searching his brain for the answer. 'Hmm, no. Sorry. What does he study?'

Luka's body suddenly jolts, and slumps face first into his salad plate. Andrew discreetly clips the GX-100 onto his own belt and pulls his hoodie over it—he must have stunned Luka underneath the table somehow. In my peripheral vision, I catch someone at the deli counter point in our direction. We're starting to attract attention, but Andrew wastes no time clipping the optex to Luka's temple, and after what feels like forever, Sam affirms that the tracking device is in place and Andrew removes the optex quickly.

14 Seven

It's true…I don't agree with my cousin's 'shoot first, ask questions later' tactics, but it looks like his run of impulsive good luck has won out again—not that I've completely forgiven him for our near-death experience in the RMN last night.

We turn a few heads on our way out of the canteen; I just shrug and walk on.

'He's tired,' Andrew says to Luka's friends at the deli counter while quickly passing by. We barely make it off campus and back to the transporter which is nestled behind a natural slope about a kilometre away.

Once we take off, Sam mundanely keeps the craft at a steady ascent until we break through the cloud cover. The windscreen automatically dims to counterbalance the sun's rays. An accelerative force jolts us forward while the aircraft creaks and settles to the vast increase in speed.

'Any update on Luka?' says Andrew from the seat behind me.

'Nothing substantial,' Sam replies, 'although he has regained consciousness.'

I swing around in my seat and shoot Andrew a look. He smiles out of one side of his mouth.

'You must be relieved,' I say, feeling the vibration of the craft under my feet.

Andrew raises an eyebrow. 'How's that?'

'We found a connection between Luka and Alan, so that kind of proves that your father is involved in all this.'

'You still doubted it?' asks Andrew.

I shrug. 'I just needed something more concrete than that vision you had. I mean, it's not you or anything—it's just the type of person I am. I prefer cold, hard facts.'

'Sometimes you gotta trust your gut, Will.'

'You still think Alan was holding back something?'

He takes a breath. 'I guess I'll go with your gut feeling on that one. You believe him?'

I remember the look on Alan's face when I told him Luka was dead. He wasn't acting. Besides, if he were hiding something, no way would he volunteer that Luka Gudjohnsen is in fact Luka Dalton.

'I believe him,' I say. 'He doesn't know anything about the Furious Angels. And for whatever reason, it looks like someone went to a lot of trouble to clone his stepson.'

Sam turns around in her seat. 'The tactical-unit lander reports a new incubation unit has been materialised in the medical bay. I thought you might like to know.'

That should be impossible, as there's no one back at the TUL—at least that we know of. Sam must have made some kind of mistake.

'*Materialised?* By who?' I say, surprised.

'The program responsible for the materialisation is Seven.src.'

'I know that, Sam, but programs don't just run by themselves!'

The craft descends with our final approach, and everything in the cramped cockpit suddenly darkens as we hit cloud cover again. A loud rumbling shakes the transporter as if something has just exploded in the rear.

'We have hit a weather system,' Sam states calmly.

The craft falls sharply, as if the air has been sucked away from beneath us. I clutch to my armrests and wait for the next wave of turbulence to hit. A flash of lightning stretches across the cockpit window, and the craft banks unsteadily from side to side. It's times like this that I find myself wishing we had a human pilot. No disrespect to Sam, but it's hard for me to trust my life to a computer, no matter how sophisticated she may be.

The cockpit windscreen brightens as we break through the grey clouds, and a torrent of rain batters the fuselage. I'd rather not see us coming in so fast, but I can't look away as we glide in over the forest. Sam holds us nice and steady until a sudden braking force drags us to a halt from behind, and we descend fast towards the narrow gap in the trees. It goes dark momentarily, and then the blue lights of the interior kick in. The rain is suddenly gone, and we find ourselves back in the calm of the vehicle bay.

Andrew and I head to the upper level, and Sam is already waiting for us on the green platform, standing between the screens while reading streams of code on the one to her left.

'You can actually read this, huh?' asks Andrew, looking over her shoulder.

'Only parts of the code, sir. I cannot circumvent the security encryption.'

Andrew takes his optex out of his pocket and tosses it to me. 'Maybe Luka's security clearance is better than ours.'

Sam scans the object in my hand. 'It may be possible to decrypt the program using this optex. Please place it on, sir,' she says.

I immediately do as she asks, but nothing feels any different.

'Your eyes are red,' says Andrew.

'Affirmative, sir,' interrupts Sam as she reads over the scrolling text on the screen. 'Seven.src was written by Executive Officer Luka Gudjohnsen. I believe the purpose of the program is to use human embryos as a means of genetic experimentation.'

Experimentation is one word I didn't expect to hear.

'I don't understand,' I say. 'We thought the incubation chambers were cloning the crew.'

'It is possible that the embryos are those of the crew,' says Sam. 'However, the program contains no data on their true identities.'

'Can't you just open the chambers and find out?' asks Andrew.

'I cannot, sir. The chambers must be sealed until the embryos have further matured, and I also would require the genetic material of the crew, which I do not have on file.'

'How can you tell then?' says Andrew. 'I mean, that this is all part of some experiment?'

'The embryonic growth is accelerated to adulthood for some purpose,' Sam replies. 'You may have noticed the embryos are approaching twelve-week maturity but were created less than three weeks ago. I believe the embryos are part of a genetic experiment because without an appropriate synaptic graft, the adult would have no memories or developed neural pathways…and therefore would not function.'

I suppose there's no point in having mature adult clones if they have the minds of new-born babies. It makes me wonder, though, why their growth is being matured. I guess Luka—or someone—was in a hurry for whatever reason.

Sam's eyes uncharacteristically narrow to a look of near confusion, and she wears a subtle frown that conveys the first emotion I've ever seen her come close to.

'Sirs,' she says, 'I have discovered an active proxy tunnel running within the firmware of this optex.' She turns towards us. 'Someone or another program is using this device to communicate with the unit lander.'

15 Time

It seems someone left himself or herself a back door to the TUL, which probably explains where this Seven.src program is getting its data. Sam can't trace the source of the communication, at least not until someone or something tries to talk to us again.

We know there are two other crew members in the manifesto who are still alive—Chris Beech and Hiro Keiko—but we don't know where they are.

It wouldn't be out of the question that either one of them is trying to communicate with us, but there are easier ways of doing that—like knocking on the door! I'm just not convinced anyone is actually on the other end of the line. We could be dealing with an automated program that's harvesting DNA from somewhere and sending it in.

Then there's Luka, who shows up at just the right time at the church, talks about his sins, and drops his visor on the floor. As far as I'm concerned, Luka's trip to the church was always one way for him. In hindsight I think he felt guilty about whatever experiments he was doing in the lab. Maybe the crossroads he spoke of was our decision to let Seven do its thing or to shut it down.

It's my best guess at this point, but either way, I'm not comfortable with experimenting on human embryos. Considering the crew members are dropping like flies, maybe it's up to us to shut these experiments down. I don't want to be the father of brain-dead clones.

I ask Sam to call up the profiles of the remaining living crew members:

KEIKO, HIRO: SYSTEMS OFFICER GRADE 1

BEECH, CHRIS: TACTICAL OFFICER GRADE 1

They're both equally ranked, but neither has anything to do with genetics. Both of them look about fourteen, around Andrew's age. I ask Sam to tell us exactly what a systems officer and a tactical officer does, but her answer is of no help. I just can't make a link between these two guys and the genetic experiment, and I don't know what their motivation could possibly be for sending more genetic material to the TUL.

Right now there's something else we can do, though—use Luka's visor to decode the programs in the G-Compiler. Sam calls up the list and starts working from the top-down.

FINDER.SRC

ANNEX.SRC

SEVEN.SRC

'Decryption of Finder.src successful,' says Sam after a few moments. 'Analysing.'

She keeps still, with her arms by her sides while her bright-green eyes scan over the endless numbers and letters on the screen. The code makes no sense to me or Andrew.

'Finder.src,' says Sam after a moment, 'was written by an AI persona, specifically Sam Casey's AI persona.'

'Isn't that you?' says Andrew.

'I have no memory of writing this program,' says Sam. 'I can only infer that a previous instance of myself wrote the program or that my memory was wiped since it was written.'

'When was the program written?' I ask her.

'Twenty-nine days ago, sir.'

If Sam is right, then there was another copy of Sam running about a month before we found this place. The timing makes it right after Andrew's father died.

'The program references the synaptic stream reader, a DNA analyser, and the communication module,' Sam states, staying focused on the code. 'I believe the purpose of this program was to identify one or more individuals and to implement a synaptic graft.'

Andrew peers over Sam's shoulder, his bright-yellow eyes trying to make sense of the text. 'What does that mean in English?'

'In abstract terms,' continues Sam, 'the program will seek out an individual and attempt to merge a specific memory with his or her existing ones.'

Andrew glances towards me. 'Then that's the program that brought us here—it's got to be.'

I nod gently but can't help wonder why Sam has no memory of writing this program or why anyone would delete the copy of Sam who wrote it. Someone definitely is trying to hide something, but I have no idea why.

'The purpose of Annex.src,' continues Sam, moving on to the next program on the list, 'was to shut down the command section of the tactical-unit lander.'

'Command section?' says Andrew. 'You mean this green platform?'

'Correct, sir.'

I suppose that might explain why the TUL was half its size when we found it.

'Could anyone have switched it back on?' Andrew asks. 'I mean, we walked up to the TUL, and it kinda just came alive.'

'Negative, sir. The tactical-unit lander read your vital signs and DNA when you selected the "deploy" option on the exterior panel. Annex.src performed an override on the deploy sequence, allowing only either of your DNA to execute it.' Her green eyes scan over both of us. 'You are the only individuals who could have deployed—or indeed, entered—this installation.'

Andrew slicks a handful of greasy hair behind his ears. 'So Finder.src was created to find us, but Annex.src was created to shut this place down?' he asks with effort, as if his brain is working overtime.

The display screens return to normal, and the streams of code clear away.

'Yes, sir,' says Sam.

'But wasn't Luka and another copy of you already here? Why shut the place down at all?'

I wonder if Sam will offer the explanation that's going around in my head.

'I do not have sufficient data to speculate, sir,' she says.

'Think about this, Andrew,' I interrupt. 'Sam writes a program that's supposed to find us, and then she writes a program that shuts everyone out of the TUL except for us.'

'The old copy of Sam kicked Luka out of the TUL?' adds Andrew.

'And Chris and Hiro as well, presumably.'

After a little more probing, we discover Annex was written two days after Finder, and Seven was created between the two. The question is why Sam decided to delete herself then shut down the TUL and wipe her own memory.

Andrew hums through a thought. 'Unless she didn't erase herself. Luka could have done it somehow. I mean, he's gotta be pissed Sam threw him out, right?'

'True,' I say. 'So maybe Luka found a way to somehow delete Sam's program…and get his revenge or whatever.'

As far as I can tell, that would make the timeline look as follows: Ken is killed in a car accident; Sam runs a program to call us here; and two days later Luka runs his program to experiment on human embryos for whatever reason. A day or so later, Sam discovers what Luka is up to and kicks him out of the TUL. Luka hacks into the TUL systems and deletes Sam. Revenge is served.

'And eventually Luka feels guilty for all his sins and gives you his visor!' says Andrew, after I fill him in on my thoughts.

I feel like we've made some progress, but we're still no closer to figuring out why Luka was running those experiments in the first place or, for that matter, what the TUL is even doing here.

Over the next hour, Sam performs further analysis of the embryos in the incubation chambers and discovers each embryo is infected with what she calls a nanocell or NC. These are tiny machines smaller than a human cell with on-board artificial intelligence and designed to be infused into human cells of various types. Sam speculates the NCs tend to repair, modify, or destroy the cells they infect. She doesn't know why the embryos are infected with the NCs, but she does know two of them are rejecting the cells and will most likely die if the NCs aren't removed immediately. She says it's too early to tell whether the newest embryo will accept or reject the infection.

The three of us stand over the four incubation units in the orange glow of the medical bay. The leftmost embryo lies in a foetal position under the skin of the blue goo, its heart beating fast. The second and third have weak heartbeats that are barely noticeable, and these are the ones that will die if the NCs aren't removed. The goo in the newest chamber lies still and level with the top of the base within the chamber. Air rushes in and out of each unit through white snakelike tubes connected to the ceiling. It's all very disturbing for me.

I look over Andrew's shoulder as he paws the glass of the dome. 'You know, it's one thing playing around with the RMN or the transporter or even stunning Luka Dalton,' I say, 'but genetic experimentation is out of my comfort zone.'

Andrew sighs. 'Will, you know that thing I said, about trusting your gut sometimes?'

'Hmm…?'

'I need you to trust mine again,' he says, downbeat. 'I wanna ask my dad what to do.'

Andrew turns around and leans back against the chamber. 'I know what you're gonna say, but before we shut this thing down, I just wanna go and…and tell him I don't know what to do and I'm sorry.'

I realise he wants to go visit his father's grave. It's the last place I want to be right now, but I won't let him go alone.

16 The Graveyard

We leave the TUL and, with our hoods raised, walk across the field through a frozen mist. It's a silent walk against the backdrop of distant thunder, and the tunnel of trees provides us a little shelter as we approach the junction.

I don't know what Andrew expects to do or find at the graveyard, but I think I understand why he's going. When my grandmother died, my mother would take me to visit the grave, and talk to her as if she were able to hear. I used to say there was no point in visiting graves because the person isn't there anymore; his or her body is just an empty shell in the ground. Right now, when I see someone younger suffering because they've lost a parent, it's hard to think that way. Maybe I've been cold in the past because it's my defence mechanism against my own father's death.

Andrew and I cross the junction and walk into the church grounds. We crunch along a gravel path to a stone archway that's guarded by winged statues looking down at us from either side. The earth is still fresh at Ken's graveside, but some of the wreaths and flowers are a little disturbed, probably from the wind.

Andrew crouches to tidy some of the mess, and I hesitate to help him at first because I'm not sure if it's my place to do so. I hesitate for other reasons too, because there's stuff here that I haven't yet come to terms with, and I don't want to take down my guard. There's too much going on right now, and this time isn't for me—it's for Andrew.

I remind myself I'm here for my cousin, not for my own grief or loss. I gently reset some of the flowers that are turned over and organise the area as neatly as I can by putting some little stones around the stems to support the tiny green stalks. Kneeling here next to the grave makes Ken's death all very real. He was a young enough lad, just turned thirty-eight with two years between him and my father. I flick my eyes to his headstone in the plot next to Ken's; it's impossible for me not to look.

PATRICK OAKLEY

DIED AT AGE TWENTY-FIVE

Stupid kid. I realise now just how young he was and wonder what my parents fought about that night before he took out the car, full of booze. I guess the Oakley's are cursed with car accidents. I never come here to visit my father because I don't want it dragging me down. I look at Andrew and put my arm around him. Maybe I'm really doing it for myself; I don't know. Andrew stops what he's doing and looks down at the earth.

I wipe some of the rain from my face. 'They're keeping each other company now, your dad and mine.'

Andrew smiles briefly, but the expression disappears just as quickly. He reads some of the inscriptions on the wreaths.

'Brother—I suppose this one's from Marie.'

It's the largest wreath. I take my hand from his shoulder and dust some earth off my palms by brushing them against my knees. A brief look around the place tells me it's pretty small, maybe thirty graves altogether, organised into rows of five or six.

Andrew stands up and pats down his soaking hoodie. 'When do they put in the stone with the inscription?'

I remember hearing somewhere it took at least a month or two.

I hear Andrew say something under his breath, but I can't make it out. He brings a hand to his forehead and stares into the scattered earth as if he can see something beyond it. The rain suddenly intensifies into a torrent as he grips the side of my left shoulder.

'We could get him back to the medical bay, back to Sam,' he says anxiously. 'She could bring him back... the synaptic graft—if we can get a sample of his DNA! Maybe that's why my dad led us to the TUL, Will.'

I don't know what to do with this, but there's a pleading in his eyes telling me he's waiting on my next word. I look down at the grave as little puddles form on the surface, bringing such finality to it all.

'Man, I dunno if that would be possible!' I shout through the torrent.

He fumbles around in his jacket, takes out his optex, and places it firmly into the palm of my hand.

'Listen to me—the embryos in the...in the incubation chambers...all they need is DNA and a synaptic graft. My dad's memories...we can accelerate the growth just like Sam said,' he says, stumbling over his words as he rushes to speak them.

I think over what he's saying, and for a moment, it seems he could be onto something, but there's a flaw in his logic: we don't have any of his father memories lying around, even if we managed to successfully clone him.

'Will, ask Sam, please. I can't do it...' he begs.

I make an attempt to reason with him, but the words don't come out of my mouth in any coherent way. I think he needs to at least try something, and I can't refuse him.

'Please, Will!' he persists.

I take his optex from him and slide it on.

'Sam, you there?'

'Go ahead, sir,' says Sam faintly.

'Sam, do you know where we are?'

'Yes, sir, approx...eighteen...dred metres from...unit lander,' she says, her words broken and drowned out by the noise of the rain.

I don't know how to phrase the rest of this sentence without sounding clinical, but I compose my words as best I can.

'Listen, there's a…' I hesitate for a second and throw a glance at Andrew to make sure what I'm about to say isn't offensive. '…a body buried about two metres down near my current position.' I wait for some kind of response, hoping I don't need to clarify any further.

'Yes, sir,' says Sam after what feels like too long.

Andrew is clinging to every word I say. I break eye contact as an unexpected thought enters my brain. Maybe we don't need a backup of his dad's memories after all; maybe it's possible to extract them from his father's body somehow. I figure it's our best shot.

'Is it possible to….to take a synaptic graft from the body?' I shout.

A moment of pause ensues again. Andrew tilts his head back and looks upwards, muttering something, his lips barely moving.

Sam crackles through just before I have a chance to repeat myself. 'No, sir…synapt…ownload…ossible due to advanced decomp…and incomplete.'

'Sam, please repeat,' I say.

'Negative, too much time has elapsed since brain death, sir,' she says with a little more clarity.

I give Andrew the bad news. He turns his back on me and takes a few steps forward. He clenches his fists with his head hanging.

I take a step closer and remove the optex. 'I'm so sorry, Andrew. It was worth a try.'

'If I'd just gotten to him the night of the accident,' he says, his voice shaky with emotion.

'Don't do this,' I say. 'You'll drive yourself crazy.'

He turns to face me. 'Why didn't I just show James my drawings instead of waiting for you?'

I shrug. 'It still would have been too late!'

Andrew wipes the rain from his face and slicks his hair back. He leaves his hand on the back of his head. 'Maybe…maybe not. You don't know.'

I put my hand on his shoulder. 'Leave this go, man.'

He drops his hand and pushes mine away.

His response takes me by surprise, but I put it aside.

'Andrew, the synaptic graft probably needs to be done really fast after somebody dies. You were never going to make it in time,' I say as best I can through the torrent.

He pushes my chest with his two hands, and I stumble backwards a little, holding my hands out to the side as if asking him with my body language what he's doing.

'It's not your fault,' I persist.

He takes a step forward and pushes me again; the impact makes me flinch this time.

'Whadda you care?' he says, out of breath.

I look at him through the rain, straight in the eyes. He's not the only one who's upset, but he doesn't know it. I've buried how I feel, and I want to keep it that way.

'Hit me then, if it makes you feel better,' I say forcefully. Deep down I think I want him to hit me, and maybe I want to hit him back.

He pushes me again and again, his face tensing up with each impact, focusing in on my chest as does so.

I stand my ground this time. He raises his hands again, but I brush them away.

'It's all so easy for you, isn't, Will? Synaptic graft?' He laughs under his breath. 'What the fuck do you know about anything? I don't know why I even listen to you—all you do is make up some big words like you know what you're talking about, but you don't!'

I wipe the rain from my eyes. 'I don't want to argue with you here. It's not right.'

He throws a look at the headstones. 'You couldn't have saved your father, but I could have saved mine.'

A wave of anger washes over me. 'You're delusional! Nothing's going to bring your dad back.'

He takes a swing at me with his right fist; I quickly jerk my head back, and he narrowly misses. Before I know what's happening, he's pointing the GX-100 straight at me. I knock it out of his hand, but he lunges towards me and tackles me to the muddy ground. I push him off and shove my palm into his face. With a quick roll, I reverse our positions, pinning him down with one knee on his chest. I pull back my right arm with a tightly clenched fist, as if I'm about to strike him.

His eyes swell up with either anger or sadness—I can't tell which.

'Do it!' he shouts.

I retract my arm a little farther but bail at the last moment. 'Don't you ever point a gun at me again,' I say.

I get back on my feet and extend my hand to help Andrew up. He ignores the gesture and recovers by himself. Avoiding eye contact, he walks a few paces to his father's grave and falls again to his knees. He takes a fistful of mud from the ground and throws it to his side.

I walk up behind him and stand over his shoulder.

He sniffles back some emotion, takes another fistful of mud, and throws it again to the side. He digs into the grave with his two hands and drags more earth away. I crouch beside him and lower his arms. The torrent of rain dies away, leaving us in the silence of the graveyard.

'You didn't come to the funeral,' he whispers.

My heart sinks. I hoped he hadn't noticed.

'I couldn't face coming out here, Andrew.'

He looks at me and blinks a tear down his cheek. I can feel his sadness like it's infecting me. 'You miss your dad too?' he asks.

It's a question I'm surprised I have to think about. I feel angry and sad when I'm here, but I supress those feelings as best I can. Back in the city, I'm safe again, and I don't have to deal with passing my father's grave every day. I know avoiding this place isn't the right way to deal with my loss.

'I do miss him,' I reply.

Saying the words out loud is strange because I've never admitted how I feel to anyone before.

Something catches in the corner of my eye, and I look to my left to find Marie standing near us under a red umbrella.

'I was getting worried about the two of you,' she says, taking a few steps forward. 'I hadn't heard from ye all morning.'

I wonder just how long she's been there. We awkwardly stand up and wipe ourselves off.

She collapses her umbrella and shakes it out, giving us a judgmental once-over.

'We got caught in the rain,' offers Andrew, before she has a chance to say anything.

Marie delicately moves some drenched hair out of Andrew's eye with her finger. Andrew immediately slicks it back behind his ears.

'That black eye of yours is looking a bit better,' she says, casting a brief but purposeful glance to me.

His shiner has changed to a fine yellowish bruise that's hidden most of the time behind his long fringe.

'C'mon' she says, beckoning us to follow her. 'I'll make ye up some lunch back at home.'

17 The Morgue

Lunch had a catch: an hour-long lecture about the evils of alcoholism. I'm pretty sure Marie knows we polished off that whiskey the other night or found Andrew's secret stash. She didn't say it directly of course, but the leading glances and 'I told you so' eyebrows from James were all the confirmation I needed. Sometimes it's best to just shut up and listen to Marie when she's talking, because she has the same stubborn streak Andrew has, mixed with a natural air of authority. Even Andrew avoids arguing with her.

That night we make a little detour and head down by the pier. Sitting there in silence for a while gives us a chance to talk things out.

Neither of us is prepared to let any of the clones die for the sake of whatever experiment Luka was intending.

'I was certain of it, Will,' Andrew says drearily, gazing out over the loch.

It's a shame Sam couldn't do anything for Ken. The worst part is that if we'd gotten to him sooner, maybe we could have retrieved his memories and cloned him. I know right now, however, that there's no point in OCD'ing on that.

I nudge his shoulder 'Tell me about my uncle.'

Andrew's eyes search for the answer like it's out in the loch somewhere. 'He was...distant...a lot,' he finally says, shaking his head. 'I dunno why he didn't come home much after Mom died. He was all alone really.'

'He worked hard, I suppose? Buried his head in the job?'

Andrew shrugs. 'I never knew he had this other life, making the TUL and the weapons and...' His voice trails off to a whisper: 'Who are the Furious Angels, Will?'

I put my arm around him because I can feel his emotion coming to the surface again. 'Maybe it's us,' I say, looking out over the loch. 'For whatever reason, your father brought us to the TUL after he died. However he did it doesn't make any difference, with...a computer program or divine intervention—who cares? He wanted you to be part of this, and he didn't want you to be alone.'

Andrew laughs under his breath. 'Yeah, I guess.'

A moment of silence follows; perhaps neither of us knows what to say.

'I'm sorry about earlier,' he offers.

'I would have done the same if I thought it could have saved my father,' I say softly.

'You were right—it wasn't the place to fight, and I didn't mean any disrespect.'

'I know...'

'All the technology in the TUL,' Andrew says, 'and we can't bring either of them back.'

I shake my head. 'Even if we could, I don't think a copy of someone is really that person.'

'What if they're our clones? What if that's us growing in those chambers?'

'Maybe,' I say, 'but either way, their fate is the same. You heard Sam…either the accelerated growth process will kill them or the nanocells will.'

Andrew nods in silence with a sullen concentration.

'That's not even what gets me,' I continue. 'What bugs me is why there are clones at all. Why was Luka experimenting like that in the first place?'

'The crew were dying. Maybe he was looking for a cure?'

'I cure for what, though? What could possibly have killed almost everyone…and so young?'

'What do I do, Will?' he says.

I'm a little surprised he's asked me that question. Up until now, he's been pretty determined to walk his own path.

'I think this has to be your choice, but whatever you decide, I support you one hundred percent.'

We reason it out for about a half hour. Andrew decides that removing the nanocells and shutting down Seven.src is the most humane thing to do. I'm glad he's made that decision because it's the one I would have chosen too.

Andrew dons his visor and gives the order to Sam. He momentarily waits in silence for her reply.

'Sam removed the cells, but something went wrong,' he says, climbing to his feet. 'She can't shut down Seven.src.'

I stand up. 'What happened?'

'Someone's blocked our security clearance from the outside. Sam thinks she's got a trace.'

***

It looks like our attempt to shut down the program attracted the attention of someone or something. I'm hoping whatever just communicated with the TUL is actually a remote automated system and not someone else we have to deal with.

We descend to the green platform.

'What happened exactly?' I ask Sam, who's looking over a large map.

'Something has tried to send data to Seven.src remotely.' She says. 'I have traced the communication to 52.481259 by -8.488134.'

A satellite image rapidly magnifies into a large, modern-looking building and its surroundings.

'It looks like University Hospital,' I say.

Sam enhances a section at the rear of the building. 'The communication originated from a subterranean compartment here,' she says, pointing at the screen.

'Subterranean?' asks Andrew. 'A basement maybe?'

'Did your father have any research links with the hospital?' I ask him.

Keeping focused on the map, Andrew shakes his head.

'Sam, what tried to communicate with Seven? Was it an automated program or a person?' I ask.

'I cannot determine that,' she replies.

'Can you get us in unnoticed?' asks Andrew.

'The hospital? Yes, sir. I can guide you directly to the source once you're inside.'

Andrew hands me my GX-100 stun weapon. 'Just in case,' he says.

Looks like he's eager to leave for the hospital right away. I clip the weapon to my belt and pull my hoodie over it.

'Remember to wear your optex at all times, or I will be unable communicate with you,' interrupts Sam. 'Shall I materialise armaments?'

'Do it,' says Andrew.

I gesture for Sam to stop. 'It's too high profile.'

'I can materialise light armour AR-1 under your attire,' continues Sam.

Andrew looks at me and smiles. 'Is that low profile enough?'

I agree, and Sam materialises the AR-1 underneath my clothes; it grips on to my skin tightly. Andrew slides up the sleeves of his blue hoodie, revealing the vinyl-like black material of the armour underneath. 'This thing bulletproof?' he asks.

'Of course,' says Sam, as she retrieves something from the orange beam. 'The fibre is resistant to nonenergised projectile weaponry and all G-class energy weapons such as the GX-100, which you are currently carrying.'

She hands us a pair of heavy-fabric gloves etched with parallel lines that resemble circuit pathways.

'What do they do?' asks Andrew, looking them over.

'They have a multitude of uses, sir. They are capable of manipulating small objects and provide an interface with mounted weaponry. I believe the former use will apply to this mission.'

After a little bit of kitting up and a crash course in matter manipulation, we drive out into the darkness of the forest and across the field. I try to make some sort of logical link between the hospital and Ken's research, but I can't find any. I'm absolutely clueless why someone or something would try to communicate with us from the hospital. Limerick City isn't exactly Silicon Valley, and I'm pretty sure there isn't a research lab in the city, let alone the country, capable of communicating with the systems in the TUL. I guess Ken could have been working with a lab at the hospital, but I'd be very surprised.

After an hour-long drive, the RMN powers down in the empty parking lot at the rear of the hospital. A wave of rain blows across the darkened windscreen.

Now that we're here, I don't want to go in. I look up at the tall imposing building and ask Andrew what he expects to find inside.

Andrew dematerialises his door, bringing the beating rain into earshot. 'A clone of my dad workin' on a computer. Then he looks at me and asks where I've been all this time!'

It might sound like a joke, but I know he wishes it were true.

I briefly visualise that scenario, and the thought unnerves me. I don't say anything. I just dematerialise my door, and we both get out.

'Sam, can you hear me?' I say through the rain.

'Yes, sir. Switching you to night-thermal vision.'

Everything lights up in a brighter shade of grey. Andrew's body glows in a mixture of a red and yellow heat signature.

We walk towards the wall surrounding the towering hospital. Little squares of light intermittently pattern the building from its many windows.

'Scale the perimeter now,' interrupts Sam.

Andrew springs up and quickly scales over the top, like he's done this a thousand times.

I try to imitate his moves but lose my grip on the wall and fall backwards.

'Apply your glove to the wall surface,' says Sam. 'It will bond with the material.'

I lunge at the surface, and the glove sticks to the wall. I bring myself to the top using my hand as an anchor. When I think about releasing my hand, it disconnects from the surface, and I'm able to jump clear the other side.

'Five seconds, hostile in your path. Maintain position,' advises Sam.

'There's the door,' I whisper, nodding towards a glass-panelled entrance directly across from our position. A faint heat signature walks by on the other side of the glass.

'Proceed now,' Sam says after a moment.

We stay crouched and move silently towards the door. A push-button keypad lights up in faint green next to it.

'Sam, the door is controlled by a mag lock. It needs a code to open,' I say.

'Look at the scanning mechanism, Officer Oakley.'

'Scanning mechanism?'

'Focus on the numeric keypad.'

I do as she asks. A series of augmented coordinates scroll over the little black box, and then a two-tone beep sounds out from the keypad, releasing the door.

We quickly step into the darkened corridor. The smell of bleach from freshly cleaned floors invades my nose.

'Seven seconds to hostile contact,' says Sam calmly.

I close the door gently behind me. As I look down the corridor, the faint rolling of wheels gradually gets louder. There are no doorways, and there's nowhere else for us to hide. This could get awkward.

'Five seconds,' says Sam.

'Any ideas?' I whisper.

'Three seconds,' says Sam.

I draw my GX- and signal for Andrew to step towards the wall and keep close to it. I do the same on the opposite side of the corridor.

A porter in blue overalls whistles a happy tune to whatever song is playing in his ear. He pushes an empty trolley through the corridor junction and doesn't even notice us before disappearing around the corner. A faint ding of an elevator rings out to the backdrop of sliding doors.

'Proceed left, second exit on the right. Then descend. Target area is empty,' instructs Sam.

The glow of a TV comes to life through a semi-open door across the hallway. I recognise some faint cartoon voices. Somebody laughs. A little boy, by the sounds of it.

'I am detecting an optex transmission signal from the room directly in front of you,' Sam's voice says in my ear.

I look at Andrew. 'How many people are in that room, Sam?'

'One young male. No threat perceived,' she responds.

I push open the door, and a child sits up in the bed. He turns his head swiftly in my direction, and I see something that shouldn't be possible. His eyes are a bright yellow from the optex he's wearing. He holds his breath, obviously surprised to see us. I'm surprised too—surprised he's wearing an optex.

'It's OK, little man,' Andrew says, approaching the bed. 'We work here.'

His face softens. 'You're angels too. You have bright eyes just like me!'

The words send a chill all over me. He's about ten, with a slim, frail build and untidy brown bed hair.

'I haven't seen you before,' he says.

I take off my glove and put out my hand. 'I'm Will, and this is Andrew.'

He grabs it weakly, and I feel like any pressure would crush him. 'I'm Chris,' he replies.

Andrew walks to the end of his bed and takes the clipboard from the metal frame.

I smile and flick my head at the large stack of books on his bedside cabinet. 'You read all those?'

'I have a gift,' he says. 'Ever since the angel came, I can read really fast.'

He leans over and takes a book from the top of the pile. 'Look, I'll show you!' He leafs through pages until he gets to his bookmark and begins to read. '*Datis retractari compellis, et ut ita dicam, quam de Scripturis exempla iudicandum...*'

He reads as if it were poetry, right down to the put-on Italian-like accent. Flawless, every word.

'Will...' says Andrew softly from the end of the bed.

Chris's eyes widen with a smile, and he looks up from the book. 'The angel helped me.'

'What angel, little dude?' I ask.

'The angel with the red eyes,' he replies.

The angel with the red eyes...I figure he's got to be talking about Luka. At least it's my best guess considering that's the colour Andrew's eyes changed to when he put on Luka's optex.

I look at Andrew and whisper, 'Maybe our friend here was next in line.'

'He's Christopher Beech,' says Andrew sternly.

'I prefer "Chris,"' says the child, who wearily sinks into his pillows.

My mind flashes back to the crew manifesto: Chris Beech, tactical officer, grade 1.

Looks like we've found the next crew member, but what's he doing in hospital, and why does he look a few years younger than he's supposed to be? Maybe this is proof that Sam was right about the whole accelerated-growth thing. Andrew clips the chart onto the metal frame. We excuse ourselves for a moment and head back to the dim corridor.

'What's wrong with him?' I ask.

'Not sure, but it says he's terminal,' says Andrew softly.

I sigh. 'Another soon-to-be deceased crew member.'

'Proceed to the doorway directly ahead,' interrupts Sam's voice in my ear. 'Descend to the subterranean compartment to the source of the transmission, sir.'

'I thought we were at the source of the transmission,' whispers Andrew.

'Negative, sir,' she says. 'I was only able to detect the energy reading from the optex when you were within range.'

I glance over to the double doorway across the corridor. The word MORGUE catches my eye.

Andrew sighs and swears under his breath. From the tension I'm reading in his body language, I'd say the last thing he wants to do right now is face dead people.

'Stay with Chris,' I say. 'I'll be back in a minute'

Andrew swallows hard. 'I'll go with you…'

'You got my back.' I interrupt. 'Besides, this'll save time.'

I walk quickly across the corridor before I have time to think about it and push through the double doors. The temperature drops rapidly as I descend to the bottom of the stairs, so I pick up the pace along a blue-lit narrow hallway and stop by some double white doors. I peer into the darkened interior through small circular windows.

'You there, Sam?' I ask, needing some reassurance.

'Yes, sir.'

The door creaks open. Overhead neon lights automatically flicker on to a gentle hum as I step inside—it's too bright for the relatively small area they light up. Quickly I turn my head to check on the invisible presence I feel behind me.

'Your heart rate is over one hundred seventy beats per minute,' says Sam.

I stand over a solitary metallic slab in the centre of the room, where a body lies covered by a white sheet. It feels like an age has passed since I came in here.

'Where's the source of this bloody signal?' I ask anxiously.

Three examination tables are lined up at the north wall. Everything is so clinically clean yet so bleak. The room absorbs all sound, which makes me even more conscious of my isolation.

The covered body creeps into my peripheral vision. My voice falls off to a whisper as I ask Sam a second time where the signal is coming from.

I hold an apprehensive breath and pull pack the sheet a little because some morbid curiosity leads me to do it. Lifeless, messy blond hair rests over a greyed forehead. I don't uncover it any further.

A subtle breeze of air wisps over the base of my neck, and I can sense something has changed in the room.

'Sam, talk to me!' I say in a single breath.

A subtle, almost inaudible creak from behind gives me a sensation that something is moving. The beat of my heart thuds around in my ear.

'Andrew,' I say softly, without looking around.

'No,' says the voice behind me.

I feel myself losing composure. I snap my eyes shut briefly then open them again. I turn around but I don't believe what I'm seeing.

'Luka?' I say with obvious nervousness.

He makes no response. His armour-covered body stands rigid, his red eyes fixated on mine like I'm the only thing in the room.

I need to say something, if only to help myself keep calm.

'I…I thought you were dead…'

His armour creaks as he moves towards me. 'You think of death in such linear terms.' He stops just in front of me. 'Did Sam send you here?' A rasp wheezes from the base of his throat. 'Our clever little AI friend,' he says, looking into my eyes.

I can tell by his sickly appearance that he's identical to the Luka I met in the church, which means this isn't Luka Dalton I'm speaking with.

I break eye contact. 'Sam traced a signal to here...Something was trying to communicate with Seven...'

I realise immediately that 'something' was Luka. I stop and swallow hard because I'm intimidated by Luka's proximity and the fact that I watched him die in front of me a few days ago.

He dismisses anything further I might say with a move to my side. He pulls back the sheet from the dead body.

My morbid curiosity makes me look, and a sickening feeling sinks to the pit of my stomach, not because of the dead body but because the body is Luka's. The same Luka who died in the church. A sunken smile sits on his face like a carving in grey stone.

'Death doesn't exist, you know,' he says, with searching eyes looking over his predecessor as if expecting to find something.

I can't find the words to respond.

Luka nods as if satisfied. 'At least he had an honourable death—born out of one life, one mind, and one whole memory, undistorted by the pains of rebirth.' He walks a few paces in front of me. 'We must express our darker purpose, William.' He tightens the glove on his hand like he's making a better fit.

'Rebirth?' I say. 'Is that when you keep cloning yourself and download your old memories to your new body?'

'An imperfect bastardised science,' he snaps. 'An infliction on those minds gullible enough to fall for its promises.' Luka crosses his hands in front him. 'I think it would be better for us both if you were to be reborn, William. Simply forget everything that's happened.' He takes a composed step towards me.

I take a step backwards and collide with a hard surface. 'Why are the Furious Angels dying, Luka?'

I need to buy some more thinking time, which I'm quickly running out of.

'Greed,' he says dismissively. 'Lambs to the slaughter, trying to fix the sins of humanity.'

'What sins?'

He raises his tone and shrugs matter-of-factly. 'Gluttony. A lust to know everything. But man was never meant to know everything—just enough to live one life.'

He makes another move towards me. I can't process what he's said because the panic in my brain won't let me.

'Andrew was wondering about his father...about the TUL and—.'

Luka shakes his head. 'There's nothing I can say that would help our peculiar situation. Imagine what would happen, William, if the unit lander were to fall into the wrong hands?' He moves closer, standing face-to-face with me. 'Into the hands of people who have no idea what they're doing?'

From his tone it's obvious that he's talking about me and Andrew.

'Then take it back. We didn't ask for it!' I say nervously. 'We just want to know the connection to Andrew's father.'

A smile disappears as quickly as it cracks onto his beaten face. He shrugs. 'Now therein lies my problem, William.' He puts a hand on my chest. 'You are much the same as I remember you.'

This Luka is obviously a clone, but how could he possibly remember me? Unless he somehow downloaded his predecessor's memories.

He reads the confusion on my face. 'The place I remember you from is far from here. It's like...' He takes a breath. 'Like looking through from the other side of a mirror.'

He moves his hand around my neck and tightens his grip. 'I need to convince our forgetful AI that it would be better if she restored my security clearance to the unit lander, or she'll be responsible for a number of innocent deaths.' He nods. 'Beginning with yours.'

I grip my hand tightly around his and try to wedge it free. His fingers feel like steel rods stabbing into my neck. I gasp for air as he lifts me from the floor.

'You and your young...friend...were Sam's idea. I think two of you are more of a chore than just the one...hmm?'

My air supply is cutting off. I pry my fingers into his hand. 'Please...Luka. We didn't do anything to you,' I say, struggling.

He shakes his head. 'You were careless, like children playing with grown-up toys. There are only seven batches of nanocells and therefore only seven chances to restore life to what I call reality,' he says venomously. 'You've already wasted four of those chances by playing God.'

My vision clouds, and I kick out my legs with my last bits of strength.

'Your actions are a stain on my work,' he continues.

I plead with my eyes to for him to let me go.

'There is no, death, William,' I hear him whisper.

I pull down on his hand as hard as I can, but his grip gets even tighter. My throat is closed. My legs feel heavy.

'You'll be reborn.' He tilts his head to the side. 'All of this will be a confusing memory.'

In desperation, I snatch the GX-100 from my belt, Luka's body jolts as I stun him. His face grimaces with the third and fourth impact but he still doesn't let go.

'Get the fuck away from him!' Andrew suddenly shouts from behind.

Luka points to Andrew with is free hand. 'Interfere with me, and I'll interfere with you.'

Luka drops me to the ground and my legs give way. I gasp frantically for air unable to do anything else.

Luka looks down on me. 'What good is your armour, William, if you don't know how to use it? I could take away your life without using weapons.'

Andrew fires a projectile into Luka's shoulder. 'Our lives aren't yours to take, you son of a bitch.'

Luka shrugs off the impact. A sudden force pulls the top of my head backwards as Luka drags me along by the hair. I jolt forward from a kick to my lower back and fall on my hands. Luka raises his arm. A heavy weapon of some sort materialises and a blue targeting beam takes aim on Andrew's chest.

'You, Andrew, are an unexpected variable I am no longer prepared to entertain.'

Suddenly the blue targeting beams disappear. Luka's eyes narrow as if he didn't expect it to happen.

I quickly scramble to my feet and run towards the door.

'Proceed to the rendezvous point immediately,' says Sam's voice out of nowhere.

With some effort I push Andrew backwards out of the room. My cousin resists like he wants to keep on fighting Luka but I succeed in getting us back to the hallway. Those red eyes are the last thing I see, looking up at me from the bottom of the stairwell. Luka stands composed with hands by his side but doesn't pursue any further. A sinister smile creeps out from the side of his mouth. In desperation, I punch the fire alarm panel near the emergency exit hoping the unwanted attention will force Luka out of the basement and away from Chris. The place erupts in a chaos of sirens.

We run to the wall, and this time the adrenaline alone lifts me over in one move. The heat from the burning RMN hits me, which is inexplicably ablaze in the empty parking lot. Sam descends in the transporter, and Andrew and I scramble inside.

Our AI rescuer swings around in her seat, while a force from beneath tells me we're rapidly ascending.

'Welcome back,' she says, glancing over us both.

'You too,' I say, trying to loosen my collar.

'What happened to the car?' asks Andrew.

'Luka's armour was emitting a dampening field, but fortunately I was able to overload the RMN's power module to disrupt it.' She nods. 'You are welcome.' Sam says confidently.

Something is different about Sam—a confidence she hasn't demonstrated before. She sits, leaning to her right, in a short-sleeve black T-shirt with the Furious Angels insignia on her left shoulder.

As I take a seat opposite, a belt materialises across my body. 'Did you update your program or something?'

She glances at me. 'No, I got my memories back.'

18 The Ark

Sam was able to fully decrypt Seven.src, which probably just saved my life. When she decrypted the program, she found her memories locked inside, purposely hidden from her by Luka.

The transporter makes a calm descent into the vehicle bay.

'So you remember everything then? You can finally tell us what Ken was doing with this place?' I ask, as the craft gives a little stopping jolt.

Sam thinks for a moment. 'You both deserve answers, but they may not be what you want to hear.'

Andrew unstraps himself. 'Tell me what I already suspect, Sam,' he says, leading the way towards the door. 'That two of the clones are of me and Will.'

The question goes unanswered until we step down to the darkened vehicle bay. The plane dematerialises into nothing, leaving us standing in the large, empty space.

Sam uncharacteristically breaks eye contact and looks over us both. 'That is technically true,' she says. 'Two of those clones are of you and Will.'

I'm surprised at her response because I still believed there was another explanation.

'The clones are made of your genetic material,' continues Sam. 'but they have no memories or personality, and they never will. They're just empty shells,' she says in a downbeat tone.

'Why then?' I shrug. 'Why did Luka or Ken or whoever clone us in the first place?'

'It was Luka,' says Sam quickly, 'but for reasons you can't possibly imagine.'

'Try me!' snaps Andrew.

Sam flicks her head towards the cavern door and back again. 'You know that most of the crew are dead, but you don't know why?'

'So the clones and the deaths of the crew are somehow linked?' I ask.

Sam nods but doesn't offer anything further.

'Luka wanted to find a cure to whatever was killing the crew,' says Andrew. 'That's the reason for his experiments.'

'Yes,' says Sam. 'But they were unethical experiments. Luka helped himself to your DNA and infused it with nanocells. He accelerated their growth, and the result is now growing in our lab.'

'And what makes us so special?' says Andrew, with a tone of disbelief. 'Why would our genes help find a cure to anything? What does it have to do with my father?'

Sam smiles weakly. 'Because you are special,' she says with sympathy. 'Your genes and Will's genes are different from those of the crew. You both are clean, uninfected, unenhanced.'

I laugh under my breath. 'Why are we different from everyone else?'

Sam takes a breath.

The floor suddenly shifts beneath us, and we ascend upwards a few metres towards a 3-D projection. It takes me a moment to figure out what it is: a gaseous cloud, like a green-and-purple nebula from a sci-fi movie. The projection fills the entire space of the room, and the nebula erodes like the northern lights waving over the atmosphere. Pulsing stars push their light through the darkness; fast particles collide and scatter debris in all directions, flying over our heads like intensely bright fireworks exploding in random places. Spiral galaxies form, taking shape around bright epicentres.

Sam walks under a projection of a black hole, around which everything seems to be rotating. She looks upwards, getting lost in the image.

'This is a giant gravity well,' she says after a moment.

I walk to her side, taking in as much of the simulation as I can. 'So this black hole, it made the crew sick?' I ask.

'No,' says Sam. 'This black hole divides my universe from yours.'

Andrew looks up with squinted eyes. 'Bullshit!' he says after a moment.

The gaseous nebula retracts from all corners of the room; galaxies spiral out of existence once again; and stars break apart, their cores splitting like atoms in a nuclear reactor. Everything returns to the source—the black hole becomes an angry, fiery red ball; a violent surface spits waves of energy in collisions of yellow.

Sam scans around her. 'This moment was the start of all things. The beginning of time.'

Before Andrew can say anything more, a thunderous rumble bounces off the walls of the cavern around us. The fiery ball collapses in on itself, as if the core is consuming the outer surface and engulfs it in a burning bright light. Ripples of shock waves accelerate outward through space; the surface of the ball darkens; and a corona forms around its mass. It explodes in a magnificent release of energy that's too bright to look at. Gas and matter catapult outward in equal measure as awesome slip steams of energy. For a moment I see something familiar to me—a splitting of an atom like the symbol on our armour, the symbol of the Furious Angels. Spiral galaxies and countless yellow stars form again and again. The simulation suddenly pauses in a freeze frame.

I look around me with a narrow-eyed confusion. 'The Big Bang?'

Sam nods. 'And what do you notice?'

'The symbol on our armour,' I say, because it's the first thing that comes to mind. 'When the stars break apart, they look like atoms splitting in two.'

'Indeed,' says Sam calmly. 'But that isn't the meaning of the symbol. You need to think bigger.'

The simulation rapidly reverses until we're back at the beginning.

Sam darts her eyes at me. 'Observe the core of the giant mass…'

The mass collapses in on itself in slow motion. The core splits in two, like a cell dividing by mitosis.

'So the symbol is describing the Big Bang?' says Andrew.

'This exact moment, to be more precise,' Sam explains. 'You understand the Big Bang as a singular entity, but the truth is…when this event occurred, it gave birth to twins.'

The simulation super accelerates, and each opposing arch of the black hole seems to mirror the other.

'In the beginning, the separation of the giant core created not one but two universes, separated by this gravity well,' Sam continues. 'We named it the Binary Universe. We call our universe the "light" and you the "dark," because from our perspective, we believed your universe was dark matter before our technology evolved to detect it.'

I think back again on the symbol: one side of it in black and the other in white.

'And you're from this…light side, this other universe?' asks Andrew.

'Yes, as is this Tactical Unit Lander obviously.'

The raised platform we're standing on melts away slowly into the floor.

'You must have noticed by now the rather huge differences between the technology in the lander and the technology you're accustomed to,' says Sam.

Over the past couple of days, I've become accustomed to getting my head around concepts I never thought I'd see in my lifetime: advanced printing of complicated machine and high-tech weaponry and armour. Right now I'm speaking with an AI who's indistinguishable from a human being, and in the medical bay are clones growing in stasis chambers, modified by tiny nanomachines at the cellular level. It's difficult for me to understand the technology or conceive how matter can be manipulated and how life can be created artificially, but I can see and touch these things. As I look up at the simulation and watching the creation of the Binary Universe, it all feels surreal—like I hear all of Sam's words but can't even begin to absorb them.

'We thought this place might have belonged to the military, some project Andrew's father was working on,' I tell her.

'Ken Oakley' says Sam with a smile. 'I was his assistant in my universe. He was like a father to me.'

I look at Andrew, expecting him to respond. Instead he looks on at the floor with sad yellow eyes.

'I know what you're thinking, Andrew,' says Sam, 'and you're correct. I didn't know your actual father—the Ken Oakley from your universe. But I wish I did.'

Andrew takes off his visor and looks up at her. 'So what am I thinking now, Sam?'

'You're probably asking yourself what the connection is between the Ken Oakley in my universe and your father.' Sam looks at me. 'And you, Will, you're wondering what's so terrible that it could kill a highly technologically advanced people.'

Sam must have been reading my mind because that's exactly what I was thinking.

'Answer my question first,' says Andrew.

'The two questions are connected,' she says. 'The Earth of my universe is dying. We came here in hope of finding a cure. The Ken Oakley in my universe was the head of a syndicate called the Furious Angels. He sent Luka and me here to find as many of the Furious Angels' counterparts as we could and to establish a base—'

'Counterparts?' I interrupt.

Sam nods. 'Counterparts are what we call our doubles in this universe.'

'So where you're from,' Andrew says, 'my father's double is still alive?'

Sam nods. 'He was alive when I left to come here. Our histories are practically identical up to a certain point in our recent past. From the brief analysis I did of your timeline, it looks like something happened in our universe that didn't happen to yours: around the mid-nineteenth century a global pandemic broke out in North Africa and quickly spread across the European continent, claiming the lives of more than fifty million people. This was a wake-up call for humanity and ushered in a new era of biotechnological discoveries. We were eventually able to cure the pandemic and make great advances in genetic therapies that vastly improved quality of life on a global level, but there was something else. As well as eradicating the disease, our scientists discovered ways to substantially increase our learning abilities. Initially this led to the formation of elite think-tanks of highly intelligent individuals. After some time, we saw new advances in technology, which led to advanced artificial intelligence and the manipulation of matter on a molecular level. The technology you see in the unit lander is a product of our advances.'

'So what went wrong?' I ask.

'There was pressure from governments to develop a mainstream genetic enhancement for entire populations. You see, in your version of Earth, many people consider access to the Internet a fundamental human right, and denial of access to that resource is considered a disadvantage. Well, in a similar way, many political people of my Earth resented that only certain groups of individuals were chosen for the intelligence upgrade. After a massive equality movement, a new bill was passed in the United Nations, declaring the intelligence upgrade to be a fundamental human right of every citizen on the planet. In 1965 Humanity 2.0 was hailed as this "new era,"' she says, making air quotes, 'for mankind and released to the general population. It originally consisted of a series of genetic treatments and therapies that resulted in a vast increase in memory, cognitive ability, reason, logic, and so on. Within five years it was refined to a simple jab—like a flu shot—and was given en masse like a global vaccine. However, there were unforeseen side effects to the therapy, which affected all second-generation 2.0s.'

'Second-generation?' I say. 'You mean kids born to parents who were upgraded?'

Sam nods. 'Yes. Almost every child born to an upgraded parent eventually suffered from severe abnormalities, including a significantly weakened immune system and shortened life-span. A hundred million kids never saw past thirty years of age, and that was just the start, because efforts to repair the treatment made it even worse, and the death rate increased. Radical religious sects grew in popularity in the late 1990s; they saw the whole thing as a punishment from God—children suffering from the sins of the parents, if you'll pardon the dogma.'

'So the Furious Angels are one of these sects?' I ask.

'No!' Sam interrupts sternly. 'The Furious Angels are a privately funded syndicate, one of many groups trying to reverse the damage we've caused. It's not a religious organisation.'

'But the text underneath the symbol mentions something about children and faith. It sounds pretty religious to me,' says Andrew.

'We found ourselves in a generation squeeze,' says Sam. 'The old die, the young die, and eventually there's nothing left in the middle, only a widening generation gap. So eventually we ended up with this catch-22 where the children of my Earth are using Humanity 2.0—the very thing killing them—to try find a cure for the genetic abnormalities caused by Humanity 2.0!'

This makes me think again of what Luka said in the morgue about greed and solving the 'sins' of humanity. I now know what he was talking about.

'The Furious Angels are what they call a high-risk, high-return initiative,' Sam continues. 'At the dawn of the twenty-first century, we discovered this universe, which is a parallel image of our own. Some major investors funded the idea of cross-universal travel with the hope of finding a solution to our rapidly deteriorating situation.

By now parents were getting pretty sick of burying their dead children, and the pressure to find a cure to the Humanity 2.0 side-effects was immense. At great cost the syndicate built a small ship called the Ark and loaded some of our best technology on board. We had only enough room for one crew member, so we had to choose carefully. Your father's counterpart eventually persuaded a colleague of his to send his son on the two-year exploratory mission.'

'Luka?' says Andrew

Sam nods. 'On our side, Luka was an exceptional geneticist from a young age. He originally studied animal genetics and completed his PhD by the age of ten. He came up with a therapy to reduce the effects of Humanity 2.0 in lab mice. It was enough to get the attention of Dr. Oakley, who convinced Luka's father to let him join our project. Eventually, because of his young age and temperament for genetics, he was selected to come to your Earth on board the Ark. The problem was that no one had ever completed a cross-universal jump before, and there were complications. First it took us ten years to actually get here, not six months, as predicted by our simulations, and Luka had to live out the prime of his life in that tiny ship. He spent a lot of that time reading the rhetoric of those religious sects and years later became convinced Humanity 2.0 was indeed the sins of our parents, and he's now hell-bent on destroying it. He doesn't just want to eradicate the side-effects, he wants to reverse Humanity 2.0 completely.'

'Where's the Ark right now?' I ask.

'In a high orbit, beyond your detection technology.'

'Forget the ship,' says Andrew. 'What about Luka? The guy who got brainwashed by all that religious stuff is dead, right? I mean, he died in the church in front of me and Will.'

'That Luka is dead'—Sam sighs, as if the thought genuinely makes her sad—'but his memories were preserved and sent to the incubation chamber in the Ark, where another clone was accelerated to maturity. The Luka you just met in the hospital is that accelerated clone.'

'So let me guess,' says Andrew. 'There's another clone in the Ark waiting to take over after this Luka dies?'

'Possibly,' says Sam. 'There's a catch for Luka: his accelerated clone won't live very long—probably just a number of days—because he doesn't have any nanocells to help counter the H2.0 side-effects. For that reason there are also many safety protocols in the Ark's computer that don't allow more than one accelerated clone of the same genetic material...but genetics is Luka's field, so who knows what's possible?'

That isn't good news. If Luka gets around the safety protocols, then we'll have to deal with a fresh accelerated clone every few days. It would appear booting him out of the TUL is only a half solution to our cloning problem.

'Why exactly did you kick Luka out of the TUL?' asks Andrew. 'The programs we found in the computer told us you threw him out of here then tried to find us.'

Sam hesitates before speaking, which up to this point, isn't like her. She pensively bites her bottom lip as she thinks over the answer to my question. I'm guessing she isn't a good liar.

'The Furious Angels have three primary directives,' she says, choosing her words carefully. 'Because we only had enough room on the Ark for one crew member, we needed to find creative ways of bringing more people from our side over here. In the end we decided to bring the downloaded memories of selected members of the Furious Angels team with us. We were supposed to find the counterparts of our seven most-senior team members on this side then debrief and clone them. Then we'd upload our memories to their clones—effectively transferring our crew's memories to healthy bodies on this side. That was our first primary directive. The second directive was to conduct controlled experiments on the living crew using our limited supply of nanocells to see if we could reverse the damage caused by Humanity 2.0 while leaving the intelligence upgrade intact. The third directive was to transmit our findings home and set up a two-way communication link.'

'But Luka didn't follow these directives, did he?' I ask.

'Not at all,' says Sam. 'He decided he didn't need a functioning crew—he just needed their DNA. He also knew the controlled experiments we were proposing on the living crew would take years to yield results. First he took a sample of your DNA, followed by Hiro Keiko, whose DNA Luka "acquired" just before I exiled him. Chris Beech, the boy you met at the hospital, is the most recent clone, which brings us to the present time. Luka destroyed the memory files we brought with us so we can't perform any synaptic grafts; we can't upload any memories; and the clones in the lab never will regain consciousness if they're accelerated.'

'So you shut Luka out because you didn't agree with what he was trying to do?' asks Andrew.

Sam nods. 'I shut him out physically, but he still had virtual access to the TUL computer through Seven.src. In fact that's the reason he dropped his visor in the church. It was the Trojan horse that he used to gain access.'

My heart sinks a little bit more when I realise we were hacked by the oldest trick in the book. We brought Luka's visor right into the TUL and let him inside the computer—just like he wanted.

'After ten years of observing him in close quarters,' she continues, 'I knew he'd never adhere to the Furious Angels' directives...Luka had no intention of reuniting the crew's counterparts on this side. He spent years on the Ark devising experiments to kill off Humanity 2.0 using our nanocells and he has no interest in merely controlling the side-effects. He wants to undo all of the H2.0 enhancements because he believes they are offensive to God. Ironically, Luka is so convinced that his work is justified, he will kill anyone he perceives as a threat.'

'Why can't Luka just do his experiments on the Ark ship?' asks Andrew.

Sam shrugs. 'Because he needs the nanocells, which are highly fragile and exceptionally dangerous. They're built into a secure stasis chamber within the tactical-unit lander, and they need to be stored very carefully until they're used. Luka won't risk moving them. As long as Luka is locked out, he can't access the nanocells directly.'

'And he can't make any more of these supercells?' I ask her.

'No, the materializer we have in the TUL doesn't do organics. We had to be careful about what we brought with us. The last thing we wanted was for the technology to fall into the wrong hands and another potential disaster to happen in this universe.'

'Luka must have been pretty pissed with you, Sam,' Andrew interjects.

Sam presses her lips together and doesn't respond.

'The Finder program...' Andrew says, hesitating, 'was written just after my dad died. I...don't think that was a coincidence, was it, Sam? I mean, my dad dies, and then all this happens?' He turns to me. 'Or am I just being paranoid, Will?'

'Ken's death seems to have triggered everything, Sam,' I tell her.

'I wrote Finder.src,' she says with a sigh, 'to bring the two of you here because I thought Luka might eventually go after you two. I thought if I brought you here and expelled Luka, maybe you'd be safe...' She hesitates again, trying to find the right words.

'We know you brought us here with that program, Sam,' I say, 'but why would Luka go after us, and why did this all take place after Ken's funeral?'

Sam sighs again. 'We came here about three months ago. I convinced Luka to at least look around for the counterparts of the senior crew members, but there were problems—differences between our timeline and yours. It's difficult to explain, very difficult...' she says, her voice trailing off to a whisper.

'Try,' orders Andrew.

She gestures as if her hands are helping her make a point. 'Chris is terminally sick with cancer, and he's four years younger than he should be. Heiro Keiko is just an infant, and Luka...' She hesitates. 'Luka was always...disappointed with his counterpart.'

'Luka Dalton?' I interrupt.

'Yes. When he found Luka Dalton, he couldn't stand to look at him, like he was an unpleasant reminder of another side to himself. To make a long story short, Luka Gudjohnsen didn't want anything to do with the counterparts of the senior crew members.' She looks over the two of us. 'Nothing to do with you two either, I'm afraid.'

'What's all this got to do with my father?' asks Andrew.

Sam looks up at Andrew. 'Because I stupidly...' she says, like she's angry with herself. 'I stupidly contacted your father and alerted him to our presence here. Even though there were differences, I believed I could debrief him and have him help me convince Luka what he was doing was wrong. Ken's counterpart was Luka's mentor on our side...I thought he would listen to your father...and that Luka would change. I'm so sorry, Andrew,' she says in a whisper. 'Maybe it was the insanity of ten years in deep space...I don't know.'

'What are you saying, Sam?' says Andrew nervously.

She takes a breath. 'Your father wasn't killed in a car crash, Andrew. Luka just made it appear that way.'

Andrew tenses up, and those familiar anger-stress lines I've come to dread appear again across his forehead.

'And he did it because of me,' continues Sam, 'because he wanted to warn me that if I brought anyone else here and interfered with his work, people were going to die. When I found a way to lock him out of the lander, I deployed Finder in secret and started all the events in motion. I thought if Luka could murder your father on a whim, he might kill others. And I couldn't stand by and let that happen. This is all my fault.'

19 Luka's Move

Andrew turns and walks away at pace. I run to catch up, but I'm not sure what to say to him or if there's anything I can say that will help the situation. Andrew has a single focus —he's not thinking about the mission of the Furious Angels or the Binary Universe or anything else Sam just told us.

Sam materialises on our way to the green platform. 'You should stay here until...' That's all she utters before Andrew brushes past, nudging her shoulder in the process. I feel bad for her because I know she's only trying to help in her own way. It's strange too, because ever since she got her memories back, the former mundaneness of her personality has translated into something more human.

Andrew ascends to the surface, and I follow.

'You don't need to follow me!' he says, running into the cold night air.

I put on my visor to counteract the darkness. 'I'm worried about you.'

'Don't be!' he shouts over his shoulder as he avoids the low-hanging branches.

It takes extra effort to keep pace with him, and I wonder where he thinks he's going. I think about leaving him do his thing, but it doesn't feel right to me.

Andrew sprints the last home stretch towards the loch then leaps onto the wooden pier and runs towards the edge. I call after him, but he ignores me and plunges into the freezing blackness of the water below. My visor automatically switches to thermal vision, and a purple-blue glow penetrates from beneath the surface. I follow the dimming glow along the pier as far as I can as the warmth drains from his body. He suddenly lunges out of the water in a quick movement and clings to the edge of the boards, making a gasp for air.

'Tell me again…what Sam said…'

I crouch and extend a hand. 'C'mon, man. You'll freeze in there!'

Andrew ignores my offer of help and pushes himself up out of the water. 'Tell me what Sam said!' He sniffles, dripping water all over the boards. His staring eyes are the only part of him that isn't shivering.

'Luka killed your father,' I say as gently as I can.

'Why? Why did he do it?' he persists with a tremble in his words.

I swallow hard. 'As a warning to Sam not to involve us in all this, because he wanted Sam to suffer for what she did.'

Andrew climbs to his feet. 'That's not what I heard,' he says through his shivering. 'This has nothing to do with my father. My father died for nothing, Will. He was a fucking pawn.'

I know he's right; Ken was a pawn, used in Sam and Luka's power struggle for a cause we know nothing about. I hold back my thoughts because I know they won't do any good.

'Then don't let your father's death have been for nothing. We'll finish this and keep Luka out of the TUL until he's dead once and for all. We won't give him what he wants.'

Andrew looks down, still holding himself, trying to keep warm. 'I want him dead, Will. I want Luka dead. I don't want to keep him out of the TUL. I want him to die, and I wanna be the one to kill him.'

'You both need to return to the unit lander immediately! If Luka is looking for you...'

The unexpected sound of Sam's voice from behind makes me jump. I really wish she wouldn't appear out of nowhere like that.

'I thought your range was limited,' I say through gritted teeth.

'I was able to slightly increase the power of the TUL projection system,' she says. 'It isn't a good idea to stay out in the open like this!'

Andrew's clothes immediately morph into the AR-3 heavy armour, and the same happens to mine, weighing me down with the weight of the thing, though at least I'm warmer now.

Sam holds out a visor in her left hand, but Andrew doesn't take it.

'You got my father killed,' he says bluntly.

Sam seems taken aback by his directness. 'I underestimated just how intent Luka was on carrying out his plan. I know I made a mess. If you only knew how I felt Andrew...' she says sorrowfully.

'You can't feel!' snaps Andrew. 'You're a machine. You're nothing but light and circuits and bad programming.'

'This isn't helping, man,' I say.

'You both need to stay at the lander,' persists Sam. 'until I can neutralise Luka's threat. I'll do everything possible to put this right!' she says, stressing her words.

'Oh will you though?' says Andrew condescendingly.

'Time isn't on Luka's side,' she says quickly, 'and if we're lucky, he hasn't found a way to circumvent the safety protocols in the Ark.'

I get the feeling Sam doesn't have a ready-made plan for this scenario.

Andrew's eyes narrow in on her. 'If we're lucky? Are you serious? You don't know what you're doing!' he shouts, clenching his fists. 'You never did. Will and I were better off without your so-called help!'

Sam tenses her lips like she's holding back the first thing she was going to say. She seems to be barely keeping her AI composure together.

'And what would you do?' she says after a moment. 'Go take some weapons and neutralise Luka?'

Andrew nods fervently. 'Yup. You got it.'

Sam sighs. 'You really think it's that easy?' Luka almost choked William to death without firing a single projectile.'

'We outnumber him three to one!' shouts Andrew.

Sam quickly matches his volume. 'You can't use the weapons! You don't know how! You know nothing about the AR-3 or how to use the optex properly. Luka is very well trained. He *will* kill you.' She stops herself from saying any more and shakes her head in frustration.

In the brief silence, I feel like a referee standing between them, but I know I'm siding with Sam. Andrew's plan sounds like suicide, but I know why he wants to do it.

'Well, we're not just gonna hide in the TUL and hope everything works out,' says Andrew, lowering his voice, 'because let's face it, Sam, everything hasn't exactly gone to plan for us, has it?'

Sam takes a moment before responding. 'That's true, Andrew.' She casts a defeated glance at me. 'And you're right, Will. I didn't plan for this.'

Looks like the optex allowed Sam to read my mind again.

'I wanted to keep the two of you safe,' she continues, 'because you're innocent in all this. Instead I've only put you in direct conflict with Luka.'

'You're not responsible for Luka's actions,' I tell her.

Sam fixes her gaze on Andrew. 'I'm an orphan just like you,' she says. 'I lost my parents to the H2.0 genetic modification and I lost my friends. I lost the memories of the crew we brought with us on the Ark, and I lost my physical body. I don't want to lose you two as well. Try to understand that I'd gladly exchange my life for your father's, Andrew,' she concludes, speaking with a humility stretching beyond her years.

Andrew looks on in silence like he's trying to weigh up everything Sam has said. I know she feels responsible for what has happened to Ken and only wants to make good, but this is all different from Andrew's perspective, and I've never been able to predict what he's going to do.

He rubs his tired eyes, barely keeping himself together. 'Look, you did what you thought was right—I get that. But Luka killed my father for nothing; he tried to kill Will at the hospital; and for all we know, Chris Beech is next. But let's get one thing straight Sam: I'm not gonna hide like a bitch. If you're telling me the three of us can't use all the weapons in the TUL to kill that bastard, then what's the point of all this? I'll do it alone if I have to.'

This is the most composed and determined I've ever seen him, and both he and Sam stare each other down like I'm not even standing between them. I know I don't feel the same way; I want to play it safe and stack the odds in our favour behind the safety of the TUL. But I also want to support my cousin, my friend.

'What do you think Luka will do next?' I ask.

Sam hesitates for a moment then says something I didn't expect to hear. 'I think it's probable he's going to track down his own counterpart, Luka Dalton.'

'For what?' asks Andrew.

'There's a procedure…a high-level synaptic graft. It can transfer a complete mapping of Luka's memories and personality traits to his counterpart, like copying memories to an accelerated clone, but we're not dealing with a clone this time. It could buy him years and also circumvent the safety protocols in the Ark.'

'So he just switches out Dalton's memories and personality with his own? He can just take over his mind?' Andrew says in disbelief.

Sam looks pensive, like she's just thought the whole thing through, and it makes perfect sense to her.

'It's never been attempted in our combined histories,' she says. 'But if he succeeded, it would buy him years of healthy life…and that's exactly why he'll probably try to do it.'

'So how do Andrew and I stop him?' I ask.

Sam snaps out of her thought bubble. 'I don't know if you can.'

'We can if you help us,' says Andrew.

20 Training

I get to the point where trying to sleep is futile. I lie on my back and wait in the new crew quarters Sam made for us within the west wall of the cavern. My anxiety keeps my arms straight by my side, and all I can do is stare blankly into the darkness.

I've had dreams in which I'm running down stairs or narrow hallway and feel a presence closing in around my body. I can't let the presence catch up with me because I sense it only wants to do harm. I concentrate all my willpower and intention on escaping from its approaching grasp but to no avail. Just before that crucial moment when I get caught and eaten or murdered, a door opens—a trigger says to my brain, 'Wake up.' In that instant, I'm free, and I realise it's all just a dream as the false sense of reality fades away.

Right now, in this room, the only thing keeping me focused through the pitch-blackness is the whoosh of extracting air vents in the rocky ceiling. I need that gentle white noise because its constant presence reassures me I'm safe. It reminds me that lying here in the darkness isn't a dream, and there's no escape—no saving hand is suddenly going to appear and rescue me.

The hardest thing to face is the realisation someone is actually thinking about killing me and his intent is very real. It makes every other squabble or past drama I've had in my short life pale in comparison. It makes me realise how vulnerable I feel. I admire Andrew and his bravery for wanting to stand up to Luka, for not falling away into a shell and hoping it all will sort itself out. He's younger, but he's got something on me.

I'm worried too for my aunt and uncle. They live simple honest lives a million miles away from the idea of binary universes and counterparts. They could never understand all this but deep down I could do with their help because I don't feel I can keep them or Andrew safe. Maybe he's right, maybe the best thing we can do is get Luka before he harms anyone else in my family. I don't know what to do.

I turn on my side and sink into the cool side of the pillow.

'Are you really gonna try and kill him?' I say.

Andrew shuffles around in his bed and rearranges himself to face me. Somehow I knew he was already awake.

'I wouldn't have cared if Luka died in that morgue,' he says. 'I'd have killed him to protect you.'

I can't help but smile to myself at the thought of Andrew wanting to protect me.

'Let Sam think of something,' I offer.

'I know I can kill Luka if I have to…You think I'm wrong, don't you?'

I briefly weigh it up, but I can't tell him he's wrong.

'If someone killed my mother, I'd want revenge,' I tell him. 'I just don't want you to have his death on your hands; he's already taken enough from you.'

White light suddenly brightens along the rocky walls of the small room. I close my eyes and groan, but the tightness of a visor materialising against my skull together with the AR-3 around my body brings me to focus.

'It's time to get up, guys,' says Sam's voice in my head. It makes me wonder if she's somehow been listening in on our conversation.

'It'll be alright Will.' Says Andrew as upbeat as he can and I admire him for trying to reassure me.

'I know it will, I got your back!' I say and tell him to send a text to James telling him we've gone camping for the day. If we're lucky he'll buy it.

After eating something Sam called food, we get up and make our way to the dimly lit vehicle bay, where she has prepared some makeshift weapons training. She scans our faces with her bright-green eyes. Her lack of confidence is infectious while her armour creaks with the slightest of movement.

She smiles as reassuringly as she can, but I can see through it.

'So are you ready to begin your training?' she says.

'What do you want us to do?' I ask.

'I want you to shoot me.'

I laugh.

'We've got no weapons,' Andrew says, gesturing to me and him.

Sam points to her temple. 'An optex is a weapon.'

'You want us to throw it at you?' I say.

Sam extends her right arm and clenches her fist; the double barrel of a mounted weapon materialises over her glove with a complex mesh of black tubes extending back to her shoulder. Mounted on the rear of the barrels near her elbow is a panel of some kind, probably for tactical information or aiming.

A faint dimple creases into her cheek as she discharges two blue projectiles into Andrew's chest. He yells out as he falls backwards on his ass. Sam pans the weapon in my direction. I raise my arm and make a fist, but nothing happens.

'Too slow,' she says.

I'm suddenly winded, clutching my chest and staggering backwards to the ground. I didn't even see the projectile discharging.

Sam lowers her arm. 'You…are…dead,' she says matter-of-factly.

'You could have just told us what to do!' I say, catching my breath.

'I don't think so,' she replies dismissively. 'You needed to feel the impact of the projectile so you'll try harder to avoid it in the future. The optex is your most fundamental weapon—a neurosynaptic interface that translates your thoughts and intentions into machine commands. It can interface with the tactile glove and act as a mobile molecular assembler for small objects, as well as tools and weapons. Everything is powered from the AR-3 armour, and that's why it can feel heavier than the AR-1 when you first wear it.'

I stagger to my feet, the finer details of what Sam said not sinking in.

'Can the visor read detailed thoughts or just basic stuff?' asks Andrew half-heartedly.

I think I already know the answer to this question.

Sam raises an eyebrow. 'Well, it depends on—'

'What am I thinkin' right now?' he interrupts.

I sigh. 'Really?'

He shrugs.

'Mammary glands, human female…perky,' says Sam immediately.

Suddenly every perverted thought I can possibly imagine involving Sam enters my brain. Everything I've been supressing since her perfect body first materialised on the command platform. I can't stop the torrent of filth coming through. I break eye contact and stare at the floor.

'Fortunately,' says Sam, interrupting my thoughtgasm, 'I'm well accustomed to extrapolating useful information from…inappropriate data.' Sam clenches her fists, her armour creaking with the slight movement. 'You have three seconds to materialise an HX-1 projectile weapon.'

'Why a HX-1?' I ask, buying myself some time.

An identical mounted weapon materialises along her other arm. Maybe this is my punishment for all the stuff I just dreamt up.

'That classification of weaponry is lethal,' she says. 'The AR-3, depending on its state of charge, can only withstand four or five quick successive impacts from a HX-1.'

'And if I have no armour?'

She raises her hands with tightly clenched fists, one pointing at me and the other at Andrew. My chest is still raw from the first impact. I immediately take a couple of steps back while defensively raising my right hand.

'It will incinerate your internal organs.' She says matter-of-factly.

Sam's armour recedes towards her body as if she's getting vacuum packed inside it. My jaw drops open; every curve on her slender frame is amplified to perfection, and if I didn't know any better, I'd swear she was messing with my head. A circulatory system of veins briefly glows in a dark red along her arms and chest as her suit attaches itself to her body like a second skin. All I can do is watch the beautiful scene unfold and wonder what she's going to do next. I sure wish she'd turn around.

My shoulder suddenly arcs violently with the first impact, and I slam into the floor. The second projectile burns its way into my chest, and I quickly hitch my knees into the foetal position as another set of projectiles flies overhead. Every sensual thought flees from my brain. I don't think I want to train any more.

Screechy footsteps move back and forth around me. I roll onto my back with a groan and watch a brief exchange of fire between Sam and Andrew. She dodges Andrews's efforts as if she already knows where the projectiles are going. Andrew dives to the side and fires again before hitting the ground. Sam flips backwards in an awesome single spring and discharges two projectiles into Andrew's chest. She lands perfectly, like a gymnast making a perfect dismount, every curve amplified against the armour.

Rolling onto his side, Andrew groans in pain. I use the opportunity to make a stealthy effort to climb to my feet, but I'm too slow.

I hold up my hands. 'I give up.'

Sam looks me up and down like she's judging my manhood. 'Are you going to tell that to Luka when he has his hands around your neck again? Raise your arm, William. You need to expect the weight of the weapon.'

I muster up some focus and turn my body to the side, clenching my outstretched fist with intent.

'Look at your hand if you have to. Think clearly, like you're giving it a direct order.'

My hand lowers with the weight of the materialising HX-1. Two heavy-duty coiled tubes stretch along my forearm from the double barrels in a brief trail of white light. The tubes connect into a small blue display at my elbow that says the weapon is in training mode. It's a strange feeling—like thinking about the object is enough to make it appear. Now I'm starting to get what Sam meant when she said the visor was a weapon.

'Now fire the HX-1,' she says, easily dodging a return projectile from Andrew with a twist of her body. 'Use your mind to give the command. Think of nothing else.'

I focus on my outstretched arm.

Sam fires again, and judging by Andrew's groan, she hits her intended target.

The projectile fires from my weapon and lodges into Sam's side while she's distracted. She immediately returns fire, deadening my right leg. Andrew fires two rounds into Sam's chest, sending her flying backwards into a flash of white light, and she dematerialises into nothing.

'I think I've proven my point,' says Sam from behind us.

Damn it, I wish she'd stop doing that.

Andrew crouches over with his hands on his knees. 'Come on! It was my first time, and I got you!'

I shake out my leg. 'I think she was going easy on us, Andrew. I'm sure AIs are tougher than they seem.'

Sam's face hardens with a wide-eyed look that almost cuts me in two. 'I'm not an AI. My memories and personality are grafted onto an AI net that simulates a human brain. Don't call me that again.'

It looks like I've definitely hit an AI nerve.

'So you were a gymnast then?' says Andrew. 'Or could all the Furious Angels pull off those moves?'

The veins on Sam's armour emit a fleeting red glow. 'First,' she says, placing her hands on her hips, 'the armour can assist you in unarmed combat, which is why you couldn't break Luka's grip in the morgue. Second, please don't speak about me in the past tense.'

Andrew uncharacteristically has no response.

The room darkens, and the three of us suddenly find ourselves inside a large yellow rectangle with a perimeter emanating a strong light from the floor. I hope this isn't some kind of punishment for insulting her.

'The AR-3 is also an interface that can communicate with your optex,' continues Sam. 'It can assist you when weaponry can't be assembled or when the environment is too volatile to discharge energy weapons. To activate the assisted-combat mode, just think about the armour. Imagine the suit sinking into your skin, like it's becoming a part of you.'

Andrew looks down at his outstretched hands. The suit obeys his thought and sticks to his body, as if it's deflating inward from the chest down.

I clear my mind and try to imagine the armour becoming part of my body, but all I can do is imagine Sam's body. Nonetheless, a sudden tightness protrudes into my neck and chest as the material deflates like a thick film receding towards me. The sensation extends to my arms, and the circuit pathways of the armour become imprinted veins against my skin until I can't tell where one stops and the other begins. A downward wave envelops my chest, and my newly imprinted veins briefly illuminate in a dark red that responds to each breath. My legs and arms feel considerably lighter, and the weight of the suit is no more, as if someone just lowered the gravity inside the room.

Andrew examines himself from head to toe. 'Doesn't leave much to the imagination, Will.'

'The armour will adjust to the movements of your body,' Sam interrupts, scanning us over, 'and help you fight more effectively. Sometimes weapons can't be discharged or are unavailable. Hand-to-hand combat may become inevitable.'

'I suppose you want us to fight you now,' I say, feeling rather exposed in the suit.

Sam raises an eyebrow. 'Indeed I do.' She throws a glance to my cousin. 'Defend yourself, Andrew.'

Andrew laughs under his breath. 'I don't know if I wanna hit a girl.'

Before I know what's happening, Sam has landed a flying side kick into Andrew's chest that sends him crashing to the ground.

Andrew exhales then swears loudly before climbing back to his feet. He shakes out his hands and raises an awkwardly rigid boxing guard with tightened fists. It's a rookie mistake—never have your body full facing when approaching a target because it gives the opponent more to hit. That was the first thing I learned in Tae Kwon Do class when I was a kid.

Sam throws her visor to the floor but doesn't break eye contact. It probably makes the fight fairer because she can't read Andrew's moves before he makes them.

'The most dangerous opponent in an armour-assisted combat is one who has no inhibitions or experience,' says Sam, turning her body to the side with her hands crossed at her groin.

Andrew throws a clumsy jab at Sam's face, overextending his arm. Sam deflects it away with a hard, swift forearm against his elbow, but Andrew keeps face and shakes it off.

He bounces on his feet and lets his arms drop to his side. 'All right, Sam, you wanna hit me?' he says in a low, calm tone.

Sam springs towards him and pumps the blade of her foot towards his chest. Andrew slides backwards and avoids it in a perfectly timed move; his body language says he didn't expect to do it.

Sam follows up with a fast punch to Andrew's mouth; the smacking sound makes me grimace. He staggers backwards.

Sam gives a sigh and takes a few steps back to her starting position.

'You need to trust the suit to defend you. Don't resist its movement,' she orders.

Andrew loosens out his jaw and returns to his starting position, full-facing his opponent again. He makes a 'C'mere' gesture with a flick of his hand.

Sam quickly steps in with a downward stamping kick, but Andrew somehow traps her foot in a perfectly executed X block. He has no idea how to counter, however, and Sam rotates fast in mid-air, twisting out of the grasp in one impressive movement and narrowly avoiding Andrew's chin with her back leg. I could watch her all day long.

She sidesteps back to the starting point and sizes her opponent up and down, deciding where to hit him next. Andrew uses the opportunity to attack with a well-executed snap kick towards Sam's stomach, but she easily deflects in what I feel is a muted move. I think if she wanted to, she could have defended a lot harder.

Andrew bounces on his feet and quickly skips in with a second forceful kick. Sam side steps backwards with a simple deflection then skips in with a fast side punch to Andrew's jaw. Andrew shakes it off quickly and counters with a jumping kick that Sam narrowly avoids with a defensive slide.

Sam's confidence this morning surprises me, like another part of her AI net separate from her personality kicks in when she's in combat mode. I guess maybe she's lucky, being able to focus solely on the task at hand without all those unhelpful human emotions getting in the way.

She spins on her back foot and swings a back heel into Andrew's skull. The smack of bone hitting bone makes me flinch. Andrew staggers backwards, but a tension of determined focus mixed with anger makes him raise his guard and square up to Sam once again.

'Now think about a counterattack,' says Sam, her calm manner sharply contrasting Andrew's heavy breathing.

Andrew—or rather the armour—snaps a perfect blade kick to the side of Sam's head, narrowly missing her. He repeats the move again and follows up with a double punch but to no avail.

'Too predictable!' Sam calls out. She turns her body side-facing and kicks at Andrew's head—a narrow miss. Then she hops forward on her back leg, throwing a kick at Andrew's face. Andrew quickly deflects the kick downward, but Sam swings a fast 180 and brings Andrew to his knees with a sweep to the back of his leg.

Sam quickly gets back on her feet. 'Too slow, too clumsy.'

Andrew drives a forceful punch into the side of Sam's knee. His angry expression tells the whole story.

Sam staggers backwards but stays her ground. Andrew recovers to his feet and throws another jab. Sam deflects the left punch and then the right; then she counters with a kick to the stomach and follows through with a knee to his face. Andrew falls to the ground.

I remind Sam this is supposed to be a training exercise. She throws a glance over Andrew to gauge his condition then shakes out her right hand like she's gearing up to dish out more punishment.

An out-of-breath Andrew stands up and skips in with a perfectly executed side kick to his opponent's rib cage. Sam locks the offending leg and pulls Andrew towards her. She forcefully punches Andrew in the thigh, raising him off the ground with the impact, then pushes his dead leg away. Andrew retreats with a backwards limp.

Sam shrugs. 'If you can't beat me, then you can't beat Luka. It's that simple!'

Andrew takes a deep breath and stubbornly raises his guard. Sam raises her guard and edges in slowly. Andrew throws a jab, but Sam intercepts, twists Andrew's wrist, locks his arm, and applies downward pressure at the elbow, bringing Andrew down to one knee.

'Do you understand now,' Sam says with a sigh, 'that you have no chance against Luka?'

21 Deadly Recon

I know Sam was trying to teach us a lesson, but it's of little use because Andrew's motivations to engage Luka have their roots deeply planted in his seeking revenge for his father, and I can't blame him for that. Secondary to those motivations, he wants to protect Luka Dalton and Chris Beech, who are equally as innocent as Ken was. I want to protect them too, but I don't know if we can or what the cost will be if we fail.

Getting out of the AR-3 is much worse than getting into it. For starters, every muscle in my body instantly aches as the armoured skin detaches itself from mine, unplugging from my nervous system one inch at a time. My arms feel like they've been lifting dumbbells all day, and even a simple action like tightening my fist is a chore. Then the price is paid for every impact I thought I didn't feel over the last number of hours.

For all the perfectly executed techniques I thought I'd never be able to do as a kid in Tae Kwon Do class—and for all the perfectly timed blocks, kicks, and punches just now—there's a debt of pain owed to my body that's now being cashed in.

I stand achingly in front of the screen on the green platform. Andrew is beside me and cracks the bones of each finger one by one, as if it gives him some kind of relief. The sound is uncomfortable for me.

Sam zooms in on a satellite image of Iceland and points to a Reykjavik suburb. 'I've been able to monitor Luka Gudjohnsen's movements to and from the Ark using the Earth's satellites as a detection grid. There was a disturbance in this grid at about four a.m., somewhere over the northern hemisphere,' she says, keeping her attention focused on the image.

Andrew instantly stops cracking his fingers. 'Why didn't you tell us this before?' he snaps.

'Because you're not ready, Andrew...The training clearly demonstrated that,' Sam says calmly.

Andrew lets out a long, pissed-off sigh. 'That's still not your call to make, Sam. He could have been doing anything to Luka Dalton.'

The screen changes to display statistics and streams of brain activity. 'I don't believe so,' says Sam. 'Luka Dalton's vitals are reading normal. He's attending college, moving around, completing his daily routine.'

'But if Luka wants to transfer memories into his counterpart, why was he in Reykjavik and not Akureyri?' I ask.

'Luka Dalton's parents live in that suburb,' Sam says after a moment.

'He's going after Alan!' exclaims Andrew.

I shake my head as I think it through. 'That makes no sense. Alan isn't even a blood relative of Luka's.'

'Well, his mom then!' Andrew barks. 'I'm not gonna just wait here until Luka kills everyone off one by one.' He glances at Sam. 'And you, don't even start with me!'

Sam ignores him as she brings up a detailed map of Earth with orbiting satellites connected together through a network of lines.

'Luka is back in the Ark, but I don't know for how long,' she says wearily.

I try to make sense of the image. 'How long does it take Luka to—'

'Two-minutes, thirty-seven seconds,' Sam interrupts, guessing what I'm about to ask. 'Luka can re-enter over Iceland from orbit much more quickly than we can get there and back. Do you see our problem?'

'There's three of us with the same weapons he has. We've got the advantage,' says Andrew.

'Even so,' says Sam. 'He has more combat training than you do.'

'We need to get to Reykjavik. Get the transporter ready!' orders Andrew. 'I want to see what he's doing before anyone else gets hurt.'

I feel the circle of debate is about to reignite in regard to how leaving the TUL is too dangerous, but Sam just lowers her head, asks us to meet her in the vehicle bay, then disappears.

I look at Andrew, who looks back. His greasy black hair covers the yellowish eye I gave him a few days ago. To think it was a big deal to me at the time—if I only knew what was coming.

'I hope Alan is OK,' I say.

'Everything will be OK when Luka is dead.'

'Just think about what I said this morning,' I say, turning to leave the platform.

Andrew isn't afraid of confrontation, and right now he's driven by his emotions to avenge his father's death. Maybe that's clouding his judgment regarding how dangerous this situation really is.

After all, we're about to engage someone who's smarter and much better trained than we are. Worse still, the stakes are high for Luka because he thinks he's saving 'his people,' and Andrew and I are about to get in his way again. I remember his words in the morgue as clear as anything; it makes me cold on the inside just thinking about it because I doubt Luka Gudjohnsen makes idle threats.

'Will,' says Andrew from behind me.

I turn around.

'Thanks for sticking by me through all of this. You didn't need to, man. This isn't your fight.'

'You would have done the same for me,' I say.

Andrew shrugs. 'I don't know if I would have. That's why I look up to you so much.'

I smile back at him. 'If our dads could see us now, huh?'

'We'll make them proud of us, Will.'

***

Sam waits for us by a newly materialised transporter. My back arches with the sudden materialisation of the armour over my body.

'I've materialised a weapon in a harness that's easily accessible over your right shoulder. It's a JX-7, a specialised cutting tool that can penetrate any material. Just point and click…that's it—no neural interface, no materialising. Understand?' she says anxiously.

'Point and click. Got it,' says Andrew.

Sam looks pensive, which makes me even edgier about this mission.

'Keep your optex on at all times,' she instructs us. 'I'll see everything you see. Go in, take a quick look around, and then get out.'

We put on our gloves and board the transporter. I use the take-off to remind myself how to materialise weapons.

'Don't materialise weapons in the transporter!' snaps an edgy Sam beside me, no doubt interpreting the thoughts being relayed by my visor.

We return to level flight and begin our fast approach—it feels quicker than usual.

Andrew puts a hand on my shoulder. 'What do you think we're gonna find in Reykjavik?'

Hopefully Luka was just paying a sentimental visit to his counterparts' parents. At least, I like to think that's the reality of this situation, because it makes me feel better. It puts me at ease to think this mission is for nothing.

'That's unlikely,' Sam says, focusing straight ahead.

'What's unlikely?' asks Andrew.

I sure wish Sam would stop reading my mind.

'Alan and his wife have nothing to do with this, so maybe there won't be anything there for us,' I offer.

'My father had nothing to do with this either, Will,' says Andrew.

Sam banks the aircraft a little. 'You should both expect the worst. You don't know how he thinks,' she mumbles.

A day of combat and weapons training doesn't give me the confidence to believe I can do this. I feel like a fake in my beefed-up combat armour with the JX whatever-it-is strapped to my back. Sam's words keep replaying in my head, and I'm analysing them with OCD precision: *Luka's got more training…Expect the worst…blah blah blah*. My stomach shifts to the base of my throat as we begin a steep descent.

'I need to get us down quickly. This might get a little rough,' says a tense Sam. Her body is rigid, and her focus is on nothing other than the grey cloud cover flying past the cockpit windows.

I turn around to find Andrew with his seat belt undone as he examines the JX on his lap.

He looks up. 'Point and click!' He registers the concern on my face and gives me a reassuring nod. 'We got this.'

The craft bumps through some turbulence, kicking in my instinctive reaction to grip my armrests. I nod at him unconvincingly.

The cockpit illuminates with a strange red-and-orange glow.

'Haven't seen that in a while,' says Sam.

The streams of colour from the northern lights wave across the sky as we rapidly descend and quickly set down in a barren rocky landscape. An isolated wooden house sits nestled within the terrain a couple of hundred metres ahead, a purple-green shimmer creeping over its sloped roof.

Sam sighs and breaks her admiration for the skyline. 'OK, these are the last-known coordinates of Luka Gudjohnsen before he left for the Ark. I'm detecting interference from within the structure, which is probably some kind of improvised dampening field. I can't go into the house with you because I don't have enough power to penetrate the field. Listen, don't communicate with me unless you have to. We don't know who's listening, and if I tell you to move, then move!'

Andrew and I turn and walk down the narrow passage of the fuselage. The sharpness of the cold Reykjavik air hits me when the door vanishes.

'You don't have to go in there!' Sam calls out from behind us.

I figure it's too late now—we're already here, about to walk out the door, and I've surrendered myself to the idea. Besides, I know Andrew won't turn back.

'We got this,' I tell her, reiterating Andrew's words of false confidence.

We make our way down the metallic steps and crouch-run along a gravel driveway, illuminated by the green hue of the northern lights overhead. The house appears well kept, with recently painted redwood panelling. Three wooden steps lead up to the front porch of the simple two-storey dwelling, and a faint light peeks through the pixelated glass of the front door.

'Sam, can you tell us anything?' I ask.

'Not much yet,' says her voice in my head, 'but a faint heat signature is coming from upstairs. Be careful.'

Andrew creaks open the unlocked front door. We creep along noisy floorboards until we get to a kitchen. Every type of pot and pan hangs from a square rack over a marble island-table in the middle of the floor. Andrew slides open a door to an adjoining dining room and peers in. He turns and shakes his head. I point upwards.

He follows me up a narrow set of stairs to a small landing, where a blue glow peeks out from behind a semi open door straight ahead. Andrew pushes past me and steps inside. A heavy weight instantly lowers my arm, and when I look down, I realise I've subconsciously materialised a HX-1. My pulse races against the collar of my armour.

'Chris?' says Andrew, his tone incredulous.

I follow Andrew and find the kid from the hospital lying on top of a white sheet in what appears to be the master bedroom of the house. His chest rises and falls with a gentle breathing.

'Chris!' says Andrew again, shaking the boy's shoulder gently.

Nothing happens.

I move to the opposite side of the bed and pull back the sheet to find hexadecimal data streams in blue text across a tablet-like device strapped to Chris's arm.

'Sam, can you see this?' I whisper.

'Optex…fully,' says Sam's broken voice through some static.

'Repeat that,' I say, glancing at Andrew.

'Place your optex…carefully,' says Sam again through the static.

Andrew takes off his visor and places it over Chris's eyes.

'Receiving….stasis…' says Sam after a moment, but I can't make out the rest of what she's saying.

'We need to get him out of here,' says Andrew. 'I'm not gonna leave him again.'

More static rings in my ear as Sam's voice speaks at a higher pitch. I can tell she's become anxious and the word *abort* forces its way repeatedly through the garbled noise. Bright light from an outside source suddenly engulfs the bedroom, illuminating the room like a picture negative.

'Move!' shouts Sam.

Andrew stretches across the bed, undoing the straps that hold the tablet in place on Chris's arm. 'I'm not leaving him behind again,' he says.

Chris's body jerks violently as the tablet comes away in Andrew's hand.

Andrew quickly backs away. Cold grey eyes snap open, and the colour drains from the kid's face as I quickly put my arms underneath him and lift him up. Andrew draws his JX-7 over his shoulder and leads the way down the stairs into the waiting transporter. Chris stops moving in my arms.

I expect company, but nothing interferes with us and we climb on board. I place Chris's still body on the floor of the craft. Diffused ultraviolet beams begin scanning; his torso inexplicably arches then falls flat to the floor. The kid takes a deep breath and exhales but doesn't awaken.

We make a sharp ascent, and a sudden push from behind knocks me to my ass; I narrowly avoid falling on top of Chris.

Sam doesn't look happy. 'He's alive,' she says, standing motionlessly over him, not at all affected by the movements of the plane which she is obviously flying somehow. A warning tone sounds out from somewhere, and she changes her focus, as if she's reading from the visor.

Andrew steadies himself against the fuselage. 'What is it?'

'A collision course,' says Sam, her eyes flicking back and forth 'Something is on a collision course with us.'

The transporter creaks with our increase in speed.

'Luka's fired on us, hasn't he?' I say.

'I believe it's an energy-pulse weapon,' says Sam. 'If it's able to get a lock on us, it could force us to land immediately.'

As the craft descends and banks sharply, she crouches next to me and pulls off her visor, followed by mine.

'We're not in range of the unit lander, and our communications are jammed.' She places her visor over my eyes. 'My backup will come online when the computer detects that I haven't returned, but I'll have no memory of tonight's events until you give me this visor.'

As the craft descends some more, the walls vibrate with the stresses of the speed we're now travelling at.

Sam looks at us both. 'You're going to have to leave soon.'

'*Leave?*' exclaims Andrew.

'I may not be able to outmanoeuvre the pulse weapon.'

'What about Chris?'

'He's stable. Listen, there's nothing to be gained by your staying here. I'll do everything I can to prevent Luka from reacquiring him. But you must go.'

The armour recedes into my chest and begins to envelop my arms.

'We'll soon be off the northern coast of Ireland,' says Sam. 'I've encoded the transponder signal of your armour so I'll be able to track your position.'

'What about Luka? Will he be able to track us?' says Andrew.

Sam straightens up. 'Have faith in my encryption techniques. They've kept Luka out for this long.' She forces out a brief smile that quickly disappears.

As the door of the transporter dematerialises, the air escapes from the cabin with a fierce intensity. I try to cling to one of the walls, but there's no grip.

'The armour knows what to do. Just think of this as extra training!' shouts Sam over the rush of the escaping air.

I stagger to my feet, and I'm pulled backwards towards the door. Andrew grips my shoulder.

'Sam, this is crazy!' I shout.

The fear of not knowing what to expect is the worst part of all, and my eyes plead with her to stop this.

Sam moves in front of me, her gaze meeting mine. 'It's safe. Just go,' she says in a calmer voice. She places her palm on my chest and pushes me out into the cold blackness.

Everything is suddenly spinning fast. My hands cross involuntarily over my chest in some instinctive impulse. The visor seems confused and distorts between regular and night vision every couple of seconds. I shut my eyes, and another instinctive impulse extends my legs behind me and locks them into place. I'm reminded of the worst roller-coaster ride of my life. I cling on to some deep feeling this will all work out.

Every muscle in my body contracts in response to an invisible force that pushes me upwards, as if my armour is repelling the ground beneath me. The repulsion suddenly subsides, and I begin to free-fall—fast. Sam's words play over and over in my brain that this is perfectly safe. I want to turn my head, but I can't move my body, and I know the ground is quickly closing in because I can feel it somehow, like a sixth sense. I yell out and open my eyes. My visor counts down some coordinates, superimposed over the distant amber lights of a town. The numbers rapidly approach zero: $-19.576...-$ $17.864...$The force from beneath pushes me upwards a second time, and a wave of cold seawater engulfs my face. My body rotates 180 as distant lights spin around before everything goes dark.

***

Andrews's bright-yellow eyes slowly come into focus. Everything is quiet except for breaking waves against the shoreline.

'You OK?' he says, kneeling at my side, coughing and shivering with the cold.

I sit up, the blood rushes to my head, making me dizzy. A desolate beach is exposed in the night-vision yellow clarity I'm becoming accustomed to.

I slowly climb to my feet and brush away as much wet sand as I can from my arms and legs. I feel fine right now, but I'll pay for that crash landing once I get the AR-3 off me and my limbs have to fend for themselves again.

Lights from the nearby town peer over a high seawall about a hundred metres ahead, telling me we're not too far from civilization.

'We must be up north somewhere,' I groan. 'Don't think we were far from the coast when we fell out of the transporter.'

'You mean *jumped*, right?' says Andrew, rubbing his arms vigorously. 'There's some shelter up ahead, an old construction site or something.'

We walk along the beach for what feels like a mile. I try to breathe some heat into my numbed fingers as I follow Andrew's lead, using the seawall as cover from the cold. I reckon it's colder here than it was in Iceland. I keep looking around because I have an unwelcome paranoia about encountering Luka again, probably because I feel exposed being cut off from Sam and the TUL.

I follow Andrew inside what appears to be a large circular storm drain; the smell of seaweed is overbearing. Large aluminium pipes, big enough to crawl through, stretch back along the deep structure for two or three hundred metres before turning a corner. Andrew and I walk inside just enough to escape the exposure, but the damp concrete offers little comfort, and we keep our arms wrapped tightly around ourselves to seal in what little heat there is. I cast a glance back to the entrance, and the visor superimposes some numbers over the circumference in an augmented reality. Farther back still, the waves break and foam through the blowing grains of sand.

'Tara Hill doesn't seem so bad now, huh?' says Andrew.

I can't help laugh because Tara Hill is paradise compared to this place. For all its isolation, Marie and James have made it somewhere I've always felt safe—I just never wanted to visit for personal reasons. Thinking about my aunt and uncle, I wonder whether Luka would use them against us if he had to. The thought makes me afraid for them, considering Andrew and I are stranded miles away from them.

'Makes you think, doesn't it?' I say, thinking out loud. 'Even with Sam flying the transporter, Luka still manages to strand us here.'

'Sam is a smart girl,' Andrew says with a shrug. 'She'll think of something.'

The staunch smell of seaweed continues to invade my nose. I look back at my shivering companion. 'She did tell us not to leave the TUL.'

Andrew sighs. 'I couldn't stay put, Will.'

I silently weigh up whether I should say what's on my mind, but right now maybe the argument is worth it.

'I agree with Sam. I don't think we should have left,' I blurt out. 'Don't get me wrong…like, I'm happy we got Chris and everything, but our luck is going to run out sometime. Do you actually want to protect Luka's counterpart if it means putting our family in danger?'

As I'm speaking, Andrew slides his JX-7 over his shoulder and examines it in his hands.

'We have to think about James and Marie…and my mother for that matter!' I continue.

'Bad things happen when good people do nothing,' he says, looking down at the weapon. 'Luka Dalton is innocent, just like Chris and my dad. Gudjohnsen can't just do whatever he wants. His actions hurt people.'

'Admit it,' I persist calmly. 'This isn't about protecting Chris or Luka or the common good. This is about revenge.'

Andrew sighs and replaces the JX-7 in its harness. 'I wonder where this tunnel leads to,' he says, turning his back to me.

'Luka obviously can pick us off whenever he wants,' I say.

'Not for much longer,' snaps Andrew.

'We can pick our battles with Luka,' I say. 'If he can get to us, he can get to our family. We don't have the luxury of making him pay on our terms, Andrew.'

He turns around quickly. '*Luxury*! Is that what you think I have? A luxury? Do you have any idea what this is like for me? Do you think I have a choice about the way I feel? You think I can just turn off like a switch and pretend I don't care that the guy who murdered my father is running around free? I have no choice, Will. I don't want to be here—I *need* to be here. I don't have your...*luxury*,' he says sarcastically, 'of thinking about everything in a rational, measured way. Remember that.'

I shrug. 'I'm just saying maybe one of us needs to be rational so we don't get ourselves or anyone else killed.'

He reaches up and takes off my visor, leaving me in darkness.

'Listen,' he says, stepping in closer, 'because I don't think you're getting this. I've already lost my dad—someone I love is already dead. If you want out, then leave, walk away, go home. Thank you for helping me. Thank you for leading me to the TUL and everything else you've done for me, but I can't stop until this is finished, one way or the other. Just walk away, Will, if that's what you wanna do. I can do this Furious Angels thing by myself.'

In the darkness, I take in every stark word loud and clear, and my heart no longer wants to put up a counter argument. Although I don't agree with what Andrew wants to do, I understand it. I also know I can't walk away from the TUL and its technology. Maybe it's not a noble reason, but it's the truth.

I tell him to give me back my visor, and after a brief hesitation, he places it firmly in my hand. 'Sometimes you really get on my tits, Oakley. You know that?' I say, sliding it back on.

He smiles a little. 'Sometimes you really get on my tits, Anderson!'

Sam's voice breaks through. 'If you two are finished talking about tits, I'd appreciate if you could come outside. We don't have much time.'

22 Ark Killer

After briefly landing and picking us up, the transporter levels off from its ascent, and Sam debriefs us.

'Luka somehow implanted nanocells into Chris Beech's body. I managed to get him back the TUL, just about.'

'But how did he implant the cells? We stopped Luka from hacking the TUL,' I say.

Sam gives me an annoyed look. 'I know, Will. The cells were probably extracted from his predecessor's body—which might explain why he was at the morgue.'

'I don't understand,' says Andrew. 'Why did the Luka who died in the church have nanocells in his body in the first place?'

Sam shakes her head. 'To supress the effects of Humanity 2.0 caused by the stresses of space travel during this mission,' she says. 'I can't believe I missed it.'

'What are the cells doing to, Chris?' asks Andrew.

'From what I can determine, half of them are programmed to begin the H2.0 upgrade process; the other half are lying dormant. I won't know anything else until those dormant cells activate. 'Chris is safe for now, sedated in the medical bay, but once those cells switch on, who knows what could happen? I'm guessing those dormant cells are going to attempt to remove 2.0 from his body. I think Luka may have found a way to extract the intelligence upgrade and Chris is his test subject.'

'A guinea pig,' says Andrew, scrunching his eyebrows together as stress lines form on his forehead.

'Did you destroy whatever Luka fired at us? Or is this going to be a rough flight home?' I ask. Though when I hear my thoughts out loud, I sound a little selfish.

'The energy weapon struck the transporter, but our backup power system was unaffected,' says Sam.

She rests her head, as if defeated, against the padding of the chair. 'Luka is throwing everything at us so he can get back into the unit lander. We can't go back there right now.'

A loud clicking unlocks a panel in the transporter floor behind us. The panel slides open, and a large rectangular black box, about a metre long, rises out of a concealed compartment. Sam nods gently, looking at the object as if she's greeting an unwelcome guest.

'That,' she says, 'is the Ark Killer.'

No fancy acronyms or obscure classification. The purpose of the thing is singular—to destroy the Ark. Sam knows too well what that would mean: destroying her only way home.

'Luka has locked a pulse weapon onto the unit lander. He's trying to drain the gravimetric power source, and he's succeeding.'

'How long—' I say.

'A matter of hours,' Sam replies, cutting me off. 'If he shuts down the unit lander, he can reset the computer core and regain access. I'm throwing what I can at the weapon, but nothing stays active long enough to do any real damage. A short time ago, he deployed three drones to disrupt power to the launch doors, which means I can't get anything in or out of the vehicle bay.'

We're now just as locked out of the TUL as Luka is. Sam masks the transponder signal of the transporter and ascends to 35,000 feet so it looks like we're a commercial aircraft. She figures it should buy us a little time but not much. The plan is crude and simple: when we feel we have no options left, we'll make a rapid descent and deploy the Ark Killer.

'So all this is about getting Chris back? I mean, that's what he wants, right?' says Andrew.

Sam taps her armrest nervously. 'He must have found a way to eradicate Humanity 2.0—that has to be why he did this. He has to get Chris back, because whatever is in Chris's body is the key to reversing the 2.0 mutation. He's made his move, and it's all or nothing. If he wins, he gets Chris and the TUL, I go offline, and if you're lucky, you two wake up in your beds with no memory of any of this.'

'And if we're not lucky?' I ask her.

'Then he'll just kill you,' Sam says matter-of-factly. 'Firing a pulse weapon from an orbiting spacecraft to the planet's surface is high profile. There's a risk that someone will detect the Ark. This is a desperate move.'

I scan over the black box behind me. 'He knows about that thing, right?'

'He's gambling I won't use it,' says Sam. 'He doesn't think I'll fire on my own ship and destroy our only way of sending his cure home, not for the sake of Chris's life, not for the sake of your memories.'

The stakes are too high for Luka; one life to him is insignificant compared to completing 'God's work' and saving his people. Luka's picture of all this is on a much grander scale, which is hard for me to comprehend. All I see is an innocent kid's life in danger and maybe Luka Dalton's life too if Gudjohnsen decides to track down his counterpart and wipe his memory.

The craft jolts with heavy turbulence.

Andrew crouches beside the weapon. The top panel of the black box dematerialises, revealing an RPG-like rocket launcher inside, with a matte-black surface and rear blue display.

'It's a nonregenerative weapon,' Sam explains. 'One shot and that's it. Point the unit upwards, and when the coordinates reach zero, you press the trigger. No more Ark.'

'You sure you want to do this, Sam?' I ask.

We begin to descend rapidly; the entire craft shakes and vibrates. I guess I have my answer.

'Where're we landing?' asks Andrew.

'Anywhere,' grunts Sam.

The craft rocks from left to right. Sam looks at the weapon with silent intent as distant green fields and hedgerows break through the clouds in night-vision yellow. The transporter's nose suddenly pitches up, accompanied with counteracting creaks from the fuselage.

I'm pushed firmly into my chair with a strong accelerating force from the rear of the craft. For some reason we're now ascending. The cockpit windows engulf in a cloudy grey before quickly breaking to night-vision darkness as we level off.

'I'm sorry,' says Sam sheepishly. 'None of this was ever meant to happen.'

'Why haven't we landed?' asks Andrew, his body jolting with the speed of the craft.

'I've detected a launch from the Ark. Luka has deployed the rest of his drones.'

'We were almost down, Sam!' I say through the noise of the unsettling creaks.

'The trajectory of the drones suggests they're heading straight for Tara Hill,' Sam says sombrely.

Andrew swears loudly.

Sam looks over us both. 'You two leave when I tell you to go. Get your aunt and uncle, and bring them back here. I'll take care of the drones.'

It's as though Luka read my innermost fears. Come to think of it, maybe that's exactly what he did, considering I was wearing the visor when I was worrying about him killing James and Marie. I'd ponder over the irony of that theory if there was more time.

'What exactly are those drones programed to do?' I ask anxiously.

'I don't know, William...lock down Tara Hill maybe as insurance, maybe kill everyone in the area.'

I've noticed Sam gets especially blunt when she's nervous. The door of the craft dematerialises, and I dread what has to happen next. Right now I might trade it all in—the TUL, Tara Hill, James and Marie—just to wake up in my own bed again and get on with my life. I look over my companions; Andrew's focused determination contrasts with the worry etched on Sam's face. Their bravery is admirable.

I need my own resolve to match theirs as I turn and face the outside. I want to see what I'm jumping into, and I want to go willingly. I grip on to what I can as my body temperature drops rapidly from the cold air outside. The transporter banks sharply to the left, and now I'm suddenly staring directly over the yellow picture negative of Tara Hill and slide towards the door. So much for doing this on my own terms.

'Time to go!' shouts Sam. 'If you can, materialise an HX-7 on each arm. The on-board targeting computer should be able to get a lock on those drones. If you don't have time to think, just use the JX on your back.'

I turn around to give her one last look.

'I'm sorry,' she says.

As I fall sideways from the craft, my vision is a blur of decreasing coordinates and rolling terrain. This time my brain shuts off for the free fall, and I wait in a state of numbness until the repulsive force of the armour lands me hands first in the backyard of Tara Hill. Andrew is beside me and quickly climbs to his feet in the night vision darkness.

Sam's voice rings through the stillness of the frozen grounds: 'Sensors indicate your aunt and uncle are asleep.' A GX materialises in my hand. 'Go stun them quickly and bring them outside. I've taken out three of the drones, but another four are coming straight for you. Hurry up.'

I quickly move to the kitchen door, but it doesn't budge.

'No time,' says Andrew, drawing his JX.

I stand back, and he fires a straight orange beam of light into the lock. A wave of heat blasts my face as the lock melts away and takes most of the door with it while the glass smashes to the floor.

A loud thudding fills my ears, and a sudden dust cloud of masonry whizzes over my head. I find myself lying on my back a few metres away from where I was standing. I guess the JX is stronger than both of us thought. Andrew rolls on his side next to me in a grunt of pain. I sit up quickly, surrounded by a rubble pile of bricks and plaster and pieces of what was once the kitchen. Water jets upwards from an exposed pipe through a blaze that has engulfed the remaining rear of the house. Everything from the kitchen door to the back windows is gone.

The ground shakes beneath us with the impact of a red projectile from somewhere above. Everything that was once frosted green in the garden erupts in flames, and the heat is sudden and stifling. I quickly realise the JX didn't cause this carnage.

'You need to move!' shouts Sam in my ear. 'I've got three drones closing in fast!'

Andrew and I scramble over to what was once the hallway. James looks up at me while staggering along the corridor, supporting his wife. I stop and look at their frightened, wide-eyed faces. I want to say something to reassure them, but before I get a chance, the tennis-ball-size white projectile shoots past from behind and hits James's chest, and then a second one hits Marie. Helplessly they fall to their knees, then face first, onto the floor.

Andrew forces his way past and lifts Marie towards him, dragging her along the tile floor to the gaping hole in the side of the house.

Behind them a circular drone slams through the ceiling, sending chunks of plaster everywhere. I'm blinded momentarily by a white dust that rises from the debris, but somehow I find the focus to raise my arm and materialise a triple-barrelled HX-7 in my right hand.

I push against the weight of the weapon, extending my arm outward and blinking dust from my eyes. A beam of white light projects from the drone, and Sam materialises directly in front of me. She walks down the hallway with the same focused expression the AI version of her used to have before she recovered her memories.

'Sam?' I say, lowering my weapon.

She doesn't respond, and my breath suddenly tightens. I look down to find her arm merged with my body, extending beyond my armour and into my chest. I can't breathe, but I audibly gasp for air. The beat of my heart thuds against her palm, and a tightening sensation in my chest forces my heart into an irregular palpitation.

I plead with Sam's eyes but still can't speak; her expressionless face is inches from mine, looking at me as if this is nothing. Her character and personality are vacant from her cold green-eyed stare. She tilts her head slightly, as if curious what will happen. Luka's words flash from the darkest place in my mind: how I am superfluous. I feel the life rip from my chest. As Sam begins to extract her hand, purposely trying to torture me, my breath ceases in one last wide-eyed plea for mercy.

A blue projectile flies past the side of my head; Sam distorts momentarily as if it just passed straight through her, but her grip becomes stronger. Andrew fires again and again. I grasp Sam's shoulder as I begin to lose my footing. I feel nothing—only the tightness of the vice crushing the walls of my heart.

A second flash of light discharges from behind me. Something explodes and sends me crashing backwards, clutching my chest. A drone hovers overhead and projects an ultraviolet beam into my body.

I hear Sam's broken words in my ear. 'It's going....to...all right...don't...'

As tears run down my face, I try to catch my breath through desperate gasps. Andrew crouches at my side. 'Will, you gotta get up!'

'Sam...' I say through the ragged breaths.

'That wasn't our Sam,' says Andrew, dragging me to my feet. The pressure instantly falls from my chest, and my heartbeat regulates. I know now it's either Luka or us as the drone that projected evil-Sam smoulders at the end of the hallway.

With a great deal of effort, Andrew and I quickly carry James outside though it takes every bit of strength I have. As we approach the door of the transporter, a second impact crashes down from somewhere above and shakes the ground beneath us. Another larger projectile rapidly descends in a red flash and pierces straight through the wing of the transporter, dissolving a wide section of the outer shell in a fiery ball. The craft plunges onto the ground, sending a wall of heat towards us.

Sam jumps down from the doorway with a HX-7 materialising on each arm and a visor across her eyes. 'I have to take out those two drones before my power module switches off. Luka is almost through to the TUL core. If he gets in, it's all over.'

We have little choice but to hoist James into the craft and lay him next to his wife.

Andrew reaches for the Ark Killer and heaves the weapon out of its case with both hands. I move my body under the unit and lock it into place with my arm. Andrew lets go of it and rests the full weight on my shoulder. A blue screen projects in front of me:

[AQUIRING TARGET LOCK]

WARNING:

NONREGENERATIVE MISSILE

[GUIDANCE: −58.26071956]

Carefully Andrew and I climb down from the craft, and a stream of double projectiles shoots over our heads. I glance behind to find Sam standing on the domed section of the transporter with her arms outstretched as she fires on two rogue drones circling quickly around our position. The drone to my right passes a scanning beam over my body and changes course rapidly. Sam aims her weapons towards it and fires—the drone explodes and lights up the sky in a brief flash of light.

The second drone fires a projectile from my left into the tail of the transporter, the blast force throws Andrew and I to the ground. The Ark Killer crashes into the rubble in front of us.

Andrew grunts and pushes himself up with two hands. He shouts out and fires waves of projectiles from both weapons, attempting to follow the path of the drone as it evades him overhead.

I scramble forward on my hands and knees. It takes everything I've got to lift the Ark Killer onto my shoulder. I turn around and scan blindly across the night sky while the coordinates rapidly approach zero.

In my peripheral vision, I see the drone change course towards me. There's no time, I steady myself and take aim. Across my display reads:

[TARGET LOCKED]

I give the command to fire using my visor. Something emerges from the wide barrel of the weapon in a blaze of red, and I immediately fall backwards.

A blast projectile from the drone scorches though the armour over the top of my shoulder. The burning immediately brings me back to focus through a surge of adrenaline.

Andrew destroys the unit in a blaze of heat and jumps down from the rubble.

'Did it work?' he says, out of breath.

'No idea,' I say, grasping my arm.

I look to the burning transporter behind us. 'James and Marie,' I whisper.

'Alive but critical,' says Sam's voice in my ear. 'Get to the RMN,' she says bluntly.

Andrew hesitates, looking on at the wreckage.

'We have to trust Sam,' I say. 'If anyone can save them, she can.'

23 Interception

I isolate my aunt and uncle's fate in the little part of my brain telling me everything is going to be OK somehow. I think over what just happened and frantically backtrack through the last few minutes, making sure there are no loose ends.

'You think that's the Ark?' says Andrew, pointing towards something that resembles a falling red star, flickering brighter as it falls towards Earth on a distant trajectory.

'Sam, I know you're a little busy, but can you confirm the hit on the Ark?' I ask.

Static rings in my ear; I reposition my visor and ask again but there's no response.

'Must be interference or something,' Andrew says anxiously. He runs a finger over the navigation screen on the centre of the dash. 'Looks like we're heading for the motorway.'

The RMN speeds up and is now well over the limit, perfectly turning with the shallow bends of the road. The deserted motorway offers up a lonely journey. I feel like we're getting farther away from the place we should be going to. It makes me wonder how much damage the TUL took if we can't go back there right now. The little voice saying, *Trust me* rings out again from the back of my mind, but I can't squish the uneasy feeling in my stomach. I present a false calmness for Andrew's sake, because when he looks at me and asks about James and Marie, I know he needs to hear that everything is going to be all right.

The car switches to the fast lane.

'Sam, where are we going?' asks Andrew nervously.

No response.

He fiddles with the navigation screen again. 'I can't do anything. It's in some kind of read-only mode.'

Whenever Andrew touches the screen and tries to select something, nothing happens. It looks like the RMN has been preprogramed to take us somewhere. I'm hoping this is for our own good, but Sam could have just told us where to go, because after everything we've done, I thought we could be at least trusted to do that.

I spot the luminous yellow of a police car's bumper sticker in the inside lane.

'Sam, we're gonna overtake the cops in two seconds,' I say.

We fly past them, and I catch flashing blue lights in my peripheral vision. The police car switches lanes and speeds up behind us.

'Pulse weapon deployed,' Sam's voice announces from the RMN's computer.

The blue flashing ceases, and the police car falls off into the distance like it just lost all power.

I spend the next minutes watching the navigation console for some clue as to our final destination. It feels like we've been driving forever—too long in fact—and I don't like the idea of leaving that mess back at Tara Hill.

Outside the limits of Limerick City, we make a soft turn right, heading through the exit for the city centre, and accelerate through a light morning fog. The RMN shakes violently as the transporter unexpectedly appears overhead. Broken static rings again in my ear, but I can't make out the words Sam is trying to speak before the craft suddenly raises its nose and breaks off.

'What was that about?' says Andrew, stretching to see where the transporter is going.

It's a little strange that it came in so low this close to the city.

'Maybe it's an escort,' I say, taking a guess.

Andrew looks at me. 'Yeah, and maybe we didn't hit the Ark after all, and Luka got access to the TUL.'

I run the idea through my head, but I reckon we'd already be dead if that happened and not on a mystery excursion to Limerick City.

The RMN ignores all the red traffic lights on the deserted foggy outskirts. A sombre mist rises from the River Shannon, hiding the high-rise hotel near the dock, and low aircraft warning lights are all I can see of building underneath. We overtake some bread vans as we turn on to the main street, which is almost deserted in a cloud of fog.

The car's speakers crackle. 'Proceed inside the church and wait for my signal,' says a monotone Sam.

'Sam, can you confirm the hit on the Ark?' Andrew asks impatiently.

We wait a moment, but the response never comes. The car clumsily mounts the curb near the Franciscan church on the main street, and the RMN powers down all by itself outside the entrance. The night vision of the windscreen shuts off and leaves us in a gloomy dawn outside the half-open red door of the church.

'I guess this is it then,' I say.

Andrew taps on the RMN console, but the screen is dead.

I look around at the deserted, fog-ridden street. 'Let's just get out of here and wait inside. Either way we're sitting ducks just waiting here.'

I push through the door; the church lies in darkness except for two candles burning at either side of the dimly lit altar. The feeling is different than when I came here a few days ago because the sense of peace has been replaced with nothing but cold morning air. A figure stands at the candle on the right; he turns and slowly descends the marble steps. The door behind us closes shut with a commanding finality. Andrew and I walk forward, each footstep echoing in the hollow interior. We stop halfway in the centre aisle; the figure stops too and stands just a few feet away, donning a red visor, the AR-3 combat armour just completing its recession towards his skin.

He stands like an exhausted shell of a young man, his face skin and bone, his eyes casting dark shadows in his sockets, like a man in the late stages of H2.0 side effects. He removes the visor and looks at us both with his dim-grey stare, as if inspecting us from head to toe—a regretful look, a sense of subtle disappointment. I almost don't recognise him, just like I almost didn't recognise myself in the mirror that day.

'These are for you,' says Luka, pointing at the candles behind him, 'in honour of you.'

It's obvious we've walked right into an ambush.

Luka raises two arms, Andrew raises his, and a sudden force unforgivingly slams us both into the glass-panelled door. The glass cracks from the impact with the back of my head, the pain stinging and severe.

Andrew discharges a blue projectile into Luka's chest, and he staggers backwards.

Andrew tries again, but this time nothing discharges from his weapon.

'Will, I can't fire on him,' he says, intently aiming at Luka with an outstretched arm.

Luka's weapons dematerialise, and he gestures toward us. 'I can't fire on you either, Andrew. It seems our clever little AI friend erected a dampening field from her transporter.' Luka takes a few steps towards us. 'But that makes her quite vulnerable to the defence drones on the roof of this building'

Andrew gets up and walks towards him. 'You killed my father. Now I get to kill you.'

I move beside my cousin and place my hand on his shoulder.

Luka glances away, shifting his stare towards the Stations of the Cross hanging on the left-hand wall. 'A Furious Angel,' he says, placing his hands behind his back, 'is one who gives his entire life, searching relentlessly for an answer. That's what they told me. Your father in this universe, Andrew, and his counterpart in mine are all part of the one spirit. I cleansed that spirit, just like I'll cleanse mine when my work is accomplished.'

'You talk a whole lotta shit, don't you, Luka?' Andrew says angrily. 'You're a murderer, and your work is already finished because we ended it.'

Andrew's armour goes into assisted-combat mode.

Luka gives him the once-over. 'Ah, Sam, always the patron saint of lost causes.'

'This is over, Luka,' I say. 'You really want to expose the TUL and the Furious Angels like this?'

He shrugs. 'There may be some rumours, nothing more. In any case, you won't need to worry about it. Sam will unlock the unit lander or I'll kill you, permanently—it's very simple.'

'Why do you need it?' I ask him. 'We took your nanocells out of Chris Beech. They almost killed him.'

'Not true,' says Luka calmly. 'I know I've found a way to reverse H2.0, and I'll go through each of you to reclaim my work. You're both nothing to me. You can contact Sam and tell her to release the command codes of the unit lander; I'll then send her the downloaded memories of your life before you encountered me. Then I'm going to kill you. But out of the kindness of my heart, I'll allow Sam to clone you and infuse your memories into those clones. You're welcome.'

'Go fuck yourself,' says Andrew.

Luka shakes his head. 'Have you ever played a computer game against a really good player? This is what's happening right now, Andrew.'

As Luka's armour tightens a little more, the red veins glow from his neck down.

'Do you know the suffering of someone who's had the pleasure of having his childhood replaced with a ten-year deep-space mission he knew nothing about? But in that mission I found the truth. Perhaps my methods were cruel, Andrew, but in desperate times we must be cruel for the greater good. You can't win. Contact Sam.' The armour creaks as Luka clenches his fists. 'Because what I see in front of me are two loose ends created by an idealist AI with more obedience than sense.'

I recede the armour towards my skin.

'We won't be contacting Sam, so this is the part where you die,' says Andrew.

'Your father was an ignorant man, single-minded...'

'Don't talk about my father,' Andrew snaps.

'...locking us all into this circle of death.'

Andrew's breathing deepens.

'Out of curiosity, did you ever find he lacked a certain…paternal instinct?'

Andrew raises his arm and tries to fire again, but Luka moves in swiftly and punches down on his elbow. Andrew falls to his knees and yells in agony, his arm deadened and flopping like a lead weight in front of him. The right jab I throw into Luka's jaw has absolutely no effect, and he quickly retaliates with a palm into the bridge of my nose. I fall backwards against the wooden pew, the blood running over my mouth. Andrew yells out again as the AR-3 resets his arm back into place.

'Like the fall of man, you've chosen the difficult path,' says Luka, calmly looking us over as if we're to be pitied.

Andrew finds his feet again and batters Luka with a smashing of quick left and right punches to his face. His opponent staggers back, absorbing the impacts as if they give him motivation. I get up and snap out a kick to his abdomen, he punches down against my shin, the pain instant and severe. Andrew puts some distance between us, venomously pushing Luka backwards to the centre of the church aisle. Andrew raises his guard, and I do the same, barely maintaining my footing due to the throbbing in my leg.

We exchange several jabs, Andrew coming from the right and me from the left. Our opponent deflects everything with vicious intent. He counters with a strike to my neck, but the AR-3 armour does its job, and instinctually I lock his arm then drive a forceful knee through his elbow. Luka grunts in a muted attempt to cover his pain, and I realise Andrew and I finally are having some effect. Andrew batters the side of Luka's skull with a series of short targeted jabs, swearing in frustration with each impact. The armour corrects Luka's arm, and he deflects my approaching kick, punching fast against my knee before bearing some more punches from Andrew's direction. Luka regains his stance and raises his guard as if we've got his attention and he's ready to take us seriously. In quick succession he deflects Andrew's incoming kick and counters in a sharp focused movement towards my rib cage, but I'm saved yet again by the armour, and the AR-3 smashes his foot away. Andrew isn't so lucky, though, and endures a strong downward back fist into the bridge of his nose. I immediately connect with a left jab and a follow-through uppercut. As Luka shakes it off and staggers backwards, I get the feeling the two of us will eventually grind him down. I catch my breath as Andrew wipes blood from his lip.

A distant rumble of thunder takes Luka's focus upwards. He clenches his fists and scans the two of us. 'My drones have just terminated Sam's transport,' he says bluntly.

The armour peels away from my skin. My visor goes dark, I quickly rip it off and Andrew does the same.

'Without Sam helping you from above, my dampening field is fully effective against your AR-3,' Luka says.

Andrew moves towards him, and I follow.

'We don't need Sam's help to beat you,' says Andrew.

Luka's armour creaks, the sound magnified by the silence of our surroundings. 'Don't be stupid! Contact Sam if you want any chance of living.'

Andrew tries to catch his breath. 'We will, after you die!' he says defiantly.

Luka lets a half smile etch out of the side of his mouth and latches on to my chest, pulling me towards him. My vision clouds with some impact, and a sensation like drowning overcomes my blood-filled nose. I lose balance and fall to the ground with a surge of pain shooting through my skull.

I make out a distorted image of Andrew lunging for Luka, followed by the sound of a brief impact. I blink my vision clear and regain my stance; Andrew swings again, but the strike is intercepted.

I take a swing at Luka's face and the impact deadens my hand. I follow it up with a second strike that deadens the other; both impacts feel like a collision with hardened steel, and my hands go numb. I realise fighting without the armour's assistance is suicide, and a voice in my head tells me to contact Sam before Andrew and I are beaten to death.

I look at Luka, bitter and distorted, the killer of my uncle and a man who would kill anyone to serve his cause. Andrew's stubborn streak seems to have rubbed off on me, and I feel the wave of a second wind, an optimism I used to get when I sparred as a kid and got kicked around the ring. The feeling told me to fight back, that it wasn't over.

'You can't win,' says Luka, straightening back up.

Andrew moves to Luka's side. I raise my guard; Luka's face hardens as if this is all some petty inconvenience to him. Before I realise he's moved, pieces of teeth bounce off the floor from my bloody mouth. I see the next strike coming, his punch disappearing under my chin and closing my throat. Unable to breathe, I fall to the floor. My optimism is instantly replaced by helplessness.

I grasp at my collar and try to loosen it. I flick my eyes up, afraid of what's coming next. Luka looks down at me. Without looking away, he smashes a side fist into Andrew's temple, dropping him hard to the ground. Adrenaline pushes me to my feet. I'll get in the way, give Andrew time. Luka looks me over like he wants to see what I'm going to do. I kick him in the ribs, and the pain of the impact shoots up my foot. He doesn't react, as if he's enjoying it. I yell out and kick him again, then kick him a third time with a louder yell that bounces off the walls of the deserted church. The bastard doesn't budge. I make another attempt, but he catches my leg, pulls me towards him, and swings a fist into my temple. I don't see the second one coming—the room spins around, and I want to fall, but he holds me in a standing position. I roll my eyes to meet his. He comes into focus with a subtle smile then lets go of my leg, and I stagger in front of him. Andrew climbs onto his back and attempts to plunge his fingers into Luka's eye sockets. In return Luka throws a reverse head butt into Andrew's face.

I stagger forward and knee Luka in the balls with everything I've got. All he offers is a grunt of discomfort. His forehead crashes into mine; my vision distorts; and blood drips down my face. Andrew reaches up from behind, wrapping his arm around Luka's neck. I yell out and smack him with numbed fists. I feel nothing. I do it again and again, uncontrollably swinging my arms into anything they can hit. Luka thrusts backwards and shrugs Andrew off with an elbow to the stomach. He then grabs a tuft of my hair, pulls me inward, and drives his knee repeatedly into my chest.

I lose count of the impacts, and my legs eventually give up, caving underneath me. Winded, I drop to the ground and lose control of my bladder. There's a hand on the back of my head, then a severe force from something hard to my face. The coppery taste of my own blood rushes down my throat, and blackened spots crowd what's left of my watery vision.

I fall against the wooden pew behind me, the strength gone from my legs. I throw a blurry look upwards because I want to see it coming, and I won't look away. I won't give Luka the satisfaction.

He turns away. He's going for Andrew. I need to get up but can't. Something in my brain won't let me. *Get up, Will*, I tell myself. *You gotta get up.* Andrew throws a punch at Luka's face, but he misses. Luka quickly intercepts and breaks his arm with a loud snap; Andrew shrieks loudly with the immense pain.

Get up, Will. You gotta get up.

My legs shake; I can't get up.

Luka throws a hard uppercut into Andrew's throat, and he falls to his knees. His wide eyes look directly at mine, and his lips try to say something—something like 'I'm sorry.'

Luka exhales and wipes his hands against his chest as if he's dusting himself off. He turns and looks at me. 'Messy business, hmm?'

All I can do is look up at him with hatred. He crouches in front of me, his eyes devoid of all sympathy, as if eons ago they lost their humanity.

Out of the corner of my eye, I see Andrew collapse to the floor.

Luka raises a finger. 'Suffering purifies the soul. Did you know that?'

I spit some blood onto the floor. 'You can kill me, wipe my memory—whatever, man—just…just let him be. Don't you owe him at least that?' I mutter.

Luka removes his visor and takes my head into his hands, his eyes boring into mine. 'I can see into your little mind.' His eyes narrow. 'I'll grant you a brute necessity, hacking away all that is in excess and leave just what is refined. How painful it would be for Andrew or for you to live with the knowledge of what has happened, retain all the knowledge you've gained but never be able to use it, never return to the unit lander, and never again see Sam, whom you deeply care for. That, my distant friend, is true suffering. I would spare you both from such a thing.'

He pushes me backwards, stands up, and makes for Andrew.

'*Please!*' I shout.

Luka grabs Andrew by the balls and puts another hand on his chest. He raises Andrew above his head, walks forward, and hurls him against the marble steps of the altar. His body cracks and flops limply to the ground. No scream, no sound.

I slide upwards against the wooden pew until I'm standing again. *I'm going to kill you, Luka*, I repeat over and over.

Luka moves towards me and grabs me by the hair; I slide along the ground behind him. As he holds my head back, I look down at Andrew.

My eyes water up, and uncontrollable tears run down my cheek.

'Be with him at his time of death. I'll grant you that grace,' Luka says calmly from above me.

A beam of sunlight hits the altar in front of me.

An angry roar echoes from the door of the church, the voice at first unidentifiable because it's usually so softly spoken.

Luka pushes my head towards the floor; I put out my hands to steady myself then turn and look behind me: Sam stands in the doorway wearing an AR-3 with her arm raised.

Two blue beams project from her arm, landing on Luka's chest.

'How could you do this, Luka?' shouts Sam.

Luka holds out his arms matter-of-factly. 'My AI friend.'

Sam takes a step into the church with the doors open behind her. 'For your sake, I hope you haven't killed him.'

'Are we not just pawns anyway? Are you not a pawn, Sam...an artificial pawn?' He holds out his hand. 'Look at you, look at what you are now—you've lost even more than I have, and yet you defend them,' he says wearily but with venom.

Sam clenches a fist by her side. 'Even with nothing, I have more than you.'

She discharges two projectiles into Luka's chest, sending him crashing backwards to the ground.

She lowers her hand. 'Will, my range is limited—retrieve Andrew quickly.'

'Andrew,' I whisper, leveraging myself upwards against the wooden pew.

Limping my way to the steps of the altar, I crouch beside him. I call out his name as I wipe the blood and tears from my face. He lies motionlessly, his head turned towards the altar and an arm hanging over one of the marble steps. I brace myself and put my fingers on his chin to turn his head.

A visor materialises around my eyes.

'He's alive…barely,' says Sam.

The two-toned whine of police sirens comes from somewhere outside.

I lift Andrew to his feet. His left arm sags down from its socket, and his head hangs lifelessly downward. He groans, trying to speak, but I can't make out the words. I carry him in my arms to the doorway and stagger down the steps of the church, then hand him to Sam, who carries him up the steps of the transporter. Two cops lay keeled over on the footpath. Four or five people gather nearby in the cold fog, wondering what's going on, but I just keep my head down.

'Retrieve Luka,' shouts Sam from the opening of the craft. 'You know we can't leave him here. There'll be too many questions already.'

I think about kicking Luka's body, but I don't have the energy. I have to switch off my mind and think of something else as I drag him out to the transporter, giving him no thought while his head smacks into the jagged-edged stone steps.

Sam takes him the rest of the way, and I follow her into the transporter. I fall to my feet with the ascending manoeuvres while coughing out some blood.

Sam scans my chest with subtle head movements. 'You're bleeding internally.'

I try to straighten myself up, but a sharp pain from my rib cage haunches me over again just as quickly.

The transporter rotates 180, and I fall back against the wall in pain as a wave of nausea rises from somewhere within. My body tingles as the fluorescent medical beam passes over my body. The sickness fades, and I feel myself getting tired.

I'm now lying down somehow, but I don't remember moving. Sam stands over me in silence. 'Andrew?' I whisper

24 Awakening

Weird thoughts flood my brain, like I'm thinking of everything in the whole world all at once. Where's Andrew? He should be here, here in Tara Hill. I look around, willing him to appear, and find him sitting within the long grass near the loch. It's greener than it usually is, just like Sam's eyes. I move closer and crouch beside him, but Luka is sitting opposite, the two of them engaged in friendly conversation. I want to get Andrew's attention, but he's distant, completely fixated on Luka's friendly expression; he doesn't remember Luka can't be trusted.

Neither of them pays any attention to my presence, like I'm not important. But we'll see who's not important. It makes me angry Luka is so casual after what he's done. It's time to finish what we started—I'll kill him while he's not looking, and I'll teach him to take me seriously. He's a dead man. I look for some kind of weapon but find nothing on my body. I think hard, but nothing materialises at the end of my arm. Soon Luka will see what I'm trying to do; this has to work...fast.

I find a JX-7 by my side, as if it appeared out of nowhere. I press the trigger, but nothing happens. Andrew looks over and smiles as if I'm a child playing with a toy. I want you to die, Luka! Why won't you die? I scream out the words, I force them out in an endless stream of diiiiiiieeeeee, as if by saying that one word, I can make it happen...I can make him pay. I hate him. I feel a hand on my shoulder I somehow know is Sam's, and I feel myself sink into the earth.

Momentary darkness gradually erodes. A gentle push on my right arm forces my eyes to open, and I blink my vision clear from the blinding blue light overhead.

Sam's visor dematerialises, and she smiles. 'Welcome back,' she says looking down at me.

I lick my dry lips, but the rawness in my throat makes it hard to swallow, and my mouth feels strange and sore. I breathe in and feel queasiness surge from my abdomen, but I stay fixed on Sam's green eyes, as if they're something I can trust, something constant. The blue light begins to fade away.

'You sustained injuries, but you're healed.'

'Andrew?' I say with a sudden panic.

'Stable…for now,' says Sam with an unsettling hesitation.

With each breath, I feel like I want to throw up, and I wet my lips with a glass of water that Sam tells me to drink. 'James and Marie?' I ask.

'I let the emergency services take them, William. They suffered heavy burns, but we will visit them at the hospital later and speed up their full recovery.' She raises an eyebrow. 'I also made the wreckage disappear before anyone could examine it in detail. If we're lucky…'

As I sit up, the blood rushes from my brain and makes me dizzy.

Sam puts a hand on my shoulder. 'You need to rest a little.'

Andrew, wearing just his underwear, lies perfectly still on an examination table next to mine, his body rigid, his arms straight by his side. I ease off from the table and stand over him. I want to hold his hand or make some supportive move, but I don't for whatever reason. His chest gently rises and falls with each breath. I twitch nervously when a sudden blue light emanates from the ceiling and engulfs his skin in a grid-like pattern of tiny squares.

I put the water glass down on my table. 'Is he asleep?'

'Will,' Sam says softly, 'the AI module is sustaining him…I'm about to—'

'What do you mean, "sustaining him"?' I interrupt.

Sam's green eyes bear down on me; her intermittent pauses offer me no reassurances, and I hope it's just bad programming.

'It means the AI is compensating for the damage to his brain. There's swelling around the cerebral cortex causing elevated intracranial pressure. I've already offset one incidence of ischemic blockage.'

With every technical word she uses, my whole body tenses up, like the medical jargon is insulting me. 'English! Say it in English!' I snap.

'Will…'

'Just tell me he's going to be OK,' I say in a calmer tone.

Sam looks down at Andrew. 'I can repair his spinal injuries, but I won't know the extent of his brain damage until the swelling subsides. Spinal repair is about to commence.'

A thin sheet of white light appears at Andrews's feet, passing up along his back while dematerializing the table underneath him. His body floats in mid-air as the blue grid extends itself around his body.

His face makes no expression or gives any indication as to any sign of life behind his closed eyes. The light vanishes, leaving only a blue glow from the grid and Andrew caged within it.

I glance at Sam, who's barely visible in the darkened room. 'When will we know?'

She takes a brief read of the displays at the back wall. 'It's difficult to predict when the swelling will give us…' She hesitates as if reconsidering what she's about to say. 'The next twenty-four hours are critical.'

I fall back against the cold metallic table and exhale into my hands. The incubation chambers at the back of the room come into my peripheral vision. Small human forms with rapid pulses etch their way upwards under the blue surface of the first two; nothing stirs in the next two, while Chris lays sedated in the fifth one.

'He's awake by the way.'

I look over at Andrew.

'I mean Luka,' says Sam.

I'm confused; I figured he died during our fight in the church. My memory of what happened there is patchy.

I follow Sam to a flat metallic table in the centre of the vehicle bay. Nothing restrains Luka's body. He's dressed in a white medical gown, his hands straight by his side, his breathing shallow. 'He can probably hear us,' says Sam, scanning over some data on a screen over Luka's head.

'Did you treat him?'

'I carried out some cellular repair. I'm also using the AI to support some cognitive functions.'

The anger I felt moments ago in my dream returns like it's just beneath the surface of my temperament. 'Why don't you just go upstairs and drive a knife into Andrew's back?' I say, snapping at her again.

Sam sighs and looks away. There's a subtle sadness in her sigh—the most pronounced emotion I think I've seen from her.

'Why are you purposely keeping him alive?' I persist.

She shrugs. 'I can't kill him, I don't have it in me, and neither do you.'

Sam seems so human right now, and if I ever consider her to be a cold AI, I'll remind myself of this moment.

'He tried to kill the two of us. He exiled you into the TUL computer. I'd say it's a little late for compassion!'

Sam shakes her head dismissively. 'It's not that simple, William, and you know it.'

I take a minute to process the stupidly of what she's saying.

'Bring up that screen again and tell me what to press.' I say. 'I'll do what you're not prepared to do. You think I can't kill him, but I can. I'm not an identical copy of my counterpart who you knew.'

A grunt of a laugh comes from Luka's mouth. 'Your friend doesn't understand your empathy. I've been a bad example for him,' he mumbles.

Sam looks down at him. '"Bad example" is an understatement, Luka.'

Luka opens his eyes and blinks a few times. 'Depends on the outcome,' he says. 'Our history may judge me on it...' He takes a breath and looks at Sam. 'Tell me, success or not?'

This little conversation is too matter-of-fact for my liking.

'If Andrew dies, I'll kill you with my bare hands,' I tell him.

He doesn't even look at me. 'As you wish.'

'You would call it a success,' says Sam. 'Your reprogrammed nanocells are destroying H2.0 in Chris Beech's body.'

Luka sits up. I immediately grab him by the throat and slam him back into the table. He gives no resistance.

Sam grabs my hand firmly. I feel her eyes burn into the side of my head.

I apply some more pressure to Luka's neck.

'Then it's accomplished?' asks Luka, gasping for air.

'You injected H2.0 into Chris and used him as a lab rat,' I growl. 'Look at me, you Icelandic son of a bitch!'

He closes his mouth and rolls his eyes towards me.

'Not so strong without all your techno shit are you?' I say.

Sam tightens her grip around my hand. 'He's going to die soon anyway. Now, if you can't do this, then go away.'

I release Luka's neck and take a few reluctant steps backwards.

'I need to balance this out, Sam,' says Luka softly.

Sam hesitates then says, 'I don't think anyone here shares in your idea of balance.'

Luka rolls his eyes at me again. 'I have to do what he can't do, Sam. Tidy away my loose ends.' He looks at Sam. 'You have yours and I have mine.'

Sam's eyes narrow. 'No, this is finished,' she says with a sudden anxiousness.

Luka sits up and speaks some indecipherable words quickly in a Latin tongue. Sam suddenly shrieks loudly and falls to her knees. Luka's body stiffens as an AR-3 morphs over him; he stretches out his arm with a two-cannoned weapon engulfing his tightened fist.

'Find a way, Sam,' says Luka, struggling to get off the table. 'Get what I've accomplished here back to our home.'

Sam bites down on her bottom lip then struggles to speak. 'Luka has executed some kind of override program. It's hacking into my systems. I can't move, William.'

I try to materialise a weapon on my right arm, but quickly realise I'm not wearing any armour or a visor.

Luka points his weapon at my chest. 'Fortunately for you, I'm going to let Sam tie up her own loose ends.'

A transporter craft materialises in the north end of the bay. Luka stands up and walks towards it, struggling with each step. He clings to the railing as he drags himself to the top of the staircase, where the door rematerializes, sealing him inside.

I move to Sam and crouch beside her.

Sam speaks in a whisper, 'He's removed life support from four of the incubation units. Chris is unaffected, but the rest of the clones are dead.'

I guess this is what Luka means by tidying up his loose ends. The transporter pitches back ninety degrees for take-off, and part of the ceiling above it dematerialises. An orange glow emanates from the rear panel, and the craft ascends into the darkness, shaking everything around me.

I support Sam's head with my hand. 'Where's he going?'

She keeps her stare on me. 'Akureyri…Iceland. He's going to find his counterpart and kill him. Will, I know the way Luka thinks. He'll try and justify it to himself as a way to cleanse his soul or whatever madness he's learned in the religious texts. The truth is, he always resented Luka Dalton. He reminds Luka of a part of himself that he hates.' She throws her eyes behind me, and another transporter materialises. 'It's programmed to follow him. I need to go offline and clear whatever he's done to my code. I'll be as quick as I can.'

A visor materialises around my eyes, and Sam vanishes, leaving my hands holding empty space. As I get my bearings and look around, the emptiness of the place hits me. I think of Andrew, but I don't want to think of him. I *can't* think of him; I need to stay focused.

I straighten up against the weight of the freshly materialised armour and call out for Sam, but nothing happens; my voice is an empty echo in an empty cavern. Emotion rises in me, but I suppress it as best I can, pushing it back down where it came from. I turn and run up the transporter steps and seal myself inside.

The computer straps me in, and I grip the armrests as the aircraft prepares for take-off. A force pushes the transporter upwards, but I feel empty and hollow—I can't even feel the acceleration. For all I know, Andrew is dead, and Sam's program is gone. I don't want to come back from Iceland; I don't want to face the fallout of this.

I stare ahead into the dark sky. It reminds me of the blackness outside my bedroom window at Tara Hill and how it unsettled me. Right now it's just what I need: nothing—I need to think about nothing. Deep down I know I don't care about Luka's counterpart as much as I should. All I care about is Andrew and James and Marie and bringing this to an end. My heart races because it's breaking in two.

Everything vibrates, bringing the aircraft into a fast descent— faster than it usually descends and coming in low along the northern Icelandic coastline. The craft comes to a stationary hover over a blanket of snow. The other transporter sits motionless to my right. From the visor coordinates, it looks like I'm somewhere near the university.

After the plane powers down, I step out of the craft and crunch along a few steps, trying to get my bearings. The bitter cold cuts through me, so I instinctively rub my hands to warm them and realise my right arm is covered with the HX-7. An amber glow from an overhead streetlight reveals freshly made footsteps leading to a large glass-paneled building in what appears to be a deserted part of the campus. Three tall flagpoles rock in the freezing wind near the entrance to my right, and a siren whines near the smashed-in glass of the main door. Four spotlights switch on when they detect my approach, but I keep walking like it doesn't matter, pushing through a sharp torrent of snow grains, and step through the glassless window frame clipping frozen shards with my armour.

I feel vulnerable and exposed inside the marble-floored concourse, which is strewn with couches and low coffee tables. A display above one of the elevators shows it has stopped on the tenth floor. As if by habit, I press the button to call it back down, but I immediately regret the move because I've just lost the element of surprise. I'll need every advantage I can get to stop Luka from killing his counterpart.

I think about what I'm going to do. I want to kill him for what he's done to Andrew, but something tells me I won't. I'll reason with him; maybe he'll listen. That's what I tell myself, suppressing anything else I might be feeling, suppressing everything that's happened tonight.

I take a few steps back, raise the HX-7 in front of me, and watch the floors count down on the red display over the elevator door: *Three…two…one…G.*

The doors part to a pleasant ding—the car is empty. I leave my arm outstretched; I'm losing my nerve. The wind hums through the building, hitting the back of my neck like an unwelcome companion watching me from behind, reminding me of that same feeling in the morgue when I realised something had changed in the room.

I look at the bleakness outside, and hardly anything is visible through the white torrent of frozen grains accumulating on the ground. The elevator door begins to close, but I intercept it and get inside. Bringing my heavy arm to the side of my head, I wait to be taken to the tenth floor, all the time suppressing an urge that builds stronger and stronger with every passing scroll of the LED display above the elevator door.

The final ding resounds, and the doors slowly slide open, but I give them a helping hand and quickly step into a white-tiled corridor with a low ceiling. Banks of wires hang out of large network switches with hundreds of green lights blinking on and off each second.

The layout forces me to turn left through heavy wooden doors labelled EQUINE RESEARCH. A faint wailing comes from somewhere inside. Without giving myself time to think, I push through to a large open-plan office with little puddles forming on the carpet from the fire sprinklers. I wipe the falling droplets away from my eyes.

Through the flickering of ceiling lights, an overturned desk enters my peripheral vision. Luka Dalton clings to the wall behind it, faced with his other self pointing the double-barrel of a HX weapon at his head.

I take a few steps closer, and Dalton casts a nervy glance in my direction. His eyes narrow a little, probably because he knows he's seen me before but can't remember where.

I raise my HX-mounted arm.

'Killing your own counterpart doesn't make up for killing someone else's,' I say. 'And it won't absolve you from your sins.'

Luka's free hand clenches into a tense fist; his body language tells me he's uncertain.

'Could you live with yourself knowing what you could have become, given different circumstances?' he asks his own counterpart.

'I don't want to die, please!' Dalton responds in his thick Icelandic accent.

'He's not you, Gudjohnsen,' I say in a raised tone.

All I can see in my thoughts is Andrew's body smashing into the steps of the altar, the scene replaying over and over.

'He *is* me,' says Luka. 'We're different sides of the same soul. He's the black, and I'm the white.' His voice lowers to a whisper as he repeats a mantra several times: 'Restoring balance through self-sacrifice will cleanse me.'

His self-righteous rhetoric is becoming impossible to listen to any further. I swallow hard and try to find the words to reason with him.

'Maybe you and Dalton are part of one soul, but try to give the less sinful side of you a chance at normality.'

Luka lowers his arm; his counterpart slides against the wall towards the floor and cries, covering his face with his hands.

'I studied the holy teachings for ten years in deep space,' Luka says, keeping his focus on Dalton. 'Maybe it could be him, William. Maybe he can take the cure to my people…' He pauses and laughs under his breath. 'That would be something, wouldn't it?'

My hand trembles.

Sirens whine in the parking lot outside, and a faint blue-red flickering peeks up through the glass wall behind Luka. The little voice within me says that Andrew is dead.

'You sorry for all your sins, Luka?' I ask him.

Luka removes his visor, looking more like his counterpart than I've ever noticed. 'May God forgive me,' he says.

'And me,' I say.

Finally I release the thought I've been holding back. My arm recoils with a triple-barreled discharge from the HX-7 that pierces straight through the chest of his disabled armour. Pieces of flesh scatter into the air as the brute force pushes him clean off his feet through the glass wall, down ten floors to the parking lot below.

Covering his ears with shaking hands, Dalton sobs uncontrollably. I fall to my knees and heave the contents of my stomach into a chunky pile on the floor. Water from the overhead sprinkler system streams down my face. I feel nothing inside. I've fallen—I've been dragged down to Luka's level.

Muffled voices come from down the corridor. I turn to face the back of the room; armed police wearing baseball caps shine white lights in my face; weapons click; and they shout something in Icelandic.

I don't care enough to offer any resistance. My mind is silent.

25 Dawn

In a brightly lit grey-bricked room, angry Icelandic once again is shouted at me. My interrogator needs to step it up a bit because he doesn't bother me in the slightest. I turn away from him and catch a glimpse of myself in a large rectangular mirror to my right. A hand forcefully engulfs my face, pushing it back, while my body arches up to counteract the pressure.

'Piece of shit,' he says.

I give a muffled groan and try to swear repeatedly at him but can't open my mouth; it seems I've taken a new liking to swearing. Through the gaps in his fingers, I can make out a tall, well-built figure of a silver-haired man wearing a dark-navy suit.

'He looks a little young,' says the suit in a weird American-Scandinavian hybrid accent. 'Leave him with me.'

The interrogator pushes my head to the side and walks out of the room while the suit sits down opposite me and crosses his legs. He gestures with a nod towards the one-way glass.

After taking a breath, he gives me the once-over. 'Some military people are very interested in speaking with you.' He raises his eyebrows as if waiting for some sort of acknowledgment. '…but you help me, and maybe I help you, hmm?'

All I can think about is Andrew and hope everything isn't lost. I feel numb, like I've been crying for the past hour, but I haven't been crying—I've been sitting in an interrogation room, compulsively analysing. The door reopens behind me and focuses my attention. Some blond lad in half-dressed body armour wraps a Velcro pad around my arm. He hands a tablet to the suit before leaving the room.

The suit reads from the screen then reaches into his pocket and puts on a pair of glasses. His blue eyes glance up at me through the top of them. 'Do you speak English?'

I wonder if there are any repercussions to answering. I try to readjust my position but quickly realise the chair is bolted firmly to the floor. Since my wrists and ankles are tied to the metal arms and legs, all I can do is face forward.

'Yeah,' I say, breaking eye contact.

'Do you know where you are?'

I don't care. I shrug. 'Icelandic jail?'

The suit narrows his eyes as if he just realised something. 'English...Irish or...something?'

I guess there were repercussions to answering—the suit slides his glasses upwards.

'OK, so you're being charged with one count of murder, one count of assault and...' He reads some more from the tablet screen. 'Then there's the breaking and entry.' He clasps the tablet in both hands and leans forward. 'So, for the record, guilty or not?'

Murder… I take a moment to process that word, waiting to see if my mind will react. It's as if the suit has physically hit me with it, and I need a moment to absorb the impact.

I make eye contact again. 'He had it coming.'

His blank expression doesn't change. 'Do you know who I am?'

I shrug and pout. 'The president of Iceland?'

'Thomas Ohlin, Icelandic Ministry of Defence.' He nods as if it's my turn to introduce myself.

I break eye contact again because I'm bored with him.

His chair creaks, and out of the corner of my eye, I see him get up and walk over to me. He crouches and leans in close to my ear. A strong smell of musky cologne hits me.

'They don't usually call me down here for interrogations, but you're a very special case,' he whispers. 'Then of course there's the matter of those two aircraft hovering as if by magic in the university parking lot.' He straightens up again. 'So, Mister Whoever-You-Are, maybe you should consider talking. It might be easier for you in the long term.'

He walks away and turns out the lights as he leaves the room.

I know it's only a matter of time before they make my ID. If they don't have an image-recognition database here, I'm pretty sure there's more high-tech stuff at the US military base outside Keflavík. This is exactly the sort of situation Luka would hate—all this attention on me and the TUL technology under a microscope. I know I should be anxious, but part of me is happy I'm pissing him off. I sit in the darkness; this is probably where I'm supposed to have a little think. Minutes pass while I run through the probabilities again: Andrew is alive—it's a reasonable assumption. I think over Sam's body language in the medical bay; I wouldn't call it tense—was it worry? What if Sam didn't get back online? Then I'm wasting valuable time here; if only I hadn't lost my visor. I should have just shot my way out of the university or jumped out the damn window after Luka. My armour would have saved me—probably.

The lights switch on again, and Thomas comes back into the room with two cups of something. A tug at my right hand and then the left frees my movement as someone behind me cuts the cable. Thomas hands me the cup, which from the smell I can tell is coffee.

He sits back down, removes the lid from his own cup, and places it on the floor.

'Can you give me a rank, a name, something?' he says, calmly stirring his coffee.

The coffee burns my lips as I sip it. 'Patrick Mahon,' I say, throwing out the name of one of my old maths teachers. It's time I put some distance between me and reality.

He leaves the stirrer in his cup as he takes a mouthful. 'Hmm, good. What are you doing in Iceland, Mr. Mahon?'

I lean forward and look at my cup between my legs. 'We're testing out new aircraft. One of our pilots went rogue, and I was sent after him.' I shrug. 'I'm sure someone has been debriefed already.' These all sound like words a military person would say. I wait for his response.

I don't make eye contact. There's a pause. He knows it's all bullshit.

He picks up a file from the floor beside his chair, flicks by the first couple of pages, and reads from the third. 'Says here your pilot friend most likely died before he hit the ground. His heart and lungs were incinerated by that weapon you discharged into his chest.'

He closes the file. 'Now this poses another interesting question, Mr. Mahon: what exactly did you shoot your victim with? That suit of yours is quite unusual.'

'It's classified,' I say.

Thomas inhales through his nose. 'Indeed,' he says, exhaling. 'Then there's the matter of Luka Dalton, the student. Does that name resonate with you, Mr. Mahon?' He peers at me over the top of his glasses.

I look up at him and smile. 'No.'

Thomas puts the file on his lap and folds his arms. 'And this rogue pilot of yours, what is his name?'

I flick my eyes to the left corner of the room. 'Christian Ryan,' I say, giving the name of my English teacher.

'Hmm,' Thomas says nodding, like someone who doesn't believe a word I'm saying. He rummages through some more files. 'You know, Patrick...' He hesitates. '...Iceland is a small place. I knew Luka Dalton's father.'

He throws a picture of Luka's body across the floor; the image shows a grey corpse partially zipped up in a body bag with a serial number written across the bottom.

'Officer Ryan, I believe.'

Thomas rummages again briefly and throws a second picture next to the first: a picture of a happy, youthful Luka minus the stress lines and the fatigue, standing next to a monument overlooking the sea.

'This is the same person, yes?' he says.

I shrug. 'I guess so.'

Thomas raises a finger. 'No, in fact this is Luka Dalton.' He folds his arms. 'Striking resemblance, wouldn't you say?'

I sip some more coffee and nod.

My eyes meet his. He knows he's triggered something.

'Luka's mother and stepfather are missing,' he says. 'Do you know anything about that?'

I hope Alan is lying in stasis somewhere and not in the morgue.

'No,' I say calmly.

Thomas suddenly becomes tense. 'I won't release you to your superior officers until this matter is resolved.'

The door opens behind me. Heavy footsteps enter the room.

Thomas's mouth breaks open, showing the whiteness of his gritted teeth. 'I haven't cleared his release.' I feel the cables being cut at my ankles as someone pulls me to my feet.

Thomas stands up. 'This is an internal matter,' he says quickly.

'There's nothing we can do. You're done here,' says a Scandinavian accent behind me.

I'm dragged out the door before I have a chance to put one foot in front of the other. I try to walk, but my legs can't keep up due to heaviness, exhaustion, and the pace we're going. The cold hits me when we get outside, but that's the least of my concerns. By the looks of it, we're in some kind of parking lot. A sharp object pierces the base of my skull, and an immediate numbness spreads over my entire body. Everything is suddenly dark.

***

'Sam!' I shout her name, sitting on my heels in the middle of a deserted vehicle bay. I instantly face the other way and see there's no elevator, just a door I can't reach near the ceiling. The RMN has no wheels, and I know I can't fix it. Why didn't I learn how to repair stuff instead of pissing around? Is it too late now? If I can find an active console, I could learn, and we'd be back in business.

There's no sign of Andrew. He's not dead, is he? I look around, but I can't see him.

'Sir,' says a voice from behind me.

I turn around and look her over. She's more human than she's ever seemed before. 'You're not how you used to be, Sam.'

'I don't understand, sir.'

'Where are your memories? Tell me you remember everything that happened! This isn't a dream!'

Sam laughs, and I do too, but I don't know why.

I open my eyes midway through a fit of hysteria, and a wave of heat moves up through me like I've contracted a fever. Something is sticking into my right arm, but I don't want to look—every time I twitch, it stings me. I glance down and find I've lost the AR-3 and a drip is feeding into my vein underneath the rolled-up sleeve of a blue medical gown. The sight of it makes me want to throw up. I want out of this place right now. I try to wrangle my wrists free of the plastic ties, but the movement makes them dig deeper into my skin. I try to calm myself and slow my breathing, but I feel the burning from somewhere inside me; it's a sensation I've had enough of, and I'm tired of cooperating. I've done nothing but cooperate since we found the TUL, and look where it's gotten me.

I take a look around—this is no hospital. Bunk beds are lined up to my left and right, with folded uniforms and black boots at their base.

With no leeway on my movement, I hang my head forward and tense every part of my body in an attempt to break away from the restraints cutting into my skin. I try to put a thought together and wonder how much time has passed. A loss of control creeps into my mind, and I'm instantly aware of my vulnerability, aware I've been violated—the drip in my arm, my nakedness under this medical gown. Screw these bastards, invading my privacy like this.

My heart palpitates with the sudden sound of battering rain thudding in the distance. I hear shouts from outside and realise I'm mistaken—that wasn't the sound of rain; it was the sound of automatic gunfire, and it's drawing closer.

A high-pitched squeal pounds my eardrums, and something heavy crashes against the floor behind me. I force my eyes shut when I hear the thud.

'Will!' calls out a voice from behind.

A deep pressure drops from the base of my skull, and I turn my head as much as I can but still can't see much.

A masked figure, dressed in heavy armour, comes into my peripheral vision and crouches beside me.

'It's your old pal Andrew,' he says, lowering his arm. He pulls a visor from his belt and drops it to the floor.

I barely contain the smile on my face. 'Smooth,' I say.

'Oh, you wanna stay?' he says, hurriedly placing the visor around my eyes. He tugs at the drip on my arm. 'What the fuck is this?'

'No idea.'

Angry shouting from behind tells us to get down on the ground and surrender or we'll be fired upon.

'Get down now!' shouts an American accent.

'Dude, you gotta get a suit on. I'm gonna pull this tube out,' says Andrew. 'Count of three: one…'

The clanking of a metallic canister skips along the concrete floor followed by another and another.

'Three!' Andrew says, pulling out the tube.

Three loud explosions and flashes of light blast out. Everything turns bright white, and I can just about hear the faint sounds of machine-gun fire through the deafening buzzing in my ears. I feel Andrew wrap himself around me, acting as a human shield from the incoming bullets. He touches the cable around my right wrist, and somehow the tightness releases immediately as the plastic dissolves to the floor.

'Dude…suit up!' he says.

Specks of green and blue move through the darkness of my closed eyes. I have to clear my mind through the chaos around me and imagine the AR-3 covering my body. I've got to suit up—if not for my sake, then for Andrew's because he's the one taking all the incoming fire, and I don't know how long he can keep that up.

I deaden my senses as best as I can with Andrew's protective grip around me. Suddenly an all-over weight pushes me down, and I instantly know I'm safe. I materialise an HX-1 over my right arm.

'The HX is programmed to fire stun rounds,' says Sam's voice in my head. 'It's good to have you back.'

Andrew swings his body 180 and fires multiple blue projectiles through the grey fog. 'Sam, I can't see shit down here!' he says.

I break off the rest of the cables, stand up, and fire through the hail of bullets, which my armour deflects off in every direction, punching holes in the metal lockers nearby.

'Adjusting for thermal. Stand by,' says Sam.

Andrew and I crouch behind makeshift barriers of overturned lockers and beds. My visor adjusts to reveal four red-and-yellow heat signatures near our position. There are two at either side, and five more lay stunned and sprawled on the floor a few metres ahead. Rounds keep coming without prejudice; they don't care we're not going down. Guns click with a sudden reload.

I lower Andrew's arm. 'Forget this, man. We're outta here.'

'We're twenty feet underground,' he says. 'We gotta fight our way back up.'

My arm recoils with another onslaught of blue projectiles from the HX-1. The stun rounds are much weaker than the regular projectiles, leaving every object they hit undamaged, except for human contact, which produces an immediate paralyzing effect on the entire body.

Andrew leads the way through the fog and bullets as the yellow-and-red figures bravely stand up from behind their cover. He takes out the left flank and I discharge a round into the soldier on the right; he drops the sidearm he tried to draw before crashing into the shelves behind and spilling their contents. There's no delay; the effect of my weapon is immediate and even satisfying.

We exit the crew quarters and clear the fog through a warm narrow corridor with insulated pipes running at either side. A blast door about a quarter-metre thick slams shut just in front of us.

I rub my arm, which is still a little raw from the drip. 'You come down this way?'

Andrew draws the JX-7 out of its harness and commences melting.

'From the roof—Sam's idea. They didn't expect it!'

The golden beam of the JX-7 reddens instantly, and the door caves in on itself in a molten mess, the heat hitting me like a wall.

Loud bangs and white flashes shake me a little off balance. Two masked soldiers in black combat gear repel down some rope behind the door, their automatic weapons drawn, and fire straight at us. The bullets whizz by as if we're invincible and burst the insulated pipes, sending steam escaping in all directions.

They're on top of us before I know what's happening; the man standing before me swipes a blade across my visor. His hand is deflected somehow, and he drops the metal object on the floor but quickly moves to strike me with his other hand. I intercept it and think about crushing the bone; the glove responds diligently and manipulates the molecular structure until his fist is no more than a limp, gooey mess. The poor bastard yells out as he drops to his knees. I finish him off by executing a downward punch at the elbow. He passes out from the pain, and I take a second to enjoy the victory. Andrew looks on after stunning his attacker with the less gruesome method of a stun round.

Sam's voice crackles in my ear: 'I've activated the service elevator to your right, five metres ahead.'

Andrew takes point, and we quickly step through the cutaway door, avoiding the sharp edges of red-hot metal still glowing from the JX-7's impact. We meet a stairwell with the repel ropes still hanging down. Andrew heads left to an old service elevator and slams open the horizontal red doors.

He gestures. 'After you.'

We both get in; the doors shut by themselves, followed by a sudden jolt and a high-pitched whirring of a motor that tells me we're ascending. Andrew suddenly wraps his arms around me and holds on pretty tight. It takes me a moment to realise it's a hug, because it's not something I expect from him.

'I thought I lost you Will!' his muffled voice says against my armour.

I put a hand on his back, but the adrenaline keeps me focused on our surroundings. 'I thought I lost you too.'

'Recommend commencing descent for wide-range pulse disrupt and drone deployment,' says Sam.

Andrew breaks off the hug. 'I think now would be a good time for that, Sam.'

'Descending...five seconds'

I have no idea what they're talking about, but this doesn't feel like the time to ask.

Andrew puts his hand on my shoulder and clenches it. 'You OK?'

I nod. 'Let's go home.' I put out my hand, and he clasps it. 'You had me worried for a while, you know.'

'Sam had to replace my spine. There's a chip in the base of my skull,' Andrew says. 'It allows me to walk until I get used to it,' he says.

The sudden thud of the elevator stopping focuses us forward again; the doors open up to another concrete corridor with walls covered in old lamps and pipes.

'Shit, is that painful?'

'I'll live.' He gestures forward with a flick of his head. 'C'mon. The embassy lobby is straight ahead.'

'Embassy?' I say, surprised.

'Three seconds to low-level pulse,' interrupts Sam.

Andrew raises his left arm as we approach the junction at the end of the corridor. 'This is where the lights go out.'

Static crackles in my ear. 'Contact,' says Sam.

The place goes dark momentarily before the yellow night vision of the visor kicks in.

We turn left through some empty offices and make for a narrow set of stairs, surrounded on either side by thick concrete walls. We begin our ascent up the stairwell, which is parted by a chrome banister that runs down its centre.

A rush of blood suddenly spins round my head as if my ears have just closed up; the ground beneath me is gone and the stairs with it. Time stands still, and I float suspended in mid-air with fragments of rock and metal scattered around me. Instantly I find myself lying on the floor, and the corridor slowly comes back into focus. I know I have to get up fast, so I push against the weight of my armour; everything is dust and rubble. Andrew turns on his side and rips off his visor, which falls away into two pieces.

I help him up to the distant sound of weapons reloading coming from above the rubble pile, which is now a small hill in front of our path.

Andrew looks down at his glove. 'It's aint workin, man.' he says. 'I can't materialise anything.'

Two grenades fly over the rubble and land behind us.

We look at each other briefly then scramble over the top of the pile into a hail of bullets from two mounted machine guns behind a hill of sandbags. Andrew jerks several times from the impacts.

I yell out and stun the shooters with an equal hail of blue projectiles. The grenades explode behind me, sending pieces of concrete and dust everywhere.

'*Shit*, that stings!' Andrew says, barely able to stand.

I put my arm around his shoulder and hold him steady. Carefully turning the corner, we find ourselves behind the embassy's reception counter. Twenty or so armed soldiers and police officers stand opposite, partly in cover behind piled-up couches, chairs, and whatever else is lying around. They load and take aim. I weigh up the odds—I know I can't hit all of them before they hit Andrew, and I'm not certain how much more his armour can take. I won't risk losing him again.

I lower my hand and contemplate our surrender, but the thought is interrupted by a deafening smashing of glass caused by a swarm of drones crashing through the ground-to-ceiling lobby windows. They dispense a brief hail of projectiles with pinpoint accuracy, and any sporadic machine-gun fire quickly dies away from isolated pockets. Everybody's down all of a sudden. Two drones stand guard, hovering near our position on three beams of blue light, while the rest descend over the rubble and down the corridor.

'They're programmed to retrieve your armour. We can't leave anything behind,' says Andrew.

The yellow night vision disappears, and the amber lights of the parking lot guide us along a path to the awaiting transporter across the fresh snow. It's time to go home.

26 The Occasion

One month later.

Andrew takes a controlled step forward while I discreetly support his left arm. Today is the first day he's tried to walk by himself without the assistance of the AI implant Sam installed in the base of his skull.

'You got this, man,' I tell him, offering an inkling of support. The tension in his face tells me how much of a struggle this is. He shuffles his right foot on par with his left then crouches to sit on the pier. I sit next to him, and we let our legs dangle over the still water.

'I'll get there,' he says.

I wave a hovering moth away from my face; they gather at the loch with the approach of spring.

'Why not just leave the implant installed? Sam said it would be OK.'

He shakes his head and looks out over the golden water. 'Nah. I wanna get back to feeling like myself again.' He looks at me. 'Can I ask you a question?'

'Sure.'

'Why did you bury Luka?'

I kick up a little water with my feet and shrug. 'I hope you're not offended by it or anything—'

'I'm not offended,' he interrupts. 'I'm just curious is all. I think it was the guilt, because you...'

I flick my eyes up at him. '...because I killed him?'

Andrew nods.

After we stole Luka's body from the Icelandic authorities, Andrew thought it might be fitting to throw him into the sea on the way home. That didn't seem right, though, and I knew it wasn't what Sam wanted either. We buried him in a grave marked by a humble stone cross overlooking Reykjavik. It seemed fitting—generous maybe but fitting. Andrew has been quiet about it until today.

'I suppose it was guilt.' I say. 'He was a troubled soul.'

He nods in silence and looks out over the loch. 'Is it time to go talk to Luka Dalton?' he says eventually.

Sitting down in front of Luka Dalton is something I've been putting off these past weeks. I know seeing his face will bring back the memories of that night, and I don't think I'm ready.

'When you're back on your feet,' I say.

We sit there in silence. I think about nothing and just observe what I see in front of me: a loch that stretches into the blue horizon, nestled between the hills. Some local kids kick a ball at the far side of the shore.

Andrew runs a hand through his greasy hair. 'I think I'll shave it all off,' he says out of the blue.

I laugh at the suggestion. 'You'd look about twelve!'

'You could shave yours too, you know. Could be our thing.'

'Our thing?' I say. 'The shaved-headed Furious Angels? Interesting.'

Andrew gives me the once-over, as if he's deciding whether or not to say something.

'You talk in your sleep.' he says finally. 'I can hear you through the walls sometimes.'

Feeling embarrassed, I look away and wonder what I've been saying. 'Just bad dreams, I suppose.' I play it down as if it doesn't bother me.

'Me too,' he says.

I keep expecting that knock on the door or some clichéd black van with tinted windows to pull up outside the cottage one day. Every car that slows down or pulls into the driveway keeps me second-guessing whether someone's going to get out and start asking questions. Nothing ever happens—it's only in my overworked imagination—but still, I don't think we'll be boarding any commercial flights to Iceland anytime soon.

A blurry, low-def video leaked to the Internet and the local newspaper showed a weird-looking aircraft and lights in the sky; it was paired with a story about the miraculous recovery of Chris Beech from terminal cancer. One quick scan under the ultraviolet beam of the medical bay wiped it all away. We'll no doubt meet him again someday soon and perhaps tell him how the cells in his body can save an entire species from extinction.

The new back wall of the kitchen is almost up now, and James cut down all the trees around the house for some reason. Sam repaired all the second-degree burns he and Marie sustained the night of the drone battle. She also wiped their short-term memory in case they woke up and wondered why their nephew shot them. The incident goes down in history as a gas explosion, but my heart is weighed down with guilt for them—I can't help it.

On the upside, it's Andrew's birthday today, so I'm forcing out a half-assed enthusiasm. I want to stay positive for him, but seeing him struggle along, trying to learn how to walk again, isn't helping me forget the recent past. He naïvely thinks no one has remembered his birthday because everyone has been so busy lately with repairing the house and everything else.

'Alan keeps calling me,' he says, falling back onto his elbows. 'He's got questions about his three days of missing time. He knows it has something to do with us, and his stepson has probably been blabbing about the ordeal at the university.'

Sam found Alan and his wife -in stasis but unharmed- in a disused hangar near the Keflavík airport. I don't know what Luka's plan for them was, and I don't really care.

'He's gonna show up on our doorstep eventually,' I say. 'I suppose we should arrange a meeting or something. It's up to you what you want to tell him, though.'

'Nothing,' says Andrew unexpectedly. 'We can go talk to Luka Dalton, but if we bring Alan into the equation, it'll get complicated. Too much exposure is never a good thing.'

I look out over the calmness of the loch. Ripples of water lap underneath the pier.

'I thought I lost you,' I say, surprising myself, 'after Sam shut down that night.' I shake my head. 'It didn't feel right when it was just me.'

The frown lines between Andrew's eyes tell me he's listening intently to what I'm saying. I know I feel an inexplicable regret over Luka's death, but I don't want to admit that in front of him. I also know an anger lies just beneath the surface of my everyday personality—an anger that I've lost a part of myself that I can't get back. The truth is, if I thought Andrew were still alive that night at the university, I probably wouldn't have shot Luka. A part of me wanted to understand his predicament, his need to find a cure for his people's genetic abnormalities. Maybe he was right and H2.0 was a step too far, maybe killing it was the rational solution. I now feel sorry for him because he was taken so young from his parents and expected to do extraordinary things and sent on an experimental mission no one understood the complexities of.

All this coupled with ten long years of being in deep space, studying religious rhetoric damning the sins of your parents, doesn't make for a happy childhood. I remember the look in Luka's eyes when he had the realisation about his counterpart, when he looked on at his other self and made the decision not to kill him. The look was hope, hope that one day Luka Dalton could deliver the cure for H2.0 back to his home. I can't help see the irony in that—how we could ever send our Luka Dalton on the same deep space mission in the opposite direction.

All in all, there's a price to be paid for everything I've been through. My scar is both the guilt of killing a man and in equal measure the anger that made me do it. It's a terrible balance of things I spend too much of my late alone time obsessing over.

Andrew reactivates his spinal implant then takes an odd-looking grey device out of his pocket. He hands me the tiny short-barrelled weapon.

'This is the ugliest gun I've ever seen,' I say.

He exhales and shuffles around, turning his back to me. 'Point it at my head and press the trigger.'

'*Excuse me?*' I say, a little too loudly.

'I'm depressed, man,' he replies.

I'm speechless.

He turns his head sideways. 'It's a razor, you dumb ass. Sam gave it to me. She programmed it to take everything off. Just point it and click!'

I swear under my breath. 'I hate you.'

He laughs. 'C'mon, before I change my mind'

'Why, though? What's the fascination with having no hair all of a sudden?'

'I'm gonna learn to walk again before it fully grows back. I need to do this,' he says.

I press the trigger, and a red beam slices through the thick black mop of hair on the back of his head. Big clumps fall away onto the pier as I move the beam over his skull; it's both fascinating and unsettling. The whole thing takes less than a minute. I give him the once-over and realise his ears are bigger than I thought, but sure enough, the new look kind of suits him, even though it makes him look his age.

Andrew smiles innocently. 'Whaddya think?'

'Twelve and a half tops,' I say.

He stands up and dusts himself off. 'Your turn.'

I swear at him with my newfound swearing vocabulary.

He points a finger. 'Do it now, or I'll do it in your sleep. Your call!'

He turns my head a couple of degrees, and I offer no resistance as I look out over the pier, thinking of something else.

'There we go,' he says, a little too sinister as the hair falls away. 'Those guys across the lake are looking over at us, you know.'

'Of course they're looking at us. You're shaving my head on a bloody pier.'

'There!' Andrew says, pleased with himself. 'How does it feel?'

I stand up and shrug. 'Cold.'

He looks at me and squints. 'Nah, it aint you!'

* * *

The day ends with more cake, reminding me of my first day at Tara Hill. So much cake. Marie takes them home from the shop if they don't sell before the expiration date. Fifteen candles sit atop the sponge layer, flickering in the makeshift kitchen that's invaded with the smell of fresh paint.

We all sit around the table: Andrew, Marie, James and me. It's the first time we've all sat down like this in a long time, and it almost feels like I'm a normal person. Wearing her warm grin, Marie pours the tea; she's a little less stressed these days because the house is returning to some sort of normality. James places his 'best dad in the world' cup on the table with his usual sense of satisfaction. He looks up and smiles as if he's enjoying the day for what it is in all its simplicity, but I catch his eye, and the smile fades into something less certain. Some memory, distant and unclear, has triggered in his mind somewhere. I have the same memory too—we're once again in the cottage the night of the drone attack on Tara Hill, with James supporting Marie as they stagger along the hallway. He's caught my eye, and I've caught his, just before the impact from Andrew's GX knocks him out cold.

At this moment I feel as though my uncle can see right through me—he can see all my guilt. His lips tighten as if he's summing me up, figuring something out. I've never seen him look at me this way before—only ever as a caring uncle who appreciated the favour of my presence here. Now that look is gone, replaced with something else, like I've become grown up in this instant, and he doubts something about me but doesn't know what it is. Marie destroys the engagement and asks Andrew to blow out his candles.

James smiles again, but the gesture is muted, and we all sing 'Happy Birthday.'

The festivities end with all of us stretched out on the couches in the living room and a strong smell of burning turf from the open fire. It all seems very simple and small as the four of us sit here like a newly formed family. Still, I feel like I don't quite belong because growing up I never had the 'typical' family.

I ask myself how long I should stay and think about my life before I came here a little more than a month ago. Thinking about it makes me anxious because part of myself is now fused with Tara Hill, Andrew, and the TUL. Besides all that, I was supposed to be back at school a week ago and my mother is getting a little antsy with more frequent texts. She's not at all mad, but eventually I'm gonna have to go home and resume my old life.

Later on, after our good nights, I stand alone in my warm room, looking at myself in the wardrobe mirror. I barely recognise the sixteen-year-old staring back; it looks like a year was taken away when Andrew shaved my head. It's not quite the horror of my first day at Tara Hill. The reflection is a younger me on the outside but a different me on the inside. Damaged and changed but definitely affected by what has happened. I can't even articulate it to myself.

I start to prepare for the nightly ordeal. I take off my hoodie, revealing a formal black shirt, the last of anything clean I have here. Next I undo the buttons from the top, down to the middle, then unclip the last one at the bottom. Finally I undo the sleeve buttons, left then right.

As I inhale, the red veins of the AR-3 glow briefly. This is my new skin, stuck to my body, and I can't shake it off. I know the difference it can make between life and death. I close my eyes and imagine myself waist-high in the calm water of the loch, the moonlight shimmering off the surface. I breathe in slowly then breathe out; the water is warm and the steam rises. This is my imaginary place, where I don't need protection from anything. I try move a finger underneath the armour at my collar; I try peel it away, but I stop myself. I'm not ready. I kick off my shoes, throw off my jeans, and lie on the bed before extending a hand to the bedside lamp.

Unknown time passes—maybe a few minutes, maybe an hour. I'm not sure whether I've slept. I force myself awake, fighting against the weight of sleep, because I feel anxious. The silence of the room isn't helping either. I've gone through so much recently, and now there's no light or sound, and the stillness leaves me nowhere to hide. I wonder if that's why Andrew always sleeps in his clothes—because he feels vulnerable without them.

But it's more than that; without the armour I feel naked because it protected me from death. People tried to kill me; I should be dead. I've killed—I had a choice, and I chose death. Burying Luka in that makeshift grave doesn't undo that. I remember the advice I gave Andrew that early morning in the TUL when I asked him if he was going to kill Luka, and I told him not to go to his level. I was right, because killing in self-defence isn't the same as choosing to kill.

I remember the screams of the soldier in the US embassy when I tore his hand in two—I chose to do that as well.

So what's the price of pretending to be a Furious Angel? Simple things like sitting around a kitchen table and drinking tea or slouching on the couch and watching a movie make me feel like a real person. I've forgotten what that's like because I've had to change so much lately and process new things, difficult things. I pad myself down and check myself for damage, but there's none, not even a bruise, the diffused light eradicating every trace. I want out; I want to walk away, and the quietness makes me very aware of my insecurity. But tomorrow I'll want it all again: the TUL, the tech, the weapons, the next thing. I wish the night would just pass.

Closing my eyes, I inhale through my nose and out my mouth. I repeat the action again and again; the sound of my breathing at least breaks the silence. I catch myself beginning to snore, so I clear my throat and open my eyes again, not wanting to let down my guard.

The door hinge screeches from my left, and the snap of the lock clicks into place. My brain switches on, and I freeze, sensing someone in the corner of the room.

'Andrew?' I whisper without looking. The veins glow again in my armour, and I glance towards the door.

'No,' says Sam timidly.

I lean forward and turn on the lamp. Her eyes squint, adjusting to the light, as she stands in her all-black Furious Angels uniform.

As I wait for her to speak, she rubs her fingers against her palms by her side. Maybe she's nervous or scared. Maybe she gets lonely in the TUL by herself. I've never thought of that until now.

'Everything all right?' I ask softly.

'There's a drone outside. I'm using its power source to extend my presence. Got the idea from Luka,' she says with a smirk.

I can't help laugh, and my heart palpitates, like it has its own memory of the night Sam's AI reached into my chest and tried to kill me.

'Almost worth dying for then,' I say.

'You could say that!' She smiles. 'Did you make some changes to your appearance?'

I smile. 'Apparently it doesn't suit me.'

She gestures towards the bed as if asking for permission to sit down. I immediately slide over to make room.

'You're so different from your counterpart sometimes,' She says.

'Oh? What was he like?' I ask out of curiosity.

Sam glances over. 'Over-logical to the point where it made him naïve. Though he was a good person.'

'Unlike me then.'

Sam shakes her head gently. 'Not true. I can hear your thoughts sometimes when you're training with your visor. You think things through, always try to be one step ahead but you have an edge your other self didn't possess.'

The idea of her probing my mind still makes me uncomfortable.

'It's going to be all right, William,' she continues, placing her hand on mine.

I swallow hard. 'What's up, Sam?' I say dismissively. I don't want to be dismissive, but I don't want to analyse myself right now either.

'You think you don't belong here sometimes, don't you? Like you're tagging along in Andrew's life. It's part of why you're unhappy right now. I would say you're having an identity crisis.'

I shake my head. 'I'm unhappy because I murdered someone. I damaged others without caring. I feel different. That's why I'm unhappy.'

'When people get pushed beyond their comfort zone, they change,' she says.

'You're a psychologist now?'

'I'm a lot of things,' she says, 'but you deserve to know who you really are, William.'

I shrug. 'And how can you tell me if I don't even know?'

She looks pensively ahead. 'Why are you here, William? I mean, why were you in the TUL computer in the first place? Why did I even send for you? Why didn't I just call Andrew?'

I laugh. 'I don't know your reasons for doing anything most of the time!'

Her downbeat expression tells me she's a little disappointed by my answer, so I try to piece together a better one. 'Look, I don't know…you needed to assemble the Furious Angels' senior crew members just like you said, and I was one of only a few candidates.'

'Yes,' says Sam. 'The senior crew members were you, Luka, me, Hiro, and Chris.'

I wait for her to finish the sentence, but she doesn't.

'And Andrew,' I say.

Sam shakes her head slowly. 'No,' she says softly.

'No? What do you mean no!?'

'There is no Andrew,' she says. 'At least not in my universe. Luka used to call him an unexpected variable, but when we came here to your side, we knew there would be differences. I needed you at the TUL because I was imprisoned in the computer core; Hiro was an infant; and Chris was a terminally ill child. Things were different for you here, so I knew the easiest way to get to you was through Andrew, and because Andrew was Dr. Oakley's son, I knew I couldn't leave him out. I programmed him into the computer core with the same access clearance as you. That's the reason Andrew had that particular recurring memory from his childhood—it was one of the few common memories you two could connect with.'

I take a moment to process this information; it pushes everything else in my brain to the side. 'Wait…' I say. 'So in your universe I worked with my uncle? And Ken never had a kid of his own?'

Sam grimaces. 'This is where the identity part comes in.'

'I don't understand.'

'Sometimes,' she says, 'Luka would tell me that knowledge is a double-edged sword. The more a person knows, the more responsible he or she must be, and I have a responsibility to tell you something.'

I sit up at the side of the bed next to her.

'The night Pat Oakley died…do you know anything about it?'

The surprise of the question hits me like a train, and I immediately retract my hand from hers. All the veins in my armour come to life in a dark red. I stand up, placing my bare feet on the cold tile floor.

'Look, I'm sorry you're lonely or whatever, but stay out of my head, Sam. Whatever thoughts you think you've read about my father are none of your business!'

Sam stands up in front of me. 'Pat was killed in a car accident. He was intoxicated and was killed instantly when his car collided with a tree.'

'Sam, my past and my thoughts are personal. I'm sick of this mind-probing shit,' I say sternly in a low voice.

'It was the same night Pat discovered he wasn't your father…'

I look into her emerald-green eyes for a moment and wait for the punch line.

'You're lying,' I snap. Although I'm accusing her of deception, I don't think she's capable of it. I stop short of asking her to leave, and I don't know why.

'After the death of his brother, Ken's guilt took him as far away from home as possible. The guilt of the affair he had with his brother's fiancé,' she says.

'That's...' I shake my head. 'It's not possible. Whatever analysis you did is wrong.' I shrug. 'My mother wouldn't have kept that from me. She...'

I think over all the awkward conversations I've had with my mother in the recent months and years. All the times she asked me to come back to Tara Hill but I'd never go. I'd never want to listen to her.

'William, I have fragments of Ken's memories, and I have DNA analysis. It confirms everything. Ken immigrated to the United States with one of his college friends, Elizabeth, who later became Andrew's mother. Elizabeth died shortly after Andrew was born, but Ken never returned home, leaving the two of you separated.'

'Then...Andrew...' I say in a broken whisper.

'...is your half-brother and not your cousin,' says Sam.

The AR-3 suddenly dematerialises. My body keels over from all the absorbed trauma of the past month, and I puke up a watery mess on the floor.

Sam places a hand on my bare shoulder. 'You don't need to hide behind your armour, and you don't need to be afraid of this place anymore or feel you don't belong. All this time, you were the key to this. Your father's death redeemed you. It not only led you to discover your identity in this universe but also allowed you to give hope to ours.'

Sam extends a hand and helps me up. I feel like I've just puked the lie of my past onto the floor, as if Sam pressed the 'reset' button and opened my eyes.

'What am I supposed to do now?' I ask her.

She smiles. 'Bring the cure home and save my people...' Her voice trails off to a whisper, her face almost touching mine.

I reach out and grasp the tips of her fingers gently.

ABOUT THE AUTHOR

Damien Mac Namara lives in Limerick Ireland. He spent several years training in TaeKwon-Do and tinkering with computer related stuff. He currently lectures in Human Computer Interaction at the National College of Ireland.

Made in the USA
Charleston, SC
14 June 2016